**Tangerine Twist**
By Suzie Carr

Second Edition Copyright 2014, Suzie Carr. Original Copyright 2011. All rights reserved. This book, or parts thereof, may not be reproduced in any form without permission from the publisher.

**Also by Suzie Carr:**
The Fiche Room
Two Feet off the Ground
Inner Secrets
A New Leash on Life
The Muse
Staying True

**Join Suzie in the myCurves Community:**
*Keep updated on blogs, book releases and community news...*
**www.curveswelcome.com**

For my Sweetheart – thank you for always believing in me and giving me the gift of freedom to pursue my dreams.

And for my Dearest Chum - I will forever be grateful to God for bringing us together on this project.

## Chapter One

My quest for a music career started the first time my fingers danced along the strings of my grandpa's bass guitar. So, it was no surprise to my girlfriend, Kelly, that I choose McFadden's Pub over her every Saturday night.

I grabbed my guitar and cell and headed out of my music room and down the hallway. I watched Kelly from behind the wall. Her back faced me. Her legs were stretched out and her hair was pulled up in a messy twist. She held a glass of lemonade in one hand and a photography book in the other. She wore her pink and white checkered pajamas with her fluffy white slippers. A half-eaten bowl of Doritos sat on the coffee table next to some playing cards still in their unfinished Solitaire pose. Comfort paired with the incomplete. Basically, a perfect analogy of our life.

I walked up to her, kissed her crop of golden spirals and said like I did every Saturday night, "Sure you don't want to come?"

She offered me one of her obligatory smiles. "Don't have too much fun without me."

To that I headed out of the door and left her alone in my apartment.

Standing at the top of my stairs and gazing out at my overgrown evergreen, I breathed in the smell of hot dogs sizzling on someone's grill. I felt slightly guilty that I was happy to be free of Kelly for the night.

~ ~

My dream to make it big started when I was a kid. Most every afternoon, I'd venture to my grandpa's house and play his upright bass. The beautiful instrument stood taller than me.

My grandpa would set out his sheet music and challenge me to decipher stacks of notes. I didn't know what the hell I was looking at. I just played the song the way I heard my grandpa play it. I'd occasionally look over at him to see if he was watching. He'd be sitting there in his patched-up recliner, sucking on his pipe, and tapping his big foot against the planked floor. I loved when he really got into it. He'd stomp and clap to my beat, wagging his head from side to side like he was one of those old men in New Orleans partying it up on Fat Tuesday. It excited me. It would drive me to play that bass with a sort of fierce intensity that stirred deep inside me. That intensity would pulse and swell bigger than his four-room house could handle. I swore the walls would start to shake sometimes.

I couldn't play for shit back then, but he always pretended to like it anyway—just like I pretended to read the notes. I'd stare at them with my eyes all squinted up. I'd sometimes drop off with a blaring headache because of it, too.

I couldn't fool him. I eventually confessed that I didn't know a C note from an F note on the music staff. He gave me shit for faking, but he eventually caved. "You'll never be good if you don't play it right," he'd said, climbing out of the recliner heaving a sigh. He pulled out his music books, laying them all out on his dining room table, and told me to start reading. It took me a while, but within two weeks I began stumbling through songs I had previously memorized, eventually ironing them out to the correct beat. Before long, I could play anything he stuck in front of me. I even mastered a few classical pieces.

I loved that bass. I loved how its body was as heavy as its notes, and how its strings were as solid as its melodies. By ten-years-old, I was itching to move on to the acoustic guitar. I wanted to play like the folk-rock musicians I'd seen on street corners in the Inner Harbor. People tossed coins—lots of them—into their cases. I couldn't imagine any other way that

I'd want to make money when I got older. I told that to my grandpa and he shook his head telling me to get my heart out of the clouds and back down to earth. "You better start dreaming bigger than that or you'll be too small for anyone to notice."

So, despite my constant begging for an acoustic guitar, he kept me plugging away at the bass, sure that was my ticket away from street performing.

At thirteen, I came across a beat-up acoustic at a yard sale. It cost five dollars. I begged the woman to put it aside for me while I raced home to grab the five-dollar bill that my Aunt Pam sent for my birthday. Within ten minutes I was back, and it was waiting for me. I tore off down the street with my new guitar strapped to my back, so proud to be a musician and feeling sorry for those who knew nothing about music. I ditched my bike in my front yard and dashed up to my bedroom with it, just to discover a broken string. I played it with its broken string anyway and it sounded really crappy—so crappy that my parents forbade me to play it in the house. So, I'd climb out my bedroom window onto the roof and play it up there. I'd imagine the plants down below were my fans. The morning glories were my loudest ones, cheering and whistling whenever I'd break into a James Taylor song. Right next to the tomato plants, along my front row, I'd always imagine my grandpa. A proud smile dancing across his face whenever I'd hit those really high notes. On my way back inside, I'd imagine waving and blowing kisses to everyone who came out to hear me play.

My childhood was one grand performance after another.

My grandpa eventually found out about my broken acoustic from a neighbor who happened to hear one of my outdoor concerts. He chided me about it for a while before finally agreeing to re-string it for me. Shortly after that, my parents warmed up to the idea of me playing indoors again.

Mom liked when I played Barry Manilow songs for her. She even bought me a book, an inch thick, of his greatest hits. We'd often rock out to "Can't Smile Without You" and "Weekend in New England."

Some pretty large dreams formed in me that summer. I envisioned a future home filled with acoustic guitars of every style, color, and make. I also saw reams of original songs spread throughout my music room that would one day earn me a Grammy, or at the very least, a shot at me gaining some real fans—ones that didn't grow leaves and attract slugs.

I think that dream really sunk in when my parents gave me tickets to an Indigo Girls concert a week before I graduated high school. After that, I would rather have died than not be a musician. Not just any musician, either. I wanted to be a musician who got people dancing in mud puddles in the soaking rain just like the Indigo Girls could do.

On graduation day, my grandpa called me over to his house. His voice hung low, like someone had wrung it out to dry in the hot and sticky Maryland early summer heat. He only lived three houses down, so it took me no more than a minute to get there. He sat on the edge of his recliner with his head drooping low. "I had to sell the bass," he said to me.

My parents walked in from his kitchen with regret on their faces. I felt like someone had died. "Why?" I asked, my throat as dry as cotton.

"It was time," he said. "I don't think you should focus on it anymore."

"You don't?" I was crushed because up to that point, I really thought I might have a future with it. It was what had gotten me through high school history and gym class—that and knowing once I graduated, I could begin my dream. In a split-second I had no idea what I would do with the rest of my life.

Then, he stood up and reached behind the recliner. I followed his hand. In it was the most beautiful acoustic guitar I'd ever seen. A big, red bow was draped around its orange sunburst body. It glistened in the dusty sunbeams that poured through his window. "You deserve to focus on this," he said.

All six strings were intact. It wasn't some particle board guitar that anyone would sell for five dollars in their front yard, either. It was one of those that music stores hung in a special room for the serious musicians.

"This is for me?"

"All these years you thought I was fighting you," he said. "Well, that wasn't the case. I was polishing you, and all those rough edges, before you got ahead of yourself."

I was worn smooth from all those years of playing the bass. That much had rung true. I hugged him. Words didn't seem to have any place.

"A person has to work hard to deserve things," he said. "You've darn well worked your butt off, and I'm telling you right now, there is no one who deserves this more than you."

I did work hard, and I really did feel deserving of my new guitar. I squeezed him and kissed his cheek. Then, I squealed.

I played it for a bit. My mom hummed. My dad smiled. My grandpa winked to the point I wondered if a lash was stuck in his eye. That was the best afternoon of my life. We sang together, ate cookies, and drank Tangerine Twists, a favorite drink of my grandpa's. By early evening, we made our way out to his patio, the four of us, giggling away, tipsy like a group of high schoolers would be on graduation night. I placed my new guitar against the sliding door while we ate burgers. I couldn't keep my eye off it.

"You've got to name her," my grandpa said. "A guitar that pretty deserves a good name."

I sipped my drink again and stared at her. "I'll think of something real special for her."

Those days seemed so long ago.

Right before my grandpa died, he had asked me to play at his funeral. I balked and he begged. I still remember how scared I was to play in front of my entire family. I was halfway through "On Eagles Wings" and I forgot the lyrics. I blanked out and mumbled. Everyone looked at me through their tear-filled eyes waiting for me to recover and to give my grandpa the dignified send-off he deserved. But, I panicked and sat down.

I never attempted to sing again. I stuck with what I knew best, jamming on my guitar.

One day, I would become the performer that my grandpa always wanted me to be. Unfortunately, the world would have to wait for Becca James to stand in the limelight. At twenty-five-years-old, the only light I stood under was blaring from the fluorescent bulbs in the kitchen of McFadden's.

Joe handed me an apron. "There's my girl! Right on time and ready to go."

I loved Joe. He reminded me of my grandpa. Joe was about sixty-five, with hair as grey as steel and meticulously combed into place. He smelled like Old Spice and almost always wore a smile, except when Red Sox fans came to town and took over his pub.

I started working for Joe right out of high school. Seven years later, he still appreciated me and counted on me to work the room, making sure everyone was pleased. His loyal customers came for the crab cakes and drink specials. Mid-week, Joe practically gave draft beer away during his extended happy hours. People would come dressed in suits and blazers from their corporate offices in downtown Baltimore and fill up on crabs, wings, and beer. Many times I'd overhear them bitching about a missed deadline or broken deal or their selfish bosses. I'd rather shovel horse shit than be a pencil pusher in a cubicle having to worry about whose ass I had to kiss to climb another rung on the ladder.

I actually considered myself one of the lucky few who knew what she wanted out of life. I had the stage and the guitar. The only thing I lacked now was a crowd who wanted to hear me play.

I took the apron from Joe and placed my guitar in the corner beside the mop. "Are Sabrina and Nat on tonight?"

"You bet they are. The place is packed."

Sabrina and Nat always drew a crowd, which was part of the reason I was still waiting tables and not owning the stage. Thanks, though, to Nat's nicotine fixes, I did get to jam at some points. Admittedly, that was not the most ideal way to get my music career off the ground, but it was a start.

I reached for a dishrag and ran back out to the bar where someone had spilled a bottle of beer all over the wooden floor. After I wiped the spill, I stuffed the soaked dishrag into the back pocket of my jeans and darted back out to the crowded floor to refill drinks.

I kept looking over at Nat, waiting for that flip of his hand. Finally, on my way back to the kitchen, lugging a tray of dirty dishes on my shoulder, he waved me over. I wiped my hands clean on my apron and untied it as I weaved through the crowd to get to him. He greeted me with a pat on the back. "Want to fill in for a half hour?"

"Sure thing," I said. "Let me just grab my guitar from the back."

Within two minutes I was up on the saucer cup-sized stage pretending to be a real guitarist—my beloved Tangerine Twist in hand—rocking out to Sabrina's country twang.

The place was so packed that every table was filled and the floor fizzed over with more rowdy people than usual. Two girls sat at the corner table near the window and scrutinized me. They watched me intently, and whenever they looked up and caught me staring at them, the prettier of the two would challenge me with a smile. Her skin shimmered, and her hair, as dark and mysterious as a wild forest, cascaded around her breasts like ivy.

She polarized the crowd. She was like the sun, daring all not to look at her directly. I tried everything to avoid staring at her. She was so damn beautiful. I pointed my eyes down at the parquet floor, up at the swirled ceiling, and across the bar to the swinging door to the kitchen. But like a magnet, I kept sweeping them back over to her for one more peek.

She caught me each time.

The other girl rattled my nerves. She looked a few years older and not as sweet and fun. A couple of wrinkles creased on her forehead like she spent a lot of time worrying about the world. When she looked at me, I felt like she was judging me like a teacher, grading me as if I were a sloppy homework assignment. I imagined her red pen slashing me over and over again.

That created a fire in me, causing me to raise my playing level. The music flowed through me like water surged through the Colorado River, powerful and natural.

They were whispering to each other. The pretty girl was giggling and sipping a pink drink. Her eyes never left me. I focused on a pitcher of beer at the table over from hers just to avoid being caught again. The heat from her stare set my body on fire. I played, and the adrenaline pumped straight from my fingers into my instrument.

About a half hour later when I was back serving drinks, they called me over to their table.

"What can I get you?" My voice quivered out of me, all choppy.

"Oh nothing," the older girl said. "We just wanted to tell you that you sounded good up there."

"Thanks," I said, flipping the blank page to my memo pad over to a new blank page.

"What's your name?" she asked.

"Becca," I said.

She straightened up and shook my hand. "I'm Gabby. And, this is Kara."

Kara sipped her drink, and raked me over with her eyes. She was even more beautiful up close.

I dropped my hand from Gabby's and offered it to Kara. Her skin was warm and silky.

"Nice to meet you," I said to her.

She fluttered her long lashes at me. They reminded me of the palms that were used to fan Roman emperors. "You've got a great stage presence."

"With a little bit of work, you could really be good," Gabby said. "Don't you think?" she nudged Kara.

Kara wrapped her lips around her little straw and nodded.

"Kara's performing tomorrow night at the Escapade. You should come and see her."

"You play, too?" I asked Kara.

She dismissed the rise of my voice with a sweet roll of her eyes then began playing with one of her long layers, the same lock of hair that was tantalizing her cleavage only moments ago. "I play a little." Her voice leapt across the wooden table to me, over the bowl of pretzels, and over their crab-shaped napkins.

"You should come," Gabby said.

"I'll think about it," I said, suddenly wishing I had a group of friends I could call up and convince to go with me.

Kara peered up at me and winked. "I hope to see you there, sweetie."

Something in the way her eyes flickered at me sent a tingle up my spine. "Maybe you will." I winked back at her, feeling sexy for a split second before I realized what I had just done.

Kara held her smile and I scurried off, bouncing a little more than usual from all the air under my feet.

## Chapter Two

When I first met Kelly, I believed I had finally struck gold. She walked by me at my friend Margie's salon and smiled. Her hair, the color of a new penny, and shining just like ice, hung straight to the middle of her back. I watched her stroll across the street and slide into a pickup truck. That's when Margie called me back to her station.

About halfway through my haircut, I summoned up the courage to ask Margie about her. She didn't know whether Kelly was interested in women, but in between snapping her gum, she told me they'd be at the Green Turtle the next night having dinner and drinks if I happened to be in the area.

So, the next night, I decided to pop into the Green Turtle. I walked in, strolled right past the hostess and straight up to Margie who was sitting alone sipping a draft beer and picking on some smothered fries. Her blonde hair was swooped back into a low ponytail and hidden under a Ravens cap. With a fry dangling halfway out of her mouth, she pulled out the stool next to hers. "Have a seat."

"Is she here?" I asked.

"Yup" Margie tucked back down for another fry and dip of ketchup. "She's in the ladies' room."

I looked behind me towards the bathroom and there was a girl sashaying up to our table with a bounce in her step, wagging a clutch by her side like a runway model parading in front of a line of buyers at New York's Fashion Week. She wore a tight baby blue t-shirt with rhinestones and blue jeans, revealing a delightful combination of curves. She walked tall and confident in skinny black heels and when she got to the table, she placed a hand on one of her curvy hips. "Hi," was all she'd said to me.

"Hi," I whispered back to her.

"Are you going to join us?" She asked, nodding to the stool Margie had already pulled out for me.

I plopped my ass down so fast, I was surprised the stool didn't collapse under the force.

"This is Kelly's sister, Patti," Margie said before sticking another cheese-dripping fry between her teeth.

I smiled politely at her and she gave me a once-over glance. I suddenly felt self-conscious in my Levis and polo shirt. Then, Margie glanced up over me again and my heart began to sputter. I knew she must've been looking at Kelly. I turned and there she was. I barely recognized her because her smooth hair from the day before was replaced by a mass of curls more thick and springy than any head of hair I'd ever remember seeing up to that point in my life. She was wearing sneakers and an Old Navy t-shirt, the complete opposite from her fashionista sister. And I couldn't have been any more thrilled by that.

When she smiled at me, her eyes sparkled and soon after we fell into an easy conversation about raspberry beer, good music, and oddly enough, the satisfying crunch of a fresh bowl of pretzels.

Eventually, Margie and Patti ended up sitting next to each other, racing through Sudoku games to see who finished first. Winner got beer bought by the loser. Margie was flat-out drunk, ranting on and on about how she should've become an FBI agent instead of a hairdresser because she obviously had some hidden strategic skills no one, not even she, picked up on. She rambled on about how they should've had Sudoku contests with large winnings, and that if they did exist already, maybe a road trip to those contests was in order. After a while, Kelly and I tuned her out.

I was immersed in everything and anything Kelly was talking about that night. When she spoke, she got real animated, flinging her hands every which way, and her baby blue eyes got really big. I decided right then and there that she'd make a fantastic storyteller. She blushed. I normally wouldn't have given a crap about weeds in a backyard or eggs frying on a stove, but the way her voice sang up and down when she talked about those things got me cracking-up and craving more and more. She could've talked about a blade of grass growing out of the slit in a sidewalk and I still would've been just as intrigued.

At one point, fortunately for me, the music got louder and I had to lean in close just to hear her. She smelled like jasmine and vanilla. I tingled every time her breath hit the side of my neck.

I was in love.

We made plans to see each other the next night to make s'mores on my deck. One night of s'mores turned into another, and before long we were each ten pounds heavier and a million times happier than either one of us ever thought possible.

That was a little over three years ago.

I slid in next to her and nestled up against her back. "Let's go out tomorrow night," I said. "I just heard of a great place we can go."

"You want to take me out?" She sat up.

I pulled her closer. "Why do you sound so surprised?"

"Do you remember the last time we went out?"

I searched my inner catalog, shuffling through card after card, and came up empty. "That's why I'm asking. I think we need this."

"I have Tommy's soccer tournament all day, remember?"

Tommy was Patti's five-year-old son, and a future All-American from what I'd been told. I'd never met him. I'd never met anyone but Patti. "That's right. How about another rain check?"

She nodded. "Yeah, sure."

I wrapped my finger around one of her long curls and thought about Kara and how much I wanted to see her again. I wanted her to wink at me and send me walking on air again. My stomach fluttered. I kept twirling her hair, and the more I twirled, the more I felt that guilt rise up in me again for being happy that Kelly had something else to do. "You probably wouldn't like the Escapade anyway."

"Are you still going to go?"

"I could ask the same thing of you."

"Becca, you know you can't come to the tournament. My entire family is going to be there. It's strange enough to them that you showed up for Thanksgiving dinner last year. I'm still fielding remarks on that one. They'll never understand."

I clenched my teeth. "Then, I'm going without you, I guess. A couple of girls from McFaddens are going to be there."

Kelly's eyes widened. "Oh? Anyone I know?"

"No. Just some girls I met. One is performing and so I said I'd go and check it out."

Kelly tied her hair back into a ponytail with the elastic she had wrapped around her wrist, trying to mask her unease.

"Maybe I should ask Margie to come with me," I added, forfeiting the chance to feed my anger with her insecurity.

A clean smile washed over her face. "That's a great idea. You'll have to beg her, of course."

Margie hated clubs even more than Kelly. "Yeah, I figured."

Kelly laid back down. "I'm going to crash here tonight. It's just been a really tough day."

"What was tough about it?"

"Got another rejection letter for some photos I sent to this small press."

I tucked the blanket around her. "Kel, you think maybe you're being too hard on yourself with this whole photography thing?"

She rolled away so her back faced me. "No, not really. I've been giving my future a lot of thought the past couple of days, and I think maybe I need to just face the fact that I'm not good enough."

"I think you need to get out and have some fun. Clear your head and then go back to it."

"It's not a guitar, Becca. It doesn't work that way. You either have it or you don't."

"So, you're just going to give up?"

She groaned. "I'm really tired."

I stood up and stared at the back of her head, annoyed that she was feeling sorry for herself and letting others dictate her future. "I'll be in soon."

I closed the door behind me and headed straight for the fridge. I cracked open a beer, sat my ass in front of the computer, and emailed Margie.

~ ~

I woke up to the smell of coffee the next morning. My stomach was growling, and all I could think about was devouring a stack of pancakes drenched in maple syrup. I called out for Kelly, figuring she was probably reading another photography book out on the sofa.

When she didn't answer, I dragged myself out of bed and searched for her. The only thing I found was an empty container of milk on the kitchen counter and a note saying she was off to Williamsburg for the tournament. She added a smiley face near her name, apologized for missing our breakfast, and told me she'd call me later.

I opened the cupboard and stared at my pathetic shelves - a near-empty container of peanut butter, a box of oatmeal, some macaroni and cheese, and a couple packages of marinade. No pancake batter. No bread for toast. Not even a packet of sugar.

At least I had coffee. I fixed a cup, black, by no choice of mine.

Then, my phone rang. It was Margie.

"Did you just wake up?" she asked.

I swallowed a bitter mouthful of coffee. "I'm not quite there, yet."

"I got your email," she said. "How about you pick me up at nine?"

I sprung to life. "Really?"

"Yeah," she said. "Don't sound so shocked."

"I just thought I'd have to beg."

"Marc's away again. I've cleaned every square inch of the house and watched all my recorded shows already. Now I'm so bored I'm playing Solitaire."

"Where is that husband of yours now?" The man was always off somewhere it seemed.

"He's in Vegas this week trying to win over a couple thousand salon owners with his charm."

"That shouldn't be too hard for him."

Marc was that person who could walk into a room of mourners and start a party. He just had a knack for turning heads, not just because of his sophisticated ponytail and devilish smile, but more so because of the way he carried himself. When he entered a room, the air parted, voices hushed. He was so tall that he had to duck to clear a doorway, and he walked with a swagger that sugared him with that bigger-than-life aura important people seemed to carry with them.

I wish I could've stepped into his shoes just for a day.

"We're hoping he can push our new shampoo line at the Beauty Expo."

"You guys have another line?"

"He's on an organic kick now. He's driving me crazy the way he's always going for bigger. I wish we could throw the products out and stick to cutting hair. This whole production process is nothing but a headache."

Margie always talked like she couldn't care less about success. I'm sure, though, at the end of the day when she soaked in her Jacuzzi in her backyard with her hundred-dollar bottle of champagne she was pretty damn content. She was a spa owner, entrepreneur, product inventor, oh hell, and I may as well toss in hair magician, too. Yet, she walked around with a chip on her shoulder, pretending that all the success was really just a nuisance that stressed her out. I've never been able to tell if it was an act or if she really was just a girl trapped in a life that she felt she hadn't earned the rights to.

Kelly was extremely envious of her. I just felt downright sorry for her. I couldn't imagine having all that and then complaining about it.

"Speaking of organic," I said, taking the segue, "how about we try out that new restaurant, The Great Sage, tonight?"

"No can do," she said. "With the outfit I'm going to wear, I won't be able to eat more than a rice cake today."

"You already picked out what you're wearing?"

"What did you expect me to do?" she asked. "It was midnight. I was alone in my big empty house playing Solitaire and your invite popped up in front of me."

"Just wear something comfortable. That's what I plan to do."

"They have a dress code," she said.

I mentally scanned my closet and panicked. I had nothing but cotton and jeans. The good stuff didn't fit anymore. "I hope you have something I can borrow?"

"The only thing I've got that's bigger than a size eight is a size twelve black dress that looks like a potato sack."

Hmm. Then, the black dress would be a last resort. "I think I can still squeeze into some eights, depending on the cut," I said. "I'll get there a few minutes earlier and try some things on."

We hung up and I poured the rest of the burnt coffee down the drain.

I sucked in my gut and ignored the image of blueberry pancakes that danced in front of my eyes. I'd eat some of Kelly's crappy oatmeal instead.

I began to pour some in a bowl and then got sidetracked with thoughts of my waistline. I wished it was tighter like it was back in my pre-Kelly days when I used to care about working out. Since then, I expanded a few inches, a few inches too much for a size eight.

In a desperate move, I dropped to the floor and crunched my abs tight for twenty-five reps. Phew, that move took my breath away. I used to be able to push a hundred of them out without breaking a sweat.

I twisted my head up to see the clock. I had exactly eleven hours to lose a couple of inches. I could've fit two triathlons into that time. I sure as hell could've managed a couple thousand crunches.

~ ~

By eight o'clock that night, the air was swollen with moisture and my hair hung on my head like a limp noodle, despite the blow-drying, the hairspray, and the mousse. I climbed out of my car and headed up the long walkway to Margie's front door. The smell of pine and earth swam together and reminded me of those nightly runs Kelly and I used to take around Lake Elkhorn when we first hooked up. We'd go later at night, long after sunset, after dinner digested, after dog walkers and bike riders vacated. We'd run against the mist of darkness, through the early construction of cobwebs, and swarms of mosquitoes out on their nightly hunt. We didn't care about spiders and blackness back then. We just wanted to be free.

I remembered the first time Kelly and I kissed. We had just finished a three mile walk by the light of a full moon. We were stretching by my car. I turned to her just as she was straightening up. A piece of hair saddled her cheek and I brushed it off. It was our quintessential moment.

Kelly couldn't get enough of those moments back then. She'd shuffle me off to a remote corner and make out with me like it was going to be the last kiss we'd ever have. Walking through a mall, she'd pull me into a bathroom and lock the stall. Walking on the beach, she'd toss me into a dune. At the movies, she'd chauffeur me up to the last row. I loved kissing her, and wanted the whole world to know. One day, when we were strolling along together through a very busy day at Savage Mills admiring some oil paintings, we came across a picture of two curvy chili peppers intertwined, resembling the shapes of two female figures embracing. I remembered thinking it was one of the sexiest pictures I'd ever seen. Caught up in the romance of the moment, I pulled her to me and kissed her right there in front of tons of people. What a tragic mistake. She tore off through my arms and ran out of the store. I rounded past a store and caught up with her behind a kiosk of wind chimes. Her eyes flared. "Please don't ever kiss me like that in public again," she said. She was out of breath and little pieces of her hair sprayed around the sides of her face.

"Why not?" I asked her.

"What if we know someone here?" she asked.

"So what if we do?"

"I'm not like you," she said. "I'm not comfortable with all of this just yet." Her words, like molten lava, spilled around us and suspended us in a new uncomfortable state.

I nodded but didn't speak. She walked off, and I just fell into pace beside her, walking, browsing, and pretending to be present when I was really wilting inside.

That memory marked the beginning of our descent down the hill of lust.

I twirled the keys around my finger as I ascended up Margie's steps. Pots of marigolds and petunias greeted me on the stoop and brought me back to the thrill of the night ahead.

Before she even answered the door, I could hear Margie's feet tapping out an allegretto tempo against the marble foyer. Through the lace curtains, I caught a glimpse of red as she opened the door. She was thirty-five going on twenty.

"Come on in," she said, feathering her hand off to the side.

I stepped in, took one look at her red cocktail dress, and crossed my arms over my chest in friendly protest. "If you're wearing that, I'm not dumping myself into the black potato sack."

"Let's see what we can do." She whisked off towards her winding staircase.

I followed her up to the bedroom wing. A mist of flowers and potpourri floated in her wake.

I didn't care if I had to wrap myself in tape to shrink down to a size eight for the night, Margie was not going to outshine me.

I followed her through the French doors and into her bedroom, which was the equivalent of four of my apartments—five if you count the dressing room that connected her room to the bathroom. I'd never been that far into her house before. It was everything I'd imagined it would be. Elaborate curtains, expensive furniture, and endless artwork that stretched out on each wall. Even in the dressing room there was a life-sized portrait of a bride in her wedding dress, veil hanging over her face so all I could see was the shadows of her features.

As I browsed her collection of shoes—which spanned several feet on both sides of her room—Margie started tossing outfits onto her chaise lounge.

I picked one up, a sexy black sequined dress. I held it up with just two fingers, afraid to even imagine my waist in it. "It's a dance club, not the Grammy Awards," I said to her.

"You can't walk into the Escapade wearing jeans." She faced me, balancing one hand on her skinny hip and the other a green paisley cocktail dress with tank straps.

I grabbed the hanger out of her hands and tried it on. I couldn't get the zipper to move more than an inch up my back. "What else do you have?" I asked.

She pulled out a printed kimono mini dress with dramatic long sleeves. "Try it on."

I couldn't get it over my head.

She pushed through a forest of clothes to get to her back rack. She handed me a royal blue strapless dress. "This is a good color for you." It was flirty with a sweetheart neckline and a cinched drop waist.

I tried it on, and it zipped. I turned to see myself and wanted to cry. "My boobs are squished."

Margie walked over to her bed and fell onto it in a back flop. She laid spread eagle looking like she'd just spent eight hours at the mall. "Let's just change into sweats and order pizza."

I stared at her for a moment, teetering on the hopeless fact that pizza and sweats were exactly what I didn't need. What I did need was fun. I also needed a drink. So, I didn't care what it took, even if I had to sew a damn outfit together, I was not slipping into cotton sweatpants with an elastic waist expansive enough for three of me to fit into. "We're going to make this work," I said, lifting her off the bed with a strong tug.

Ten outfits later, Margie dug out a punchy orange, silk drape skirt. I adored it right away. She paired it off with a simple white top and strappy sandals.

I tried it on and it almost fit. I was shy about an inch around the waist. I thought about leaving the button undone. Margie had a better idea.

She straddled an elastic over the button and looped it through the hole and back around the button. "I've seen a few people do this when they're not quite ready for maternity clothes. It'll give you that extra inch or so."

I was mortified. I couldn't believe how much I'd let myself go. Staring at my button contraption, it dawned on me that comfort was not the friend I'd always thought it was.

She turned me around to the mirror. I squeezed my eyes shut, afraid to feel worse.

"You look adorable," she said.

I opened my eyes.

I did look adorable. I spun around in circles, feeling sassy for the first time in years. Margie doted behind me like a mother seeing her daughter in a wedding dress for the first time. Her hair was swept back into a soft knot.

"Just put on these sandals."

I examined them. "How am I going to fit into these?"

"Squeeze," she said. "No pain, no glory."

If what Margie said was true, then I should've been receiving more glory than a queen that night because by the time I faced the red-carpeted steps of the Escapade, a blister had already formed on one of my big toes. The pain blinded me. "I'm going to need one hell of a drink," I told her.

"I was thinking more like four or five," she said with the straightest face. She walked ahead of me up the steps, swinging her hips side to side and stealing a lottery's worth of winks and smiles from every man within a twenty-foot radius.

She didn't even notice.

People packed the club wall-to-wall, a sea of glitter and fancy drinks. We'd be lucky to catch a small glimpse of Kara. I pushed us straight ahead to one of the many bars. We ordered a couple of Cosmos then headed to the dance floor and claimed a spot directly in front of the stage. The club pulsed with laughter, house music, dancing. Sweat mixed with perfume and cologne to form a hungry, sexy film over the crowd.

Through an opening behind the stage, I caught a glimpse of people mingling. I strained to see Kara or Gabby, but the mimed figures were shadowed and faceless from my viewpoint. Before long, the lights dimmed and a sole spotlight centered on stage. The crowd waited to breathe.

Then, Kara passed through a tinseled curtain. She looked like a bedazzled angel. She walked towards the middle of the stage to the microphone, fingering a melody on her guitar, and sporting one hell of a sexy smile. Her chocolate colored hair bounced around playfully, flirting with her guitar strap. She sang her first note from a place deep inside, sending me into a bobbing spin.

Maybe it was the way she tilted her head to the side when she sang, or the way her lips grazed the mic, but I was spellbound. She massaged the crowd, getting them to loosen up and sing along with her. Even those by the front door were hooting at her, clapping on cue. What she didn't have in range, she made up for with her charm. During about the sixth song, I looked over at Margie and she was fiddling with her cell. I could only assume texting Marc. "Tell him he's missing one hell of a show," I said.

She looked up, shocked like I had caught her stripped down to her underwear. But a second later, she caught her bearings and laughed. "Yeah, I just did." Then, she went right on texting completely ignoring the show.

Kara played a few James Taylor, Alyson Kraus, and Billy Joel covers. I was so wrapped up in her that I hadn't even noticed that Margie had slipped away. I figured she had probably scurried off for more drinks or to talk to Marc.

After a half hour passed and Kara was wrapping up her last song, I started to get a little worried about losing Margie in the sea of dancers behind me. But then, Kara pulled me out of my fear when a crazy blue light began to shine all around her. She was tilting her head back and hitting a high note for the first time that night when all of a sudden she lowered her head, then slowly and dramatically opened her eyes and locked onto me. Then, she broke into the sweetest lullaby voice and sang the last line of the song straight to me as if no one else was around.

I didn't even want to blink out of fear I'd lose valuable seconds with her. She broke our stare when she bent forward in a bow. I desperately wanted another sip of her sultry act. She curled back up and eye flashed me.

My heart twirled around inside me, sending ripples everywhere, even through to the tips of my pinky fingers. When she walked off stage, I stood breathless.

Just then, I felt a tug. Margie snuck back up to me. "Sounds like Kara finally hit an interesting note. You must've inspired her," she said.

"I want to go say hi to her. Do you mind?" I asked her.

"No," she said. She scanned the room as if looking for someone. "Let me just say bye to a customer I ran into."

"I'll wait for you over by the door."

"Just go in. I'll catch up in a minute." She took off in a gallop, skirting around people.

I followed her track until she slipped out of sight. I circled towards the backstage area, scouting it for any sign of Kara or Gabby. I wanted to see her. I had to see her. So, I swallowed my nervous twitter, checked to make sure my elastic was still looped around my button, and entered a room backstage with a dozen round banquet tables, emptied of linens and littered with a few beer bottles and crumpled napkins stained with the remnants of salsa. Twenty or so people stood around in small circles, talking and laughing. The room was dingy and smelled just like my childhood basement did after heavy rain. Not exactly the classy backstage I'd imagined.

A bag of opened nachos sat lonely on a folding card table with a jar of dip off to its side. A guy wearing a Hawaiian shirt and khakis opened a fridge in the corner and pulled out a couple of long neck bottles of Corona, handing one off to a feminine man with the longest fingers I'd ever seen.

Kara was by herself on a metal folding chair, changing the strings on her guitar. Her legs spiraled out in front of her, glistening, one crossing over the other. I walked towards her with small tiny steps. When I was a few feet in front of her, she looked up and smiled. I wanted to tell her how great the show was, how much I loved her voice, how I wished I could hit the riffs she could hit, but I couldn't find my tongue. It twisted up like a wind swell in the back of my mouth.

Her eyes twinkled.

She placed her guitar in its stand by her chair. It sat like a queen, tall and honorable with solid mahogany back and sides and a delicately engraved hummingbird pickguard. Its gold hardware, fancy rosewood fretboard, and bridge added to its royalty. I couldn't take my eyes off the cherry sunburst finish. "I've always wanted a Gibson Hummingbird," I finally said to her.

She picked it up off its stand and handed it to me. "Go ahead and play it."

"I couldn't." I handed it back to her.

"Play it." She wedged it back in my hands.

It wasn't until I sat down and hoisted the guitar strap over my shoulders that I realized Margie had ducked into the room. She stood with some tall guy in a suit and shiny shoes over by the doorway. She was laughing and standing close to him. He offered her a sip of his drink. He held the glass while she placed her lips against it. He didn't take his eyes off of her. I wondered if Marc knew the guy.

Kara leaned in towards me, bringing me back to the moment. My hands shook, and I felt a rush of heat come across my face. I plucked the strings and caught her eyes studying my fingers. The Gibson sang like a chime, light and breezy. I strummed and out rang a deep, rich thundering tone like a big choir in a cathedral. The work of art I was holding in my hands could definitely sing.

Next thing I knew, Kara lifted another guitar from behind her. She started playing "Dust in the Wind."

She sang the first couple lines of lyrics then stopped. "Sing with me."

"I don't sing."

She teased back into the melody again. "I bet you've got a voice hiding in there." Her eyes swaddled me.

My throat dried up.

She broke into a higher voice, welcoming me to harmonize.

I began by humming.

Her eyes twinkled again.

I joined in low, treading beside her, taking refuge in her lead. Gosh, she was beautiful. Her skin resembled the smooth surface of a nectarine, so soft, curvy and fresh.

If it wasn't for Gabby eventually calling Kara over to speak with some bald guy in a turtleneck, I could've stared at her for a thousand more songs and not grown tired. She placed her hand on my shoulder. "I'll be right back, sweetie."

I smiled up at her and nodded. She slid her hand down my back and walked away.

I nearly wet myself.

I watched her flounce across the floor, drinking in every one of her strong steps.

I played a little longer with her Gibson, every once in a while looking up to see if she was watching me. We stole half a dozen glances from each other.

At one point, I looked over at Margie and that guy. They huddled closer. He was touching her arm and running his fingers upwards parallel to her breast. Margie giggled and whispered something to him. He flirted right back. Margie fell into his embrace, then quickly pulled back when she realized I caught her. Within seconds, the guy walked away and she came over to me.

I felt numb. The world had just flipped over on its side. If Margie and Marc couldn't make it, who could? "Was that your customer?"

"Yeah," She shrugged and twitched the corner of her mouth. She wouldn't look at me.

I wanted to come right out and ask her the obvious question, but wasn't sure I wanted to know that secret. "Does Marc know about him?" I couldn't keep it in.

"It's not how it looked," she said.

It seldom was. I thought of Marc and wondered how I'd ever be able to look him in the eye being armed with the new knowledge. "Maybe we should just go."

She started to sputter something about me not understanding what she's going through. I couldn't listen to her. I just stood and placed the Gibson back on its stand, then turned to leave. But, Kara and Gabby were walking towards us.

"I'm really glad you came," Kara said, stopping within inches of me. Her dark eyes curled up at me, lassoing me right in. My face flushed. I fidgeted not sure what to do with my hands, my feet, and my erratic heartbeat.

Gabby turned to me. "Kara and I were just talking and wanted to see if you'd be interested in stopping by a private party she's playing at this Friday night. Maybe play a couple of songs together and see how the audience reacts."

"Me?"

"You're quite a muse for my sister."

Sister? That news shocked me somewhat because they couldn't have looked less related. Gabby had deep-set wrinkles like a roadmap on her forehead, her lips were thin and crooked, and her eyes were small and far apart. She didn't have a drop of Kara's sex appeal.

I looked from Gabby to Kara and back to Gabby who was stretching her eyes wide waiting for my answer. I was afraid she'd pop them right out of her head.

"You're serious?"

"I think the fans would relish the harmonizing," Gabby said.

"I don't know. I don't want to screw with Kara's gig."

Gabby handed me a memo pad. "Jot down your info. I'll send you the details."

I caved and gave her what she wanted.

A few minutes later, on our way back to my car, Margie wrapped her arm around me. "What do you say we both keep quiet about tonight? You don't say anything to Kelly about what you think you may have seen and I'll promise the same."

"I've got nothing to hide."

"I saw the sparks from across the room."

I bit down on my lip, trying to conjure up a defense to my girlfriend's best friend. "Like you said to me earlier, it wasn't how it looked."

Margie just nodded. We walked in silence, alone with our speculations.

It wasn't until much later, when I climbed into my empty bed, that I began to worry how Kelly would really feel about me landing my first real gig with one of the most beautiful women I'd ever seen.

## **Chapter Three**

I sat on a picnic table outside the *Baltimore Weekly Magazine* building, waiting for Kelly to spring through its mirrored doors on her way out of work. The tired sun filtered through the canopy of willows, creating a hazy glow around a Japanese maple tree hunching over the grass in front of me. A family of Canadian geese flew in a perfect triangle overhead, piercing the air with their squawks. A biker raced down the street, pedaling against the light breeze that was circling off the lake.

Two days had gone by since I had seen Kelly, and I still hadn't figured out if I wanted to tell her about my gig. I was afraid my good news would just make her feel worse. I thought about lying to her and telling her I had to go help my parents paint the inside of their garage. She'd never think to invite herself. She hated painting perhaps just as much as she hated the spiders that hung from the cobwebs in the garage's rafters.

Kelly swung open the doors and stopped, waiting on a lanky girl with chalky legs and a square figure to catch up to her. They walked slowly. Kelly was fully engaged, nodding her head up and down with each of the girl's hand gestures. Kelly was giggling, and then she tripped over nothing but air. Her arms flailed out like tentacles as she twisted off to the side, rolling onto the grass in a lopsided somersault. A sandal flew off and landed in an Azalea bush. Anyone driving by surely got a free show of her panties. I cupped my hand to my mouth and tried hard not to laugh, which was so difficult because everyone around was pretending they hadn't seen her flip in the air like a clumsy circus clown, either.

Kelly was cracking up when the girl offered her a hand.

I loved that klutzy side of her. The first time I'd seen her fall, I knew she was a keeper. We were camping in West Virginia in the Shenandoah Park, and we decided to get an early start on a day hike. The sun was just rising above the tree line and the air still swaddled the morning dew. We set off on what I anticipated would be a romantic day in the woods, stopping at each turn to smell the wild grass and admire the shades of nature. Then, she tripped over a branch. I brushed the dirt off her arms and she giggled. It was the cutest giggle I'd ever heard next to that of a baby. No more than five minutes later, she tripped again, that time over a tree root. She landed on all fours, and when I picked her up and saw the dirt circles and tiny dents on her knees, I felt so sorry for her. But she still laughed at herself. She must have tripped, whacked her hand on trees, and hit her head on low lying branches like fifty times in just the first hour. By the time we got back to camp, set the fire ablaze, and roasted our marshmallows, I had nicknamed her Bumbles. After that, whenever she succumbed to a clumsy move, she'd curl up into my arms and seek the comfort of her pet name.

I'd swear she purposely ran into walls and stubbed her toe just to hear me call her Bumbles.

It dawned on me, as I watched her stumble up to her feet, that I hadn't called her by that name in quite some time.

Some guy retrieved her sandal from the bush, and when he handed it to her, both she and the girl practically convulsed right there on the lawn. They were laughing that hard. I decided to join in the fun. I walked towards her laughing as well, and when I was close enough, I called out to her.

She turned and smiled really bright. The pale girl handed over Kelly's lunch tote to her and said her goodbye. Kelly skipped towards me. "What a surprise," she said, with her cheeks flushing the color of rose petals.

"Are you all right?" I asked, still giggling.

"Yeah." She scanned the ground looking a bit dazed. "I think so."

"I just thought we could go for a walk or something."

"That sounds great." She stepped closer scanning my face as if looking for a secret hidden between my freckles. "It's been a few days. I was beginning to miss you."

"I missed you, too," I said, grabbing hold of her hand. "Let's toss your stuff in my car and take a stroll around here. Get your mind off of this place." I grabbed her lunch tote and walked her towards my car.

We walked slowly at first because of her sandals. I didn't mind because a light summer breeze blew in just as dusk was starting to descend on us. I took us down past Howard Community College and past the pretty townhome communities with their flowerbeds and brown picket fences. We were passing one of the busy intersections on the route when I finally asked her how her day went.

"A new person started." She picked up her pace, her sandals clacked with new force. "She's the new assistant photographer."

"The same position you applied for?" Kelly spent a whole weekend drafting and redrafting her resume and then taking new photos to add to her portfolio. She photographed the white lilies on my front flower bed like twenty times before satisfied with the shadowing and focus.

"Yep. I was told I didn't have the proper training." She marched onward. "Matt, the photography director, told me I should brush up with some courses and then maybe I'd be ready for the next opening."

"Well, that's encouraging, isn't it?"

She sighed. "It'll take ten years for the next opening."

I widened my step to keep up with her. "Maybe you can do some freelance stuff in the meantime?"

She wrapped her hair in a ponytail. "Can we change the subject?"

"Sure," I said. We walked for a good five minutes without speaking. I examined the blades of grass stretching out along the sidewalk cracks, the pebbles strewn out in front of me, and the remnants of berries shaken from the trees.

"Have you gotten my messages? I've tried calling you for two days now," she said.

"Yeah, I texted you back," I said, doling out a total white lie to cover up for the fact that I didn't have a clue how to tell Kelly about the gig and not make her feel worse.

She stopped. She stared at a sycamore tree on the other side of the road. Her lips, a thin, straight hundred and eighty degree line, sat still on her blank face. "You're lying."

"No. I'm not."

She creased her forehead and kept walking. "That's weird, then, how I never got it."

I reached for her hand again and we walked, swinging our arms rhythmically. "It happens."

A truck went by blowing diesel and dust into the air. One of her golden strands waved in front of her eyes and I brushed it away, tucking it behind her ear. "You're beautiful, you know?"

She shook off the compliment. The tips of her small, proportioned ears flushed a deep shade of red.

I stopped her, lifted her chin with my hand, and decided then was as good a time as ever to tell her my good news. "I've got a gig Friday night."

The sun held its position above the poplars just long enough for me to be able to see the delicate trace of a smile etch itself on her pretty face. "You have a gig?"

"Yes. I do." I shoved my joy back down, waiting for her to embrace it.

Her eyes brightened, and she showed me the perfectly white teeth and rosy cheeks that she'd kept hidden from me for some time. Even her curls seemed to spring back to life. "Wow. A gig."

"It's just a small backyard party," I said. "There'll be someone singing and I'll play guitar just like at McFaddens."

"I'm really happy for you." She bit her lower lip as she said that to me, her eyes squinting at something more than just the setting sun. She fidgeted with her necklace. "This could really lead to some great things."

Ever since the very beginning, I would dream up an elaborate scenario of how we'd celebrate my first real gig. First, no matter where I was in the world, she'd hop on a plane and get to me as soon as possible so she could spin me around until we got dizzy. Then, she'd shower me with all sorts of things like flowers and a party, and more photos of me on stage than could fill one hundred memory books.

"I hope so," I said, settling on her smile instead.

~ ~

The driveway to the gig house was hidden by a grove of trees. Thankfully Gabby had sprinkled a few landmarks in her email to me, so when I saw the deer crossing sign I slammed on my brakes and wheeled onto the driveway. Gabby mentioned it was long, but after a half mile I started to panic, thinking I'd turned at the wrong crossing sign. I couldn't be late for my first gig.

I sped up and rounded the curves with a skill that I never knew I had in me, brushing by the tree branches and ditches like they were just other cars riding alongside me on the interstate. Then, finally the trees opened up and I could see the faded blue-jean sky ahead. Cars were snarled in tight on each side of the driveway. I could see the white octagon-shaped house in the distance. Three stories towered on top of each other, dwarfing the maples that protected it. A man in a suit stood at the top of the driveway and flagged for me to reverse. I took one look over my shoulder at the winding string of cars and the narrow path I had just survived and panicked again.

I stepped out of my car, and he jogged towards me. "You'll have to back it up. There's no more room up here." Cars piled in a heap in front of the house's eight-car garage. I'd be lucky to make it through the maze on foot.

"There's no way I can drive in reverse," I told him.

"I'll take it back for you," he said.

I was just about to hand him my keys and ask him why he couldn't have been standing at the beginning of the driveway to warn guests of the tangled web of cars ahead, when his face fell flat. I looked back and four more cars had approached.

"Oh, this isn't good." He wiped his brow with the back of his hand. "All of this for a twenty-year-old girl's birthday party." He stomped off towards the other cars. "Just leave your keys in your car," he yelled over his shoulder to me.

Part of me was relieved that the gig already had a flaw. That eased some of the pressure for me. I couldn't totally screw it up all by myself now.

I put the keys back in the ignition to my Civic. I caught my breath as I stared up at the geometric mansion. Its white pillars seemed to reach up to the early moon. A dazzling chandelier hung in the center window like a giant diamond. Balconies the size of my bedroom perched out from the house, each with its own set of chaise lounges and overflowing flower pots.

It was a warm, clear night. The full moon was climbing the twilight sky and operating like a spotlight. I could see the tennis and basketball courts, and the Olympic-sized pool off to the side. A group of people stood out on the back patio and smoked. Their voices bounced off the forest of trees lining the outskirts of the property.

I opened the backdoor of my car to get Tangerine Twist. I swept her up into my arms and kissed her case for luck. "It's you and me, Tang. Let's not screw this up."

I scanned my outfit one last time, praying what I had bought would work. The long tunic and skinny jeans looked great on the mannequin.

I stood amidst the rich chaos surrounding the octagon palace; a train of cars piling up behind and a stately mansion worthy of tour groups, gift shops, and entrance fees in front.

I smoothed my hand over hair to tame any fly-aways from the drive over, then walked towards the house, shouldering Tangerine Twist on my back. I passed by a red Mustang with a glittery license plate that read *KMUSIC*. My stomach flipped.

~ ~

I knocked on the red door. A butler ushered me. I expected to see marble and lots of glass; sterile and stiff. But, instead plants filled the colossal space, breathing warmth and a sense of comfort and casualness into it. A mural of a garden, with stone steps and ivy and roses crawling up its archways, blanketed the walls. Thoughtful lights illuminated mini waterfalls and weathered pottery making it look like a sunny summer day when the sweet smell of flowers and the buzz of honeybees peaked.

The foyer stretched what seemed to be the length of a football field, opening up to French doors. People filtered in and out through them from the back patio.

"Are you Becca?" the butler asked.

I nodded.

"Kara is waiting for you out back," he said.

I drew a deep breath and followed him. The smell of teriyaki and marinara wafted through the air. Waiters in tuxedos skirted around holding trays at shoulder height, offering stuffed mushrooms and coconut shrimp. That's when I realized I had forgotten to eat that piece of pizza I had tossed into the microwave before jumping in the shower.

Kara was talking to a group of people when I walked out onto the patio. She wore a simple black dress that hugged her body and a turquoise beaded necklace draped down past her chest. Her hair, smooth and straight as glass, fell to the mid of her tanned back. Soft accent layers brushed over her cheeks. I had never seen someone look so sexy and sun-kissed in all of my life.

When she saw me, she immediately excused herself from the group and drifted my way.

"I'm so glad you could come." She stretched back and checked me out from head to toe. "Nice outfit."

My face flushed. "Thanks. I wasn't quite sure how to dress for this."

"Well, it's perfect." She clapped her hands together. "Listen, I really appreciate you coming. My usual guitarist is 'finding herself' somewhere out in the jungles of Brazil."

I couldn't imagine what kind of an idiot would purposely choose to trek over fire ants, anacondas, and the grounds of indigenous tribes instead of hang with Kara. "Well, I'm glad I could be here to help."

She started towards the stage area where her Gibson stood proud, the spotlights gleaming off its steel strings. I towed behind her. Her ass cocked side-to-side in a slow provocative beat. She talked to me over her shoulder. "I thought we could pick up from where we left off the other night. Maybe jump into those songs again and then get a little daring as the night progresses?"

I would've been willing to stand on my head and whistle Dixie all night if that's what she wanted. "I'll follow your lead."

~~

Once on stage, I pulled Tang out of her case and found a note from Kelly wishing me luck and letting me know I deserved this moment. She had sprayed my favorite perfume on it, Beautiful from Este Lauder. I chuckled softly, then tucked it in my front pocket. In an instant, I felt justified to be happy.

Kara was talking to Gabby off to the side. Everyone seemed to be checking her out, and she didn't seem to notice.

I sat on the stage and studied the small cliques of people before me, munching, drinking, and laughing. Their ages ranged from twenty to seventy. Some wore elegant gowns, while others dressed down in dark jeans and accented t-shirts. The scene looked like a Sunday evening in the Harbor, minus the paddleboats and Lady Baltimore ship. People snaked about grazing on the energy around them. A pair of Yorkies chased each other under a table overflowing with sushi. A swarm of pretty girls flitted about sipping champagne. A group of men wearing golf shirts smoked cigars and sipped brandy. Hundreds of people swirled around the expanse of green grass and pavers, talking and smiling. A few curious people passed by and stretched their eyes up to me, inspecting our guitars, our lighting, and our microphones. If they stood close enough, they could probably catch a good buzz off my adrenaline rush.

Kara walked over to me and sat.

"Are you sure it's okay for me to be here?" I asked her.

"Of course, sweetie." She sat forward to tune her Hummingbird. Soft glitter sparkled along her cheeks.

I adjusted my foot against the stand. Then, Kara adjusted her mic and reached over and adjusted mine so it was level with my mouth. I tapped it and it knocked back. My throat tightened. I looked over at Kara and she curled up the corner of her mouth and winked. My breathing sped up.

"What do you want to start with?" she asked.

My heart labored on, pounding and dancing wildly under my tunic. "Anything is fine."

"How about a little John Mayer?" The tiki torches reflected specks of caramel in her eyes.

"Sure." I wanted the answer to come out light and breezy. Instead, it rolled out like a powerful thunder clap, boisterous, echoing, and pounding against the stillness between us.

"Do you need the music or can you play by ear?" she asked.

"Music sheets just get in the way."

"Girl after my own heart." Kara broke right into counting down our first four beats, then fingered the opening of "Your Body is a Wonderland."

I sat mesmerized by her beauty, the way her fingers cradled her pick, her hair cascaded down around her breasts, and her eyes fluttered with the melody. I slid my fingertip across my pickguard waiting for the right moment to interfere. I noticed Gabby standing off to the side. She plowed her arms through the air in propeller fashion obviously annoyed at my just sitting there drooling over her sister like a rabid fan. So, I feathered my strings ever so lightly, catching up to Kara's count.

I picked alongside her, easing into the moment the way I would slip into a cold pool. I floated my attention over to Kara and was suddenly spellbound with a yin yang tattoo extending up the back of her neck. As she started to sing about candy lips and bubble gum tongues, I started to relax and really feel the song.

The crowd tightened in, their loud voices hushing to whispers— whispers that Kara's guitar easily treaded over. My light fingering murmured in the background. Then, Kara stepped it up. She jammed on her guitar, improvising, going way off in a jazzy tangent. I strummed along trivially, admiring her, timid to mess with her sound and amused with her bravado. Her fingers, powered by some mighty force, generated a friction so sweet and seamless, it cut through the air like a butter knife to Kobe steak. I stopped playing and just watched, my jaw dropped down to my lap. Even the Yorkies stopped chasing each other, the men in the corner quit puffing on their cigars, and the chatty people sealed their lips and nodded their approvals to each other.

Hundreds of eyes reached out to Kara, engaged. Mine did too.

She slipped back into the familiar melody, finishing on pitch. Then, she turned to me. "Play with me," she said.

Oh God how I wanted to. I'd give anything to be that worthy. "I think these people will start throwing shrimp at me if I cut in."

She wrapped her hands around the mic and leaned her lips in close to it. Then, she curled her eyes up to the attentive crowd. "My friend here would like to play you a song, but I think she needs a little coaxing." Her voice echoed across the yard, bouncing off the tall shrubbery. "Who wants to hear her sweet voice as much as I do?"

A string of claps ricocheted, then fizzled.

"What's it going to be?" she asked me.

I wagged my head in defiance. My tongue suddenly paralyzed itself.

Kara covered her mic. "What's wrong? You look like you're ready to faint."

"I don't think I'm ready for this," I said to her. The little hairs on my arms stood up saluting the humid evening as if begging for reprieve from me.

"Just feel the music and forget everything else."

I must have flushed ten different shades of red, embarrassed to be so scared of something that was supposed to be so natural to me. I just nodded, afraid to fully commit. Nausea crawled up the back of my throat.

"I've got your back," she said, placing her hand on my knee.

I involuntarily folded mine over hers and squeezed. "Thanks. I just have to catch my bearings. Just start anything and I'll jump in."

Kara clucked her tongue, slipped her hand away, and set out to perform a Sheryl Crow song.

I just stared down at my black boots, following the edge of a line of dust on it from the driveway. I tried to steady my breathing while counseling myself to toughen up. Singers sing. Guitarists play guitars. I wasn't going to make a living as a performer by analyzing tracks of dirt on my shoe.

Well into her second line of "Soak up the Sun," I drew in a sharp breath and dove in head first, desperate to save myself from drowning in a sea of regret. At first, I sort of flapped around in search of my footing. My voice teemed out soft and breathy from my throat. I glanced at Kara, and a certified smile was dancing clear across her face. The deeper I dug inward for strength in my voice, the wider her smile stretched. The spokes in her eyes spiraled to life, pushing me to dig even deeper. I balanced on Kara's notes, resting gladly against the shadows of her lure until I was brave enough to take the plunge, open up wide, and let the music flow between us.

The music just took over, picking me up and slinging me over its shoulder and carrying me off like a lily pad on a rapid. Kara and I balanced against each other, connected by invisible tethers. She pulled, I followed. I leapt, she was right behind me. We acted, the crowd reacted. We trekked out of the song's normal melody, the crowd applauded. We reached for a higher range, the crowd went wild.

I felt like a puppet, dangling, yielding, flexible, and completely safe knowing Kara had the strings and could swoop me up and place me back on stage, should I fall from grace and forget the lyrics. My fingers were moving, my voice was rising, and my spirit spinning around with Kara's on the craziest high.

The energy radiated. People started to dance with their arms weaving around their partners' waists. Others bounced their heads to the beat, their primped flips and tousled waves bobbing against the evening sky. I knew, I just absolutely knew, that this was the moment my grandpa had spent countless years prepping me for—that slit in time when the average transformed itself into that intangible force, a force so intense it couldn't be faced head on or it'd blind a person.

Kara crooned her guitar to the crowd, and they devoured her, scraping up every morsel of her golden flecked skin, taut arms, and delicate face. Sex appeal dripped off of her, and I had a front row seat with my mouth opened wide, ready and able to drink it all up.

At the end of our song, she circled up around me, cocking her head just enough for me to catch a glimpse of a freckle right below her left eye, and whispered, "I think they liked you."

She grabbed my hand and I stood, bubbling over in her soft caress. We bowed together. The crowd went nuts, clapping and whistling.

I couldn't imagine experiencing anything more beautiful and satisfying than this.

This was my calling.

~ ~

Later that night, I climbed into my empty bed and hugged my sheets tight. I closed my eyes and tried my best to fall asleep. Three hours later, I was still lingering on Kara and the warm ripples running through my body from the curious glances she passed my way all night long. I was hungry and starved for more euphoria.

I stretched and headed over to the fridge for a drink. That's when I saw my cell teetering on the counter and heard the voice message alert beep. It was Kelly. She ranted on and on about a corkscrew she was buying at a Pampered Chef party she was at and begged me to call her back to let her know if I wanted one of my very own. Her words slurred. Giggles bubbled in the background, and she ended the call with a hiccup. I flipped my phone shut and stared at it for a moment wondering what possessed her to get drunk. I'd only seen her drunk once, and that was only because someone had spiked the punch at one of Margie's spa parties.

## Chapter Four

I remembered the first time I had made love to Kelly. I had planned our special moment like a bride would plan her wedding night. I even went as far as to arrange for someone to come into our hotel room ten minutes before we planned to arrive and spread rose petals over the bed, light a few dozen candles, and turn on a CD of piano music. I wanted our first time to be perfect. All that prep work took her breath away when I opened the door for her. She started to cry instantly, falling into my arms and cradling her head against my chest. We made love for three hours that night. She confessed later while we were in the shower lathering soap bubbles onto each other's breasts, that it was her first time ever having an orgasm, and that she was already fully addicted to them. So right there, water cascading over us, we made love again, shaking with pleasure in each other's arms.

Now I couldn't remember the last time we had sex. Maybe three months ago? Or had it been even longer? I'd stopped counting, as well as initiating. We just sort of fell into a comfortable mode where instead of devouring each other, we gorged ourselves on sweets, salt, and countless hours of reality television and lifetime movies.

Loud meringue music bellowed out of the Dijon colored stucco walls at the El Dorado restaurant, Kelly's and my favorite place for Mexican cuisine. Authentic and rich in flavor, the place churned out lots of satisfied customers.

I sat across from Kelly, trying my best to snuff out some of the leftover capriciousness from my incredible evening with Kara. All I had to do was think of Kara and I could feel my eyes start to sparkle, my cheeks blush, and the corners of my lips pull upward. These were feelings I hadn't experienced in quite a while. I felt light, breezy, and flirty.

We both dunked our chips into the salsa at the same time. She tapped her chip against mine in a friendly sword fighting move. I rescinded, dropping my chip and holding my hands up in a pardon. She giggled, scooped it up, and gobbled it.

"So, did you have fun last night?" I asked, eyeing her bright crimson painted fingernails, an odd overcoat for her typical filed, naked nails.

"I don't even remember." She took a sip of her iced tea. "The girls from work are crazy and persuasive. They got me drunk."

"I heard."

She smirked. "I can't remember the last time I had such a good time. I woke up with one hell of a headache this morning. But, it's gone now."

She reeled another chip into her mouth and crunched down.

I fidgeted, took a sip of my soda. "I've been trying to get you drunk for years now. So, what gives?"

She cornered me against the back of my seat with her baby blue eyes. "I was just having fun. Bonnie invited me. You were at your gig, so, I went. But, you know me. I hate parties. Probably a good thing I was drunk." She reached for another chip and dunked it. She swirled it around, gathering up huge chunks of tomato. She feathered it into her mouth and some dribbled down to her shirt without her realizing. I chuckled and handed her a napkin. She smeared it until she looked like she had taken a shot to the chest at close range. She tossed the balled up napkin aside and continued to dig in.

We chomped away and in between talked more than we had in the past couple of weeks. We carried on about the Red Sox and about the corkscrew she ended up buying me for the wine I was starting to guess she'd be drinking with me. Long after our waiter served us our enchiladas and beans, we were still talking on and on about trivial things like how the tomato plants in her garden were starting to bloom, and how my car needed some new floor mats and more Freon eventually. We talked about the party, the food served, and the way her friend's apartment was decorated.

We covered just about everything; in details so clear I could taste and smell them. Then, she clasped her hands over mine the way she used to do when she was ready for a serious talk. "So, tell me how last night went. I want to hear every detail. Did you get a standing ovation? Did you play Led Zeppelin? Did you sing?"

And just like that our world seemed to rotate back on its axis. I told her everything, about the dogs running around with bows on their heads, the applause, the cheers, and the harmonizing. I left out no detail. Well, except for one. Kara. She didn't need to know everything. She just needed to know the stuff that'd keep her smiling back at me.

~ ~

The next afternoon, I drove to Elkridge State Park, and with Tangerine Twist buckled to my back, I walked out to the fishing lake. I loved sitting on one particular wooden bench and watching the insects skim across the water. A forest dotted the far lying outskirts, while wild rhubarb and morning glories fenced in the shallow end. A dry-rotted log sat like a stoic lifeguard to my right, serving as a refuge for tired birds. A few years back, I had carved "Becca loves Kelly" into the log. Despite being faded a bit, and crowded by other carvings, it still popped out at me.

Elkridge Park was one of those few peaceful spots in Maryland spared by the influx of transients. It was a mental pilgrimage of sorts, a place to escape from society. The adjoining river stretched for miles, leaving enough room for everyone to enjoy the tranquility of nature, complete with an orchestra of cicadas providing the background soundtrack. That was the perfect place for me to come and practice complex classical pieces.

Clouds as wispy as cobwebs floated in the sky, and humid air rolled in over the tops of the trees. I breathed in the smell of moss and pine, as I buried my toes into the squishy sand. I fiddled the strings, sliding into rhythm with the insects. I starting playing a new song I'd been working on for months. Chiseling away at it, smoothing out its edges and polishing where I thought it really needed to shine, I was motivated to turn it into something Kelly would love.

Two hours had passed before I looked down at my watch. I could've sat there all day, basking in my good mood. Life was good. And it was only going to get better from here.

~ ~

A little while later, I drove to Margie's salon to get my hair cut. Swollen and frizzy from the humidity, I felt like I had a head of cotton candy. I wrapped it tightly into a ponytail and walked into Capella's Salon and Day Spa, excited to tell Margie about my gig and about Kelly coming out of her funk.

The scents of mint and lavender curled around me. Margie was blow drying someone's hair. The receptionist offered me a cup of tea with honey and a squeeze of orange. She sided that with a slice of cinnamon swirl cake.

I sat on a wicker couch and observed. Stylists peppered the air with conversation. They wore black aprons, white shirts, and pencil skirts in a rainbow of colors. Not a strand of their hair missed an ounce of style. Products lined a series of shelves stretching the length of the waiting area and securing a line of privacy for those receiving pedicures. Each bottle lined up perfectly on glass so clean they looked like they were floating. Even the fake rhododendrons gleamed.

A young girl, not more than eighteen, ushered me to the shampoo chair. We brushed by Margie, and she half-smiled. Her eyes sunk deep, appearing more hollowed than a gutted Halloween pumpkin.

"Use the smoothing shampoo and conditioner on her," Margie said to the girl. A hint of rasp trailed her words.

I was just about to stop and ask her if she was feeling okay, when I noticed Marc's empty station. At that, I just kept moving my feet ahead, instantly dreading the reason.

A few minutes later, with my hair sleeked back in a towel, I sat in Margie's chair waiting for her to finish hugging her client goodbye. My eyes darted to Marc's empty counter. Everything, down to the brush holder, was void of him.

Margie scooped up a towel from the floor, then dragged herself over to me. The sag of her mouth served as an obvious preamble of the words to come. "He left me."

"What happened?"

She stepped in front of me and whispered, "I fucked up." She sighed.

"The guy at the club?"

She nodded. "Brian had texted me while I was in the shower asking if we could get together, and Marc read it. Then, he tossed the cell into the shower with me."

I nodded, treading that line between judging and understanding.

"It was just coffee," she said.

"Marc didn't believe you." I said, declaring it more than asking.

"No. He said he's done with me. That he can't trust me anymore." Her chin trembled.

I bit my lower lip. "I'm so sorry," I said. The words hung out to dry, lonely and frazzled.

I scanned his empty station again, wishing the picture of the four of us at Nags Head would reappear right below the Matrix sticker. "Maybe he just needs some time to see that he can trust you."

"Marc's not like that." She stepped back around my chair and started combing my hair, pulling it and hurting my scalp. I just gritted my teeth and let her. She started chopping through my hair, texturing it like a maniac. Tears spilled down her face. Her mascara smudged. She sniffed and wiped her face with the back of her hand, gulping back deeper sobs.

"When did this happen?"

"The day after he got back from his trip."

I grabbed her arm to stop her frenetic chopping. "How come you didn't call us?"

"It's embarrassing," she said and zoned back into my haircut, probably wishing she could jump inside my jungle of hair and hide.

She combed, cut, re-combed and re-cut over and over again until I felt like I had lost ten pounds of hair. I sat as still as the dry-rotted log on Elkridge Lake, taking on a carving of my own. At one point, my cell vibrated in my pocketbook, but I was too afraid to move. Every two minutes it buzzed against my wallet, acting like an impatient alert, screaming at me to pick it up. But, I waited until I was clear outside the salon's doors before I dared to check it.

An unrecognizable number.

"It's Kara. Free for dinner tonight?"

In those seconds it took me to catch my breath, I lost all sense of reason. Before I knew it, I was texting her back and asking her where.

~ ~

Around four o'clock that afternoon, Kelly unlocked the door to my condo and entered with an armful of grocery bags. I helped her set them on the counter, but then a carton of eggs slid out and sailed down to the floor. Kelly and I both dove for it, clunking our heads together and falling flat on our asses. Yolk puddled around us. Kelly plucked up two that survived the impact, holding them in the air like they were rare gems. "This was all I needed anyway." Yolk spilled down her arms and into her shirt.

So there we were, splattered and battered, stuck to the floor with nothing to do but stare at each other and giggle like a couple of school girls. "What were you planning on making with these?" I asked her.

"Cookies."

"What's the occasion?"

"Nothing. I just thought I'd make you some."

"You don't have to do that," I said, following her around the breakfast bar into the kitchen. My sneakers squished. I strung out a six-footer piece of paper towel from the roll.

"I thought we could rent a movie and stay in tonight. Cookies will hit the spot, don't you think?" She started to pull the milk, mix, and butter out of the bag.

"I actually got invited to get something to eat with that girl, Kara, from the gig."

Kelly poured soap into a bowl and stuck it under the faucet. "Oh." She plucked up the sponge and started to scrub the bowl. "I probably should've called you first, I guess, huh?"

I could've replaced her crooked smile by asking her to come out, too. I knew that's what she really wanted me to do at that point. "I didn't know you were going to stop by."

"It's no big deal." She wiped her hands on her sweatpants. "Where are you going to go for dinner?"

"Some sushi place."

She wrinkled her nose. "Have fun with that." She punched my arm lightly, and a stream of runny yolk drizzled in the wake of her fist. "Oh, I'm sorry." She reached for a towel and smeared it a little deeper onto my bare arm. "I'm making a huge mess."

I stopped her. "I talked to Margie today."

"Oh? How's she doing?"

"Marc left her."

"What?" The spokes in her eyes cranked and twitched. "When?"

"A few days ago, I guess."

"She told you?"

"She was pretty upset. She was hacking away at my hair."

She skimmed it with her stunned eyes. "It looks fine." She stole the paper towels from my hand and scooped down. She smeared them against the floor, working the eggs into a slick mess. I was certain my floor would never be the same again.

~ ~

On my way to meet Kara, I stopped by Walgreens to pick up my PMS prescription. Lately, my periods had taken up war, firing assaults against my vulnerable belly so fierce even Hitler might have turned his head in weakness. Kelly kept telling me to stop drinking coffee, cut out the chocolate, and forget the martinis. I'd rather suffer the havoc wrought on my innards than give up those treasures.

I walked down an aisle and grabbed a Hershey bar before stealing a glance at myself in the oval mirror dangling dangerously close to a set of fluorescent bulbs above. That night was the first time in years that I wore anything more than mascara and lip gloss. I barely recognized myself; plum lips, flushed cheeks, and smoky eyes.

I breezed up the aisle towards the line formed at the pharmacy counter. The tech was cashing out a plump lady wearing a tight red dress, which buckled in all the wrong places. I glanced over to watch some kid wailing off to the side, pulling at his mother's skirt as she sat with her arm corked into one of those blood pressure machines. A few feet closer to me, an older gentleman, with eye glasses as thick as ice cubes, was reading the back of a bottle of Chromium Picolinate. Right in front of me was a young girl smelling of coconut oil. Her cinnamon hair was pinned to her back in a ponytail. Her bathing suit strap was tied in a bow at the nape of her neck. A few speckles of sand glistened around her sun-kissed shoulder blades. She reminded me of a young Kara with the subtle tilt of her head, the gentle curve of her hips, and the confident way she caressed the air around her.

Kara. She was probably driving in her Mustang, already on her way to meet me.

My stomach leaped into a series of pirouettes.

In less than fifteen minutes, I'd be sitting across from her, a mere two feet of table separating the two of us.

My head swirled way too euphorically.

~ ~

I showed up at Palagios restaurant with knees as slack as wet noodles, and wobbled up to a man behind a marble podium. He looked up over his glasses at me, inspecting every square inch of my pathetic attempt to look cool and collected.

"Do you have a reservation?" he asked, his steel hair every bit as hard as his stern face.

"Yes," I said through my coat of nerves. "I think it may be under Kara Travers?"

He nodded, pushed his glasses further back against his nose, and scribbled something on his list. "Follow me."

My heart sputtered, while my heels tangled into the spongy charcoal fibers of the carpet. I followed him past his stately perch and into the dining room where a sea of blue blazers and slinky black dresses hovered. Waiters walked around stiff as plywood wearing fake smiles. The room smelled like lemon grass and garlic.

The last time I entered a place as stuffy as that I was ten-years-old and at my aunt's surprise fortieth birthday party. We all got decked out in frilly party dresses and fancy suits. My mother's hair looked like a bee hive. My dad's resembled a shiny coat of paint. They smelled like they had bathed in Old Spice. All of my extended family was there, even including the relatives my mom was always damning to hell or praying would be struck by a meteorite. My aunt walked around like she had a metal rod sticking up the back of her dress. Every time I snuck a glance at her, she was tilting her head way back and cackling. The people around her just sort of arched their eyebrows high at each other waiting for my aunt's head to make landfall again. That night was a blur mostly because a bunch of us kids snuck beer into the coat room and got drunk. It was my first time drinking, and I got violently sick. While the older cousins cracked themselves up imitating the adults, I huddled against a coat rack, shivering like a bum on a New York City street corner in the middle of a blizzard and promising God I'd never drink again if he'd help me to stop throwing up.

The maître d led me towards an archway. Through it, I could see Kara huddled up near Gabby, engrossed in conversation. Gabby's hair, wild with big curls, clogged my view of Kara. She towered over her sister like an annoying weed, choking out any chance for us of kindling that innocuous flirt I had dreamed up on my drive over.

I moved closer, and now I could see new caramel highlights trickling through Kara's mocha hair. When she turned her dark chocolate eyes up towards me, I melted into a gooey mess, barely able to move my feet forward.

Kara stood and extended her hand, and I instinctively leaned forward and planted my lips on her soft cheek.

"Thanks for coming," she said, her face still close enough to mine that I could feel her breath wash over me.

"You're welcome. Thanks for inviting me."

With pleasantries put aside, she pulled out a chair for me before folding into hers again.

I looked at Gabby. "Hi," I said, nodding and offering her sister a smile, trying my best to squash the unjustly perturbed feeling that she was even there.

"Hey, Becca." A lopsided smile sprang up on her face as her voice rose a decibel too high for the intimate setting.

A waiter with a British accent brushed up to our round table and handed us each a wine list. Gabby studied it. Kara tossed it to the table, flipped her hair behind her shoulders, and widened her eyes at me. She reeled me in with an amused look that was dancing across her face.

Breath cut short, I buried my face behind my wine list, pretending to study it hard just like Gabby. I read each wine silently, unable to recognize a single one. I'd just point to one and pray it would end up being fruity.

When the waiter returned with his arms folded neatly behind his back like a well-packaged dress shirt, Gabby handed him her wine list. "We're going to take a bottle of the Veuve Clicquot."

He gathered our wine lists and floated off.

Gabby turned to me. "You'll love it. Trust me." She smiled. "It's intense, well-balanced, with a remarkable fruity structure."

I just nodded and fled to my water glass. I was out of my league on all fronts.

For the entire meal, Gabby droned on about her life. I nibbled on my sushi, wishing I had chosen the porter house steak, while she filled me in on her life story. She graduated from UMUC's business management program with a bachelor's degree. She wanted to be viewed as more credible, so she continued on for her master of science in business management, and while taking a marketing course discovered her love for promotions, specifically in the music industry. Her semester long project was to promote a mock event, so she chose to go a step above and beyond, rolled up her sleeves, and promoted the shit out of a gig for Kara. Projected attendance was one hundred. Actual attendees topped out at over four hundred. She credited her barter methods and knack for selling herself for filling most every seat in the Martin's West ballroom. Fast forward to today and her goal was to become one of the most successful promotions managers in the music industry. She was using Kara as a stepping stone; bringing her from a no name to a star. So far, the local scene had generated some significant buzz. A few groupies had created a fan Web site for her, detailing her every move on stage and listing her gigs for as far as they went. For now that was just three months out. The plan was to make that a solid ten months by the next year. Oh, and the other exciting plan that'd shoot her to the outer extremes of promotional success, furthering her chances of becoming known on a national level, was to get an album cut and get it played on the radio. Kara just needed a hook; something to set her apart from the others; and something with more of an edge that'd really make her pop.

Gabby finally took a breath.

All that will happen, she insisted.

Kara meanwhile was sucking her wine down and on glass number four already. I knew that because the entire time Gabby droned on about her life,

I never let Kara out of my peripheral sight. I could tell you how many times she nodded, nibbled on her salad, and even the number of times she blinked. I wondered how it could be that Kara looked every bit as fresh as she did at the beginning of Gabby's exhausting diatribe. By the time I dug my dessert spoon into the quarter-sized dollop of sherbet, I was physically incapable of smiling or nodding at Gabby any longer.

"Now all that being said, Kara and I are sort of in a predicament," Gabby said, her voice softer, slower, and more punctuated.

"Predicament?" I asked, the four syllables stretching way beyond normal rhythm.

"That's right." She paused and sat up straighter, bracing her wrists against the table. "Bottom line is we've been told by a few producers that Kara's single act is good, but that if she had someone to back her up, play off of her, and bring new harmonies to her music, her career could catapult. We need a duo partner. And we want that to be you."

"Me?"

The room grew quiet as the three of us sat staring back and forth at each other. I started to fumble with my fingers under the table. I dropped my napkin and licked my lips. I could've restrung my guitar in the bubble of time that sat between us.

"You're perfect." Gabby said. "The other night at that kid's party was my test for you, and you passed. You got the thumbs up from one of this region's hottest music producers."

Kara sat with her arms folded across her chest studying me. Her eyes twinkled. She winked at me, and I think my heart may have skipped a half beat.

"Are you interested?" Gabby asked.

I felt alive in a non-terrestrial way, like I was a flower growing in elapsed time and blooming petals larger than life. The room buzzed. And, even though my feet still rested on the carpet, my spirit lifted up to the ceiling and soared around up there with the beams and paned windows. My world had just opened up, and I was more than ready to start exploring it. I could barely keep my ass against the cushioned chair. I wanted to throw my hands up in the air and run through the restaurant whooping for joy. I'd heard of people who got lucky like that. Out of thin air, someone handed them their dream gift-wrapped and ready to open. Up to that point, I'd never even won a dollar scratch off ticket.

I didn't know the protocol on how I was supposed to react. My legs bounced and my heart leaped in my chest. I could hear Margie in my head telling me to calm the fuck down, negotiate, and scrutinize the details. But, when the screeching yelp barreled out from between my lips, fueled like a cannon, it ran over Margie's cautions and shot me up into a standing position. "Are you kidding?" My palms slapped the table like a couple of bricks. "Of course." Another cry of joy escaped. "Shit. Yes. Of course I'm interested."

Kara lounged back in her seat sporting a sexy, naughty smile. Her lips curled up, her eyes cradled a flirt, and her cheeks flushed. The only thing that could've heightened her to an even more dangerous level of sexiness would have been a cigarette dangling from her plump berry-toned lips.

A simple tilt of her head sent me reeling. That was when I sat back down again, clinging to the chair's arms for balance.

"Okay, let's discuss logistics," Gabby said. "First off, we'll need you to sign a twelve- month contract with us."

"Sure, I'll sign whatever." My heart raced.

"Just to be clear, I'm your promo manager. What I say goes. You need to trust me. As you can imagine, I have a vested interest both personally and professionally. Kara's my sister and her success is pretty damn important to me."

I nodded.

"Professionally, this is my chance to prove to the music industry that I have what it takes to take a couple of artists from middle of the road to super stardom."

"I totally understand," I said, floating away on the magic carpet ride.

"Of course, now we'll have to work on your image a bit, but that shouldn't be too big of a deal. We've got to do something with that haircut. You'll also need to get a few performance pieces for your wardrobe. I'll draw up the paperwork and propose a payment plan by tomorrow night. Are you still working at that bar?"

"Pub," I said. "And, yes, I am."

"Quit. First show is in a week. Kara and I have a family thing to attend over the next day or two, so we'll start rehearsing mid-week."

I started to run through the things in my mind that I needed to get through. Tell Kelly. Quit McFadden's. Go shopping.

"We're going to hit the ground running. It'll be a lot of hard work and hours together."

I nodded, never letting go of the smile dancing across my face as I imagined late nights in the studio jamming with Kara. Gabby blabbered on about typical gig expenses and wardrobe for several more minutes, but I didn't hear any details. I just kept nodding and pinching my arms to make sure I was not dreaming. I tried my best to stay grounded. I sped from zero to one hundred in five second intervals, all while trying to figure out what I did to deserve all of this.

## Chapter Five

"Are you home, yet?" I asked Kelly. My joy overflowed into my cell, short-circuiting the air waves. I pictured a satellite tower sparking and lighting up the night sky with my excitement.

"I got home a few minutes ago," she said. "What are you so excited about?"

"I'll be there in a half hour to explain."

"Can you give me a hint at least?" she asked.

"Nope. Sorry. See you in a few." I chuckled then hung up.

I sat there in my recliner and lingered on my good fortune for a few minutes more, afraid it would disappear if I stopped replaying the night in my mind. I plucked up my jotter pad and pen from the end table and scribbled my name, exaggerating the B and J.

Too legible.

I tried again, squishing the letters together in fancy swirls. At arm's length, my signature looked like a real autograph, which sent a nervous jitter coursing through me.

I looked around my condo and even it seemed different to me now, like we didn't match anymore. The trusty couch that Margie was ready to toss into a dumpster three years ago sat against my pale orange living room wall like a stranger, showing its age and complacency. Some of the seams on the cushions bulged, exposing fuzzy white stuffing, like an unkempt beard lacking the melanin of youth. No matter how many times I vacuumed and spot cleaned the worn burlap, it remained hostage to the years behind it, unwilling to move forward and at least try to look like something worthy of company. The longer I stared at it, the more it annoyed me. It was dull and oppressed, willing to collect dust as I would soon speed by it now on my way up to bigger and better things. I climbed off my recliner and patted it. "I think it's time you retire." I imagined brown leather in its place.

I walked to the front door, flicked the light switch off, and left the couch sitting in the dark as I stepped out of my old confines and into my new life.

~~

Kelly's parents' house was lit up like a Christmas tree. Every window glowed with a fake candle that her mother plugged in each night. Kelly's beat-up Volvo hugged the side of the driveway, mere centimeters from the lush grass her father painstakingly nurtured all summer long. Their tidy household was one to be envied by those who didn't know any better.

She was sitting on the front stoop. Her arms twisted in front of her, draping between her legs.

When I climbed out of my car, she popped up and ran towards me. "My parents are due home any minute, so do you want to just take a walk?" She reached down for my hand and skipped forward towards the street before I could answer. When we rounded the bend of her yard she finally stopped and asked me. "So? Fill me in."

On the drive over I imagined a climatic build-up where one adjective perched on top of another until the excitement buckled under the pressure and buried us in a pile of good news. But, now that I was standing there in front of her, I couldn't contain myself a second longer. I just blurted it out, leaving the fluff at our feet. "I just joined a duo. I have my first official gig as Kara's partner in a week."

First Kelly squealed. Then, to my delight, she jumped up into my arms, wrapping her arms and feet around me. I cradled her and swung her around, fueled by the bright and shining future ahead of us. "This is it. No more waiting." I eased her down and stood face-to-face, swinging our arms in front of us. "She even asked me to sign a twelve month contract."

"A contract? Really?" Her smile strained. I could see it even through the dark spears of night that fell between us, a quick and deadly prick to my bubble of joy.

"Yeah, it's standard." I said that like I'd signed a dozen of them already.

She dropped her hands. "Wow! Okay, so tell me about it."

I cradled my hands around her waist.

A car approached.

She jumped away from me, waving as her neighbor passed by.

When the dark protected us again, she inched back up to me. "So, tell me."

I told her everything. About how I'd have to quit McFadden's, attend practices, buy new clothes, and write new songs, and about how great our future would be.

She soaked it all up, nodding when appropriate. My bubble was expanding beyond limits. Then, she asked. "So, when do I get to meet her?"

~ ~

The next day, I sat hostage in front of my laptop, waiting for Gabby's email with the contract to pop into my inbox. By ten o'clock in the morning, I had already consumed a pot of coffee and eaten two breakfasts—first one scrambled eggs and wheat toast, second a blueberry muffin, freshly baked in my oven at six a.m. upon waking to wait out the ridiculously long morning.

Bloated and strung out on caffeine and sugar, I climbed off my balance ball and dug my guitar out of her case. I worked a bit more on a new song I started. I wasn't feeling the melody the way I intended, so I reworked it, raising the capo a few frets to get a richer, higher pitch. I also played with the scale a bit more.

By two-thirty, slipping some cleaning into my practicing, I managed to scour the tub and facelift it with a fresh bead of pure white waterproof and mold-resistant caulking. I created a seamless spine that could withstand my hotter-than-hell showers for at least another six months.

When I still hadn't heard from her at four o'clock, I called out sick to McFadden's. I had no choice. Until I saw the contract, signed it, and delivered it back, I couldn't risk quitting. And, I certainly couldn't face Joe until then because my guilt would obviously sit on my face like a beacon. When I had spoken to Margie earlier that morning and told her my incredible news, she questioned how I'd be able to swing quitting my stable job for a pay I didn't even know would be there each week. I told her not to worry without getting too specific. Not even Kelly knew that I'd saved ten percent of my tips every night and invested lump sums of it in CDs over the years. Call it my secret cosmic superstition, but when I first started saving, a warped fear settled into my brain that if I'd told anyone about my investments, I'd jinx my dream. I interpreted the threat rather seriously, because after all, that money was my ticket to freedom—to bigger and better. If I spent modestly, I could last six months without a paycheck. Even as Margie probed me for more details on my monetary plan, I refused to disclose any particulars until I was certain Gabby and Kara would cement what they offered me the night before. I didn't want to mess with the cosmic work at hand. So, I simply told her I had complete faith the money would come flowing in right away. She told me I was a complete idiot and offered me a three month nest egg.

At six minutes after nine o'clock, Gabby's email sailed into my inbox, fanning me with a larger than life tailwind that practically blew me off my balance ball. I opened it and read Gabby's right-to-the-point address to me,

"Read, sign, and fax back. Mail originals to the address above. Practice session scheduled for six p.m. this Thursday, Vibrations Music Studios."

I held my breath for the minute or so that it took to print out the two page contract. Pretty much it just summed up to my agreeing to practice, perform, and travel as necessary with Kara for the next twelve months of my life. Translated into a language I could savor, what that really meant was that for the next three hundred and sixty-five days of my life, I was guaranteed a chance to live out my dream. I signed on the dotted line, just as I had practiced, placed it on the fax machine, and sent it off.

After jumping in place for several minutes, while clapping in between muffled screams into a pillow, I took a deep breath and called Kelly to report the start of our new life.

She didn't answer.

~ ~

The instant I turned on my cell phone the next morning, I had three urgent messages from Kelly who begged me to drop what I was doing and call her the second I got a chance. I looked at the clock and it was only six a.m. I called her, and before the phone could launch into ring number two she answered, sounding just as desperate to speak with me as she did in her voice messages. I could picture her with hair pulled back in a messy ponytail, wearing pink and white checkered pajama bottoms with an oversized Ravens t-shirt and pacing the floor.

"Have you seen my portfolio book with the pictures of Tommy's tournament?" Her voice hinged on frantic.

I glanced over at the coffee table where she left a pile of her photography bibles from her recently aborted funk period wondering what the hell could've been so urgent about pictures of Tommy kicking a soccer ball. Her breaths echoed in my ear, pushing me to clear through the cobwebs and snap into wakeup mode. I leapt over to the couch, unaware that I had left the blinds wide open the night before and was standing in my illuminated living room giving the entire neighborhood a free peak at my Hanes bikinis. I crouched low and looked for the portfolio, even though I had no clue what it looked like. I didn't even know such a thing existed. "I just see your books."

"Fuck."

In all of the three years I'd been with Kelly that was the first time I'd ever heard her say fuck. "I'll look better and give you a call in a few minutes."

"This is really important, Becca. My boss is giving me and Bonnie an opportunity to submit some photos. They need a cover shot of a kid playing soccer. This is my chance." She drew a breath. "I know I left it there."

"I'll look and call you back within ten minutes."

First thing I did when I hung up was drop down on all fours to scan the entire room. Fully committed to finding it and setting my day on a course I could appreciate, I studied the room from wall-to-wall. At first, I saw only a couple of popcorn kernels and a Popsicle wrapper under the couch, and some crumpled up napkins wedged under the foot of the end table.

What followed was a series of unfortunate events that pretty much shot to hell any luck that my day, or my future for that matter, would rise above that disastrous moment.

I climbed up and scoped out the room from my five-and-a-half-foot height, traversing around the room knowing Kelly was probably biting her nails down to nothing. I made it all the way past the couch and love seat, rounded the recliner, and was just about to survey the book shelf in the hallway when I stubbed my big toe on a ten pound dumbbell. The pain blinded me, forcing me to leap around screaming my own version of fuck repeatedly. I hopped on one foot, clamping my fingers around the toe I now suspected was broken. Then all hell broke loose. I fell, crashing into Tangerine Twist. The rest went down in slow motion. The tile sped towards me. Tangerine flew away from me and slammed into the foot massager Kelly had given me for my birthday. The cracking noise was deafening. My hand smacked the tile, then the rest of my body fell on top of it. When the crash ended, I convulsed into a series of stuttering sobs, the kind that emanate from the deep recesses of the belly. Two extremities, one obviously more important than the other, throbbed like a spike driven through my skull. My thumb—the one part of my life that I needed more than a leg—pulsed the color of an angry sky right before a severe thunderstorm. It doubled in size. Freshly filed just the night before, the nail that doubled as a pick for the past fifteen years now was nothing more than a jagged series of valleys and hills. Next blink, I searched out Tangerine and she lay face down on the tile, her burnt orange back warning me not to turn her over. I reached over and slowly lifted her. A crack, a good twelve inches long and as mute as a flat line on a heart monitor, had killed her.

Then, my phone rang.

Furious, I took that damn cell phone and flung it so hard against the wall that debris splattered back towards me. Five seconds of hell all because of a fucking book of pictures.

I cried for two hours, curled up beside my battered Tangerine, cradling my broken thumb between my hands and my swollen toe with my feet. Tang, my phone, and I, bruised and shattered, sprayed out in the room like victims of a war we didn't intend to fight, peripheral casualties in the wrong place at the wrong time only now to suffer the unconceivable consequences.

Bleary-eyed, I eventually dragged myself up, got dressed, and drove to the emergency room to get my finger set, feeling numb to the bone at my indelible loss.

By the time I'd gotten my thumb and toe squared away at Howard County General Hospital, purchased a new cell phone and gotten back to my condo, Kelly had already come and gone. She had tacked a note to my kitchen bulletin board telling me she found her portfolio, asking me what happened to Tang, and begging me to please give her a call as soon as I got in.

I removed the note from the corkboard and shredded it into a million pieces as best I could with my thumb splint. Four weeks until I could graduate to a flexible gauze cast. Prognosis: no guitar playing for at least eight weeks. I plopped down on the couch, propping my taped toes on a pillow and sinking into my broken night.

On Thursday, after dodging half a dozen calls from Kelly, I emerged from my condo and headed off to break the news to Kara and Gabby.

~ ~

At five-thirty, I pulled into the parking lot of Vibrations Music Studio. From the street, the studio didn't look big enough to house a store, all its inventory, plus a dozen teaching and recording studios. The stucco building squeezed in between an antique store and an ice cream parlor, the quintessential necessities of any Main Street in America. Parking was located in the rear. Along the side of the building, which seemed to stretch on a whole city block, were blown up snapshots of musicians jamming on guitars, beating drums, and rocking out. Psychedelic colors swirled in the background. Past the loading dock, I found a spot next to a minivan. A dad and his son climbed out. The boy carried a clarinet case. He smiled at me, fellow musician to musician. The dad, a balding guy in a suit, rushed him along. No time for niceties. I could hear his inner thoughts drumming, drop the kid off, follow up on emails over Blackberry, shuffle the kid home, pop a frozen dinner in microwave for him, then rush out and meet up with the board members to discuss how to spend corporate dollars. I'd rather break all my fingers than plow through my day like that.

Once they were out of sight, I watched a pigeon fly into a drain up on the roof. It kept popping his head up and down as if expecting I'd be brazen enough to climb up and snatch whatever it was he was trying to hide.

I looked down at my bandaged wound, imagining all sorts of fissures, broken blood vessels, and torn nerves and tendons all vying to work together again. I wished I could believe in that new age crap just that once. Let it prove my skeptic-self wrong.

Thirty minutes was a long time to kill. Too much time to think.

I should've warned Gabby and given her some time to sort through the options instead of just showing up with my broken thumb, swollen to oblivion. She'd take one look at me and write me off. She struck me as that type of person, quick to snap someone's dream like a twig if it interfered with her own. The Don Vito Corleone of the music promoters.

I folded my arms over my chest, reclined a bit, trying to relax before the bad news axe chopped me up into a million useless pieces. I felt like a patient waiting for test results that would tell me if I'd live or die.

Time dragged on. An eternity later, I still had ten minutes to go.

I couldn't decide whether to be early, on time, or five minutes late.

I did the math. It would probably take me three minutes to get out of my car, stroll really slow to the front of the place, and find our practice room. I figured I'd set out at one minute past six o'clock. That would put me in front of her a random four minutes late.

I blew out a deep breath, watched the clock switch from five fifty-two to five fifty-three.

My thumb throbbed. So, I elevated it on my console, holding it up like a wine glass ready to clank another in a toast.

I stared at a tree over the hood of corporate man's minivan and watched a squirrel traverse up its trunk with a shelled peanut in his mouth. He darted his head around, on full alert, as if waiting for someone to come along and fuck with him. I'd bet no one would dare. I bet if his girlfriend asked him to look for her hidden acorns, he'd have the smarts to not ram his foot into a rock, because he wouldn't be preoccupied with what her mental state of the moment was. Nothing would stand in the way of his coveted nuts. Every squirrel for himself.

Smart squirrel.

At five fifty-eight, I had to get into that building and get the moment of impact over with. Get what I deserved, one way or another. We'd see what the fate of the universe had in store for me. I never prayed much, but I damned well prayed my ass off as I climbed out of my car and tottered forward.

When I walked into the front door, an older man with curly gray hair greeted me.

"Practice rooms?" I asked.

He pointed up to an animated sign of a guitar. Lightning bolts fired out of its cartoon body. "Just follow these signs with Jazzy on them."

I followed the trail of Jazzy signs through the retail part of the store. Hundreds of feet of glass cases lined the wall to my left. Inside them were karaoke machines, amplifiers, microphones, recording devices—virtually everything you'd need to have a really cool party. A couple of teenaged boys jammed on electric guitars alongside a gigantic speaker. Some crazy, high-pitched heavy metal song sprang out of their fingertips, accompanied by head bangs, flips of hair, even the exaggerated furled lip of a rock star. When I passed by, they both looked up long enough to smile sheepishly at me, like I'd caught them sneaking a shot of their daddy's whiskey. Their cheeks even blushed.

I closed in on the end of the retail store to a gray door with no window. Jazzy pointed me forward. I opened up to a room the size of a football field. Lesson rooms draped each side. Off key notes rained through the air, followed by a couple of rambunctious teachers showing off the real way it should've been played.

In the heart and center of the room sat thousands of musical instruments and accessories. A musical candy shop. To the far end of the room was a knotty pine loft with half a dozen recording studios. Every door was shut, sealing out the noise with its sound proofed walls. Recording lights shined above every one.

Everyone wanted a record deal.

As I neared the end of the room, I entered one more doorway. Trusted Jazzy guided me through it, and escorted me towards a punk girl sitting behind a tall counter. She was playing jacks. The wall behind her listed three rules of the practice studios. *No smoking. No drugs. No bad vibes, and that includes music.* Her pink spikes grew red at the tips. An earring hung from her lip and reminded me of a barbed wire fence. I wondered if it hurt. I wondered what it would feel like to kiss someone with a jagged hoop earring cut into her lip like that.

"Hi," I said all casually. "I'm here for a practice session with Kara and Gabby Travers."

"Go through the door, last room on the left." She said that without ever taking her eye off her jacks.

I was shaking now. A gnawing nervous tick traveled in me, making me want to throw up.

I should've told Gabby way before that.

I pulled open the door and headed down a narrow hall to the last room on the left. Other than the occasional drumbeat or bass, the hall was surprisingly peaceful.

75

I stood in front of the door for much longer than a minute, trying to hear them, to work up the nerve to knock, and to turn that steel knob to enter. I wondered if she'd be wearing her hair straight, wavy, up, or down. Would she be wearing something casual like a tight pair of jeans and a fitted t-shirt, or something flirty and daring?

I knocked.

Kara said, "I'm coming."

Kara opened the door wearing a low-cut fitted t-shirt and a flirty skirt and sandals. "Hey," she doled out to me with a voice that could stir a sleeping tiger.

"Hey," I said with a half swallowed chuckle.

She opened the door wide, and I walked in past her with my thumb deftly hidden in my pocketbook. "Is Gabby coming?' I asked.

"No, she wanted to give us a chance to work together tonight. She won't really have much to do with our practices. She wouldn't know a C from a G."

The room, as silent and weightless as outer space, closed us off from the rest of humanity. My thumb, ballooning in my pocketbook, suddenly felt heavy, like gravity pinpointed its exact location and zeroed in on it. I stole a peek around the room and saw yellow ochre-colored walls, posters of Dave Matthews, Eric Clapton, and Jimi Hendrix, an electric guitar on a stand in the corner, wires haphazardly strewn around the floor like snakes, and charcoal gray commercial grade carpeting, the kind you'd find in a doctor's office. "Listen, I need to tell you something," I said.

She propped up on a stool, exposing her smooth, creamy legs. "Sounds serious."

I propped up on the stool next to hers, our knees a mere inch from touching. I managed to find my voice. "It sort of is serious." Her sweet eyes brimmed with curious twinkles. I dug out my thumb from underneath the rubble of gum, receipts, sunglasses, and various trinkets, holding it up like a carcass.

She leaned forward on her stool. Her sculpted ass rested dangerously close to its edge. She nurtured my broken thumb with her sweet eyes. "What happened?" She massaged the sterile gauze with her long sleek fingers, crooning over it like one would a cute injured puppy or baby bird.

I collapsed right into her sympathy. I looked straight into her mocha latte eyes and exaggerated the truth. "Rammed my foot into a thirty-pound dumbbell and then smashed into the ground, thumb first."

She stroked my immobilized thumb. "You poor thing. Does it hurt?"

"Yeah, a little."

She raised it to her mouth and soothed it with a kiss, seemingly unconcerned with what that injury would mean to her future career plans. Selflessly, she focused solely on my well-being. "How long before you can play guitar?" she asked.

I felt clouds of panic start to form, swirling around, engulfing me, and sweeping me away from the moment like a dust ball. "I'm hoping not too long," I said.

She cradled my thumb in her hands. "Listen. I'll talk to Gabby. All you have to do is focus on singing for now. We'll make this work." My impending singing catastrophe loomed like sandbags in my mind. As far as Kara knew, I could sing the National Anthem in front of hundreds of thousands of fans without as much as a breath out of gear. I could pretend to be cool as mint and deal with the foggy lyrics and the tunneled access to small quantities of air. Unlike at my Grandpa's funeral, I could hide behind Tangerine. Maybe nobody would notice the blue plastic plate cradling my thumb or the inexplicable crater on Tangerine's front board. How many details could a spotlight bring out? To me, I had only one choice. Pinch my noise and swallow the nasty grains of fear.

"Singing it is, then," I whispered, hovering between exhilaration and dread.

Kara continued to stare consolably down at my swollen extremity. "Have you been icing it?"

"Yes." I loved how her upper lip formed a perfect heart shape.

"Taking anti-inflammatory pills?"

"Yes." Her nose sloped like it was carved by Michelangelo himself.

"We need you better." She tapped the tip of my nose. "So, we've got to take real good care of that thumb."

Not wanting the doting to end, "I broke my toe, too."

She darted her eyes down to my open sandals and to the taped toes. "Oh my gosh." Her hand, soft as spun silk, now cradled my wrist.

I could've devoured her attention all night long, swung upside down from it, and flipped round-and-round on its strength and beauty. "I guess I've got a clumsy side to me."

"Well, clumsy, what do you say we get started before you do anymore damage?" She plucked up her Gibson from a stand. "How about 'Hey There Delilah'?"

I nodded and perched forward on my stool.

"Use the microphone so we can record it to see what we'll need to tweak."

I pulled the mic off its stand and clung to it for dear life, as she progressed forward with the intro. On cue, I broke in softly, singing to Hendrix and his banded afro. Halfway through my second verse, Kara stopped.

"Listen, you're a sexy girl." She paused and looked up at me, her golden flecks sparkling like jewels. "That's your selling point." She paused again, and up went her curvy lips, arching like a tiger in heat. "You can sing. But, you need to take it to a different level. You've got to expose that sexy side because that's what will win over the guys…" she paused. "…And the girls." When she spoke her words blew out of her lips so effortlessly. "Make that crowd fall in love with you."

I nodded, quick and dotted, like a bird pecking bread crumbs.

"I'll show you what I mean." She took my mic, and then closing her eyes, she gingerly brought her mouth right up to it. She carried her voice almost to a whisper. "When you sing into that microphone, sing like you're making love to it," she said, her top lip sliding down the mic's round knob.

My insides quivered.

"You can do it," she said, standing up and locking the mic into the stand. "Come here."

I rose on command. My arms brushed against hers, that's how close we stood. "Put your mouth up real close to it."

I did. I could feel its rough texture on my lips. I closed my eyes.

And then, I melted at a sudden rush of warm air. Kara's mouth grazed the other side of the mic. Her breath flowed directly into my mouth. I closed my eyes and pictured it—our two hot mouths separated only by a tiny knob.

"It's just you and the mic," she whispered. "Make love to it."

My body trembled, smoldering in a fit of lust. I was ready to kick the stand across the room and take her right there. I sang the verse, that time more raspy and provocatively, fueled by her hot breath.

"That's good," she said, backing away. "Let's work it out."

She wasted no time. She broke out into the song, and I simply fell right into place beside her, as comfortable as if I were lounging in bed in my pajamas. I sang with a new hunger, and I must say, I nailed it. I kept looking over at Kara, and she followed in harmony, making love to that microphone in a way that sent delightful shivers through me. She brushed her lips against it, dripping her sexiness all over it.

The music flowed between us. When she sang, she flirted with the words, making me wish I were one of them. Her body pulsed to the music like an instrument all its own. She didn't miss a beat. And neither did I.

Prayer answered.

## Chapter Six

On my drive home from practice, a sense of ease seeped through my veins like liquid gold, filling in all the cracks from earlier and heightening my love for everything by a few thousand notches.

The clear night swaddled me in a perfect song. The stars sparkled brighter, the traffic flowed, red lights turned to green, cars pulled to the right lane when I approached from behind, and balmy air blew in through my window void of humidity. In one, quick, natural step, I managed to just slip into that elusive pocket of space where everything glowed in a pristine light.

Life had just handed me a free pass to everything good.

When I got home, Kelly was sitting on the couch with her legs folded. A plate of fudge with a red bow tied around it sat on the table in front of her. She took one glance at my broken extremities, gasped, and jumped up. "What happened?"

I twisted my wrecked hand up for her to get a closer look. With resentment sealed over by the magic of the last two hours, I melted into her embrace. "I broke them. My thumb, my toe, and Tangerine." I walked out of her hug and over to Tang. I picked her up and cradled her broken body with my one good hand. "She's completely destroyed."

Kelly's eyes, spilling over with renewed remorse and horror, combed over the smashed fret board. "We'll get her fixed."

Enveloped in a deep, strange sense of calm, I placed Tang down on her stand. "Nah." I walked away from Kelly towards the kitchen, tossing my answer over my shoulder. "Even if we could, I doubt she'd ever be the same again."

Kelly's feet tapped against the tile floor behind me, chasing to keep up with my hobble. "Becca, sweetie, I'm really sorry. I never meant to have all of this happen. I just needed the portfolio, and I knew it was here."

"It's okay."

"So, your practice, how did it go? They're not going to drop you now are they?"

"Nope. Kara was really sympathetic about the whole thing." I opened the fridge, pulled out the milk, and chugged right from the carton. I just kept on chugging, ignoring Kelly's puzzled stare. "I had a really good practice and want to just focus on my upcoming show this weekend."

She traced her finger along my splint. "How are you going to do this duo thing with your thumb broken?"

I pulled it back out of her reach. "I'm not playing guitar for a couple of months. I'm going to sing, instead."

"Sing?" she asked. "But, I thought you were afraid to–"

"Shh." I placed my bruised pointer finger over her glossed lips. "I'm going to sing. Let's just leave it at that."

Her eyes grew as large as quarters. "Okay," she said, nodding.

~ ~

In the two days that followed our practice, I got my life in order. I shopped with Margie, who generously bought me ten outfits with matching shoes. When I told her I couldn't accept, she begged me to let her treat me. She confessed she viewed our shopping spree as therapy. On the way out of the mall, I actually saw her shoulders relax and a small smile creep onto her face. She cut my hair back into shape, after she had texturized it to shreds at my last appointment. Then, she slobbered gooey chocolate gel coloring into it, covering up the pink highlights she'd given me in early spring.

Kelly cooked me dinner two nights in a row probably to make herself feel better about my thumb, toe, and guitar. She massaged my back, my feet, my scalp, and even tucked me into bed both nights with a kiss and glass of wine. Gabby called to give me the gig details and to let me know that I needed to complete a W-9 form and bring with me, signed and dated. She never mentioned my broken thumb, and I didn't either. Kara emailed me the sheet music of a single she wrote, "I Can Presume," asking me to learn the lyrics so we could sing it together on stage. She ended that sentence with three exclamation points.

I told Joe that I'd no longer be able to work for him. He responded with a bear hug, a kiss on the top of my head, and the reassurance I could come back anytime. A day later, he begged me to come down to see him because he cited I forgot something in the back room. I walked in one hour before the Friday night rush, and everyone I had worked with over the past seven years greeted me with big smiles, a sheet cake two feet long, and exuberant cheers. We devoured red velvet cake and gulped it back with draft beer. Right before the Friday night crowd filtered in the pub, Joe handed me a twelve pack of personalized guitar picks in my favorite color, orange, and told me to make him proud. Immediately following that, Kelly drove me home in my car, Maggie followed in hers, and I bawled the entire way.

Then, Saturday night finally arrived.

Kelly drove. I rode shotgun. Margie curled up in the backseat. The hot, summer air smoldered through Kelly's open window. Margie complained to Kelly that my hair would frizz. Kelly closed it. I opened mine, unwilling to sit in a pile of my own nerves with no air to break it up. We bickered like that for the first fifteen minutes of our drive to Tambourine, the site of my first paid crowd.

We drove out past the farmlands of Eldersburg and headed west towards Frederick. I bounced my legs up and down, shaking the car, lending me to the question of how I'd pull this off. The memory of forgetting my words at my grandpa's funeral splintered in between the fragile slits of seconds and minutes. As cars passed us by, I focused on their license plates, desperate to pluck the nightmare and its residue out before it could lodge itself in too deep.

Five-hundred-and-fifty tickets sold.

I closed my eyes and saw faces, marked with expectant smiles, shattered into gazes of horror as I fumbled for the right pitch, the right melody, and the right words.

I opened my eyes, combed the dusk sky for reprieve. The silos glowed in the setting sun. Shadows bounced. The cow dung stench stung. My heart bucked.

I glanced at the clock, willing for a little more time to catch my breath, get it together, end the chaos in my mind, and remember the lyrics to Kara's song.

I stared at another license plate willing the words to flitter in and etch solidly.

Margie carried on about a client. Kelly chuckled. My breath tangled somewhere deep in my lungs.

By the time we pulled into the parking lot, I had sketched out the entire night. I imagined that I'd introduce Kara and Kelly. Kara would flirt. Kelly would hate her instantly and get all jealous and insecure. Gabby would protest my broken thumb. I'd trip over my new heels when walking out on stage, falling flat on my face, then rising to a trickle of blood dripping from my broken nose. I'd prop up on the stool next to Kara. She'd start strumming magic, and my voice would crack like a thirteen-year-old boy. I'd be one verse behind, trying to think of the next, ending on nothing more than a mumble and turning ten shades of red. I'd faint. I'd find myself back at McFadden's the next night, bruised and tattered from my broken career, shoveling slices of left-over red velvet cake in my mouth in between serving up beer battered fries to Red Sox fans.

~ ~

As instructed in Gabby's confirmation email, we walked into Tambourine through the back door. The dark room was decorated with tapestries and area rugs. A bright lamp lit the far end of the room, offering me a glimpse at the parquet floor. Muffled voices of ticket-holders buzzed through the large cracks under the double doors in the neighboring room. Gabby's high-pitched shrills exploded over them. She was cackling next to a table piled high with chips, dips, and brownies. I caught a glimpse of her brown hair, curled up in tidal waves, when she tilted her head back in laughter. A man dressed in a dark suit, and no sign of a smile, brushed past her. She stopped the cackling and followed him. The headliner band, The Styles, with eyes charcoaled dark and hair frayed out in feathery wisps, sped by us out the back door, probably to take a smoke break. In their wake, Kara stood, smoldering hot in a black embellished t-shirt, blue jeans that probably cost more than my car, and a thick brown leather belt with a swirl design. She crossed her arms over her chest and curled her lips up into a sexy smile for me. She winked, and my heart immediately shifted into overdrive.

Kelly grabbed my hand. "Is that her?"

"Yeah," I said.

"Wow. I didn't expect her to be so ridiculously pretty."

I wished I could've fast-forwarded the next few moments. The panting, sniffing, and staking out of territory ensued. Kelly's hand tightened in mine. I wished Kara could've worn an oversized sweater, or flat shoes, or a baseball hat on top of all those loose waves, anything to make her look less threatening.

What unraveled next was like an innocent scene straight out of an episode of *The Brady Bunch*. Kara extended her hand to Kelly first. "Hi, I'm Kara." Kelly smiled nicely and shook her hand. "Hi, I'm Becca's girlfriend, Kelly." Not an ounce of shock spread onto Kara's face. Not even a blink. A lovely smile glowed as she continued to exchange pleasantries. Kara, the used car saleswoman on her best behavior, sold us on her reliable smile, her comfortable style, and perhaps more than anything else, her all-around charm. She didn't even flinch when Kelly dispelled the truth that I wasn't in the market for a newbie. No momentary lapse interrupted her smile. No tension appeared on her face to indicate that my hitched status disappointed her in the smallest of fragmented ways. She just ushered us to a table of liquor and started pouring ice into our tumblers.

"Oh, and make sure you have some of the taco salad," she said specifically to Kelly. "I made it myself—it's all organic." Kelly shook her flushed face no, folding in on herself. Margie and I stood back with our ice-filled tumblers. Kelly in her retro t-shirt, fitted, worn-in jeans, and flip flops looked as uncomfortable as a new kid at school, while Kara, tuned-up to perfection, sipped a margarita and stole all of Kelly's confidence. Kara over exaggerated her smiles, while Kelly fidgeted with a strand hanging from her belt loop.

I never gave Kelly's casual, no-frills style much thought until that moment. There I stood, rattling my ice cubes, wishing she could've at least thrown on a pair of heels and a top that looked a little less like she was ready to go out for pizza.

Margie ended up exchanging my tumbler for a shot of Tequila. I downed it and asked for another. By my third, I was ready to go. At that point, the room started to spin just enough to make me happy. Margie pulled Kelly away from me. And Kara put her arm around my shoulder and giggled in that sexy tone of hers. "You're not getting nervous are you?" She squeezed me closer to her. I snuggled up, settling in for my long night ahead with her, completely numb to much of anything else. "Not anymore," I said.

Linked together, we walked to a set of stools next to a mirror lined with lights. In the glow, her face sparkled. A tress of her hair feathered across her cheek, and compelled, I brushed it back behind her ear. That was when Margie coughed and I turned back to see her tugging Kelly towards a vintage orange couch at the other end of the room. Red wine, as dark as blood, brimmed Kelly's glass, spilling over into small puddles at her feet. She swilled it and half of it disappeared in a blink.

"How long have you been going out?" Kara asked, her eyelashes curling at just the right angle, almost like they were waving me into their embrace.

I meant to say three years, but all that sprouted from the unwanted question was a shrug. A moment later I decided to add, "Long enough I guess."

"She doesn't look like your type."

I could feel the hot air blow over me like a steam pipe venting its pressure, shaking me down to the grind, and pushing me forward with no railings to stop me from taking that step over the edge. "What do you think my type is?"

Kara simply tilted her head to the side and teased me with one of her nods. With one look she managed to turn my world upside down. The illusory curtains opened around us, shining new light onto the dark room, and I cuddled up to my cozy buzz as we immediately plunged into warm-up mode. We crooned like experts, Kara with her guitar and sculpted beauty and me with my raspy voice and broken extremities. I concentrated on how expertly her fingers flirted with those steel strings. I wondered how they'd feel tickling along my skin.

Ten minutes later, when I was still trying to catch my breath, Gabby halted in front of us, ordering our lineup at the double doors like we were a thirty piece orchestra. "Listen up," she said. "There'll be a blonde man wearing dark-rimmed glasses at your one o'clock position." She pointed her overdone eyes at me. "I've got two words for you."

I nodded, waiting.

"Impress him."

She walked to the double doors, and we followed. My nerves really kicked in then. Kara reached down for my hand and whispered, "Remember, make love to that mic."

Before I could swallow down the lump lodged in my throat, the house lights dimmed and the crowd fell to a hush. The doors opened. The crowd cheered. I looked back and Margie shot me a thumbs-up. Kelly chugged more wine and eyed Kara's curvy waistline. Next thing I knew, Kara yanked me forward onto that wooden stage and strutted the shit out of her long legs, spotlight bound with me hobbling alongside her feeling every bit like her underling.

A single halo of light shone down on the stools front and center where we headed, hand-in-hand. Our heels clacked against the wooden staging on a four beat rhythm. I don't think I could've clapped as melodically, even if my life was at stake.

When we got to the stools, I blew out a sharp breath and plopped my ass down. My moment arrived. Over five-hundred people waiting to hear what I had to sing. If I pulled it off, maybe one day, Kara and I could be the front-runner on the tickets.

My knees knocked. My heart galloped. Tiny shivers of delight danced up and down my spine. I looked right at the blonde guy with the dark-rimmed glasses, exactly at the one o'clock position. His eyes were as drained as the bottom of my shot glass. I looked at Kara who offered me a sweet sidelong glance.

"You ready?" she said, stoking me with her beautiful caramel eyes.

By the time I completed my nod, her beauty and grace settled on me and I actually felt like I could skydive out of a plane at that point. The nerves straightened, replaced with a sinewy vibe that sprayed that fine mist of confidence I desperately needed. I just wanted to claim that moment, fling my hands up in the air, and whizz down the rails of fearless abandon with the woman. "Hell yeah," I said, grabbing the mic and getting set to make the craziest love of my life.

Kara didn't waste a second. She broke out into her song. Her fingers danced across the strings, sweeping us off together over everything earthly. I simply tossed my voice out there for all to hear. I squeezed that mic between my two hands and belted out upper ranges I had never even attempted before that, knowing Kara could cradle them in her sweet lullaby tone if necessary. I made some serious love to that mic, to that song, to that crowd who, by the end of the song, were standing on their feet convulsing in a storm of cheers and applause.

I remembered every single word.

Fueled by their energy, Kara and I continued to croon to them. Song after song, the lyrics flittered into my head with ease, leaving room for me to focus on my delivery. We had them cooing. Even the glasses guy clapped and smiled at us. By the end of our final song, dripping in sweat, vibrating at a higher level, we stood and bowed. Then, she grabbed my hand and together, we bowed again and again. The crowd thundered in front of us. My life couldn't have been written any better.

I soaked up the moment, letting it seep deep within the farthest reaches of my inner core. My grandpa's spirit hugged me. Tears welled up in my eyes. I squeezed Kara's hand, and sure enough, her silky soft skin really was planted against mine. For the briefest fraction of time, I stood taller and mightier, able to take on the northeast winds of the change in my life's course. And just as quickly, the wind managed to whip me off my feet when, without the slightest bit of warning, Kara wrapped her arms around me and hugged me real tight. She smelled like mint and flowers. The crowd rose to their feet. I just knew Kelly would be cringing.

She pulled away and held my hand up in the air with hers again. "They loved us," she said before bowing one more time and strutting off stage. Her heels tapped the floor one breathtaking stomp at a time. I followed her straight back to the orange couch. She turned to me with eyes blazing, and in one swift move, kissed me straight on the lips, firmly. I felt my soul come crashing down, my heart racing, and my body turning to a pile of mush. She bounced away, giggling.

I watched her dance from one person to another, man, woman, didn't matter, and kiss them firmly on the mouth and on the cheek, leaving everyone as breathless and stunned as me. She kept beaming about the great night.

Kelly buckled when I stood in front of her. Her face upturned in a grieving backbend. She simply offered me a crooked smile. She stuffed her hands in her front pockets. "Good show," she said, before turning to walk over to Margie who was touching her freshly kissed cheek.

I should've shuffled after her, placated to her insecurity, and tried to be the good girlfriend. Instead, I landed my gaze on Kara again. Our eyes locked.

Oh God, did I need help.

~ ~

The three of us piled back into the car not more than ten minutes after the show ended.

Kelly rode shotgun that time. I drove. Margie sat like a statue in the backseat with her head creating a stable blind spot. I opened the window to clear the air of the pungent stench of tequila, cigarettes, and greasy food that clung to our clothes.

"So, you really think I did a good job?" I finally asked two miles down the road, while stopped at a traffic light. The blaring lights of a Seven Eleven bounced off Kelly's winced face.

She sighed, nodded, and bit her lower lip, staring at the red light as if willing it to change. "Yeah, I did. You looked right at home up there."

"You okay?" I asked.

Kelly parted her lips, but sealed them back just as quickly, shaking her head side to side instead. "I'm fine. I just have a small headache from all that cigarette smoke."

The light changed to green. I gunned it. With twisted up tension, I drove toward another traffic light that was turning yellow. I plowed right through it as it changed to red. I never did that. Two seconds later, sirens wailed behind me. My heart jerked.

The cop car pulled up close to me. The lights from the sirens blinded me. "Great." I put on my blinker and pulled over.

I lowered my window all the way and a few seconds later the cop asked me for my license and registration. I pulled the packet out of my glove compartment. I was shaking so violently, I couldn't separate last year's insurance card from the current one, so I just handed him the entire package.

"You were racing through the traffic light and going forty-five in a thirty mile an hour zone."

I bowed my head. "Sorry."

"I'll be back. Sit tight here." He walked away.

For ten minutes we sat in silence, then the cop finally came back to issue me a ticket. "Slow down or next time it'll cost you even more."

I took the ticket and my packet back from him. "Yes, sir." When he walked away, I handed the packet over to Kelly. "Could you put this back, please?"

She eased it from my hands and shoved it in the compartment, slamming it three times. "What the hell's wrong with this damn thing?" She yelled at it. She continued slamming it, each one more exaggerated then the next. I lost count, but I would guess it was around her tenth attempt, that it finally caught. "Piece of crap." She hit it one last time and the door popped back out at her. She left it dangling at her knees when I pulled back on the road.

Margie scooted up. "Whoa, kiddo. Take it easy." She slapped both of our shoulder blades, centering us into a group hug. She rested her head against mine and sighed. "I know this is going to be an adjustment for you girls, but trust me. Everything will be okay," she said as if finishing up a previous conversation.

I imagined Kelly must've griped to Margie about me and Kara. Margie probably spent the entire time consoling her and telling her what a good girlfriend I was. That I'd never hurt her. That she had nothing to be jealous over or feel insecure about. That's what friends did for each other. They lied to keep peace.

Kelly rested her head against Margie's, so now the three of us looked like a crooked post knocked down, weathered within seconds by the fast moving torrent of change. We drove away from Frederick, and for a good ten mile stretch, remained hunched together like that, for Kelly's sake more than mine.

Kelly was the first to speak. "I'm scared."

"Of what?" I asked her.

"Of what all of this change is going to do to us. I mean already, look at you. You're wearing these sexy clothes, your hair is all perfect, and you're wearing lip liner." Her face scrunched up. "You're already different."

I exhaled. Margie squeezed my shoulder blade, as if urging and begging me to relieve the renewed pressure. "You need to trust me," I said.

She nodded.

The three of us drove forward together, forming the wake of a silence that beat so forcefully, I doubted aspirin would be enough to take its edge off. "Do you have any of your migraine pills with you?" I asked Kelly when we approached our exit.

Materialized before I could even put on my blinker to exit, she plopped three pills in the palm of my waiting hand. I swallowed them while taking the sharp curve, without water.

## **Chapter Seven**

About four weeks into my new job as a musician, I drove up to the teller window without having to ask for a withdrawal. Gabby had signed my first paycheck as a professional. My heart leapt when I turned it over to the teller. I celebrated an hour later with a new pair of sandals and my first ever pedicure outside the walls of Capella Day Spa.

Kara and I were building fans faster than even Gabby had projected. That was all due to a simple equation: Gabby brilliantly arranged the venues, Kara and I rocked, and the places begged us to come back. By the end of our second month, we were performing five nights a week and receiving requests from fans to hear our originals.

Kelly and I saw very little of each other for those first several weeks. If I wasn't performing, I was practicing or doing good deeds for credibility's sake. During the day, Gabby had us working the pro bono scene. We'd play at community events, charitable functions, high school pep rallies, college quad parties, and anything to get free press. We landed the entertainment section of *The Post, The Sun,* and *The Times*; our photos plastered across the local event Web sites. We even had a favorable review from *The Out Takes*, a regional gay/lesbian tabloid.

Every once in a while, I'd come back to my condo and find Kelly sleeping in my bed with her body stretched from one end to the other. I'd nudge her, she'd moan, and fall back asleep. I'd end up sleeping on my couch, cuddled up to a soft pillow, imagining the whole time it was Kara.

What a tease Kara had become to me. Night after night, as I was warming up, I'd watch her caress the long neck bottle of a funky beer and flirt with her guitar strings. She'd catch me and her eyes would twinkle, then her petal lips would turn up slightly. All signs she approved. Provocative images would filter in of her lounging in my bed. The moans I imagined coming from her tickled the farthest reaches. Those long fingers embracing me, pulling me to her, and luring me towards her soft inner thighs and to ecstasy.

The firestorm inside melted my good judgment, my inhibitions, and my fears. We'd sit within inches of each other and all I could think about was how much I wanted to fuck her. Soon, visions of us pretzeled up together popped up all the time – when I was buying my morning coffee, reading the newspaper, doing my physical therapy for my thumb, even when Kelly and I were sitting in the front pew at St. Paul's Roman Catholic Church.

I was a horny mess.

Eventually, I started flirting with her. Of course, my definition of flirting would be considered by some to be nothing more than friendly banter. Nonetheless, I started touching her arm more when she cracked a joke, winking when she'd make an offhand comment, and twirling my hair when I was sure that she was looking.

She consumed my every waking thought. I couldn't make it through a bowl of cereal, a quick trip to the grocery store, or a television show without her sneaking in and absorbing every last bit of my thoughts. I started to ache whenever I thought of her out on a date. She dated quite a bit, from what I overheard Gabby say to a restaurant manager one day. Girls and guys lined up to ask her out. She never went out solo. She never paid for lunch or dinner. She never opened her wallet to purchase a drink. She didn't even know the customary amount for a tip.

She was a goddess with a universe full of admirers.

That was probably why we were selling so many tickets, and how Gabby managed to get our first single, "I Can Presume," into the hands of DJ Raz from Tops 106. Every night on the drive home slot, he would play a new single and drivers would call in and give their grades. The higher the grade, the more coverage the song would get on the station. Of course, to even get the guy's attention, Gabby had to present the single in a basket of various liquors and assorted crackers and cheese. She researched and learned his favorites. He never promised to play it, but Gabby said she got good vibes.

Around my third month, my thumb had healed. I'd eventually get Tangerine fixed. But, until then I had purchased a second-hand replacement from Vibrations to get me back in the groove.

Then, around month five, Kelly had decided to come to a show. She was helping me cut a loose string from my shirt when Gabby ran into the backroom screaming, holding a radio out in front of her like it was a platter of caviar. "I Can Presume" blared over her screams. Kara joined her screams first, then me.

"It's official," Gabby screamed over us all. "There's no turning back from here."

She turned up the volume to its max, and Kara ran up to me. We jumped around, knocking over tables and chairs. Brushes and lipstick rolled around at our feet. Kara swung me around like the matador in a Paso Doble dance. I clung to her, laughing and spinning and dizzy in love with the news. She twirled me around, dipping me this way and that. Our song filled the space with beauty. I had lived for that moment, and when it finally became a reality I felt ready to explode with joy. I looked over at Kelly, and she hung back watching me dance with Kara. An uneasy smile rested on her face, one that I knew took an awful lot of patience to keep steady for my sake.

Not long after, I had a night off because Kara and Gabby had to go meet up with their family for a wedding in Philly. I was driving to get some wine for the bubble bath I was planning to take and our song came on the radio. I opened my windows and turned up the volume. I immediately called Kara. It was magic. Her voice from well over a hundred miles away melded with mine.

To celebrate, I had purchased a bottle of expensive champagne instead of the wine and invited Kelly over. When she told me she couldn't make it because she had already made plans, I called Margie. She was there within an hour. We polished off the champagne within forty-five minutes. Feeling giddy and drunk, we decided to get a limo and ride around from telephone pole to telephone pole hanging flyers Gabby had designed about an upcoming gig. Kara and I needed to fill two thousand seats. As we ducked in and out of the limo, Margie started to fill me in on Kelly. Apparently, she was out with the photography staff of the *Washington Times* at a political event.

"When did she make friends with these people?" I asked.

"She's been out with them several times already. Her and her friend Bonnie from work applied there. The Times can't offer them anything, yet, but were willing to take their work on spec." She paused. "How do you not know this?"

I just shrugged.

We drove onwards and I ordered the limo driver to stop at a liquor store. I stocked up on beef jerky, Doritos, Cokes, and a quart of Bacardi dark rum, the staple before each show. Kara and I would sip that concoction to warm us up. It numbed me enough to not worry about screwing up.

Back in the limo, I untwisted the cap and took a shot of it straight from the bottle, then handed it off to Margie.

"I think I'll just stick with a Coke, thanks."

"Come on, we're celebrating." I clanked a glass in front of her, which she politely nudged away.

"Kelly was right. You certainly have changed."

And what followed after that comment were a few defensive wisecracks from me and an hour long ride back to my condo on mute.

I stared past her and out the window. I rested my head back and watched as headlights bounced off trees. I was swaddled in a sea of rum, wishing it were Kara in front of me instead of my judgmental, hypocritical friend.

~~

In the days following my night out with Margie, I fretted about challenging her and Kelly on the comment about my change. I was changing, and it was a good thing. I didn't feel like defending that to her or to Kelly. So, I just went about my busy life, riding those waves of change that were catapulting me from small pub girl to artist on the radio. I felt kind of bad for Kelly because every time she'd call, I was either in the middle of writing another song, heading out to a gig, or trying to catch up on some sleep. Life was getting so crazy for me, but I always managed to at least talk with her when she called. Then one day, when Kara and I were meeting with Gabby about some paperwork over at the recording studio, Kelly called me again. That time, I let it go to voicemail.

"Your girlfriend?" Kara asked.

I nodded. "Yeah. I'll call her back."

I did, but not until eleven o'clock that night long after the three of us finished up our meeting and downed a couple bottles of Riesling. I was eating a pile of pancakes and a side of bacon when I called her from a worn out booth in Frank's Diner. Fluorescent lights poked down, helping to sober me. On the second ring, I gulped a mouthful of coffee that was much too cold. I waved at the waitress, an older woman with spokes of gray spraying the rest of her wiry black hair. She acknowledged me with a sourpuss of a smile, armed herself with an almost empty pot of coffee, and came to my rescue. As she was pouring the sludge into my cup, Kelly picked up.

"Hey, did I wake you?" I asked, then winked at the waitress when she dropped two more Splendas down on the table.

"I couldn't sleep."

"So, how are you doing?" I asked, rhetorically.

"I'm fine. I had just called to see what you were up to. I thought maybe we could've gotten together for a bit if you had some free time after your practice."

"Sorry about that. Time just slips away when I'm in practice mode."

"Any chance I could come over right now?" she asked.

I had at least another hour before I could drive. "Now?"

"Yeah, now," she said.

"Do you feel like eating breakfast?"

"Not really. I just want to talk."

"I'm not going to be home for at least another hour."

"You're still out?" she asked. "It's almost midnight."

I didn't want to tell her I was drunk. The last thing I needed was a lecture. "I'm at Frank's, and I'm still waiting for them to bring out my food." I slopped another forkful of pancakes into my mouth.

Silence.

Then, "Okay, fine," she said. "I'll come by in an hour."

An hour and a half later, with the Riesling settled in my bladder instead of my head, I drove back to my condo. I walked past Kelly's car, which already had the late fall frost settled on her windows. I took that as a clear indicator she'd been there much sooner than we agreed.

I sprayed some breath spray on my tongue and entered. She was working on a Sudoku puzzle, snuggled under a blue and purple afghan she had painstakingly crocheted for me a few years back.

"I'm sorry it took me so long to get home."

"Traffic bad?" she asked, her eyebrow raised up to mid forehead.

"Miles of backup," I joked, trying to lighten the knotted tension. "People were dancing on their roofs, flashing and mooning each other."

She chuckled softly. "We need to talk," she said, a peaceful smile rested on her face.

I sat down beside her. "About what?"

She wrapped her hand around mine. She was shaking. "I don't want you to get angry. I just want you to listen to what I have to say."

I nodded, bracing for the judgments, the impending arguments, and the attacks to who I've become over the past five months. I stared at her trembling lips and drafted my rebuttal. I'd acknowledge that I was changing. Who wouldn't in my position? My life was moving full steam ahead. Hell, I felt sexier than I had in years. I was charged with a motive, alive with a bustling career, and blessed with music, good food, and fine liquors. I might have been changing, but I was changing for the better. I was living the life I deserved, finally. All that hard work was paying off. And, well, if Kelly couldn't deal, that was her fault, not mine. She'd have to lighten up and join in instead of worrying so much. "Okay, I'm listening."

"I love you." She brought her fingers up to my face and cradled my cheek with them. She stared into my eyes. Speckles of moisture brimmed under her blue irises. "Okay?" I relaxed, figuring she'd use her reverse psychology on me, the way she always did whenever she wanted her way.

"And, it's because I love you that this is really hard for me to do."

I tensed again. When I breathed, my chest rattled.

"Becca, I can't do this anymore."

"This?"

She stole her hand back. "This," she said, waving at nothing. "Pretending to be happy with the situation."

"The situation? You mean the money coming in? The fans running out to buy my single? The incredible times you choose not to partake in?"

"I don't like this new you," she said.

"Well, that's fucked up." I didn't like the tingling in my fingers or the tightness in my chest.

"It's not you anymore. I don't recognize this person you're trying to be. I wish you could see what a fool you're making of yourself. You're not a party animal. You're not a flirt. You're not ego-driven. You're not selfish and self-absorbed. You're that girl who plays guitar and entertains people with her smile and beautiful voice."

"I'm not selfish or self-absorbed."

"But you are now," she said.

My blood started to boil. "I think you should leave before I say something I'm going to regret."

"This is what I didn't want. I didn't want to make you angry."

"How did you expect me to react? You think I can just snap my finger and go back to the way I was before all of this happened? I don't want to. I like who I am now."

"You're selling yourself short trying to be someone you're not. This new you isn't natural or even likable. And, if you're not willing to open your eyes to see how you're hurting yourself, then I don't want to be a part of this anymore."

My insides flared. "So, you're breaking up with me?"

She sat there silent, her non-response saying it all.

My chest panged. My throat dried. The tiny hairs on my arms stood tall. "Then, get out." I stood up and pointed to the door. "Seriously, get out. I don't need you anyway."

She went to the door, opened it, and then turned back. "I'm not the enemy here. I really do love you and just want what's best for you."

"Get out," I screamed.

She closed the door.

I grabbed my shoe and belted it at the door. Then, I tore off towards the kitchen, rounded up my scissors and huffed back to the afghan. I cut the shit out of it until ragged pieces of yarn clung to each other, bracing for the end of life as they knew it.

~ ~

I didn't sleep at all through the night. I walked. I ran. I climbed the steps at the Catonsville Community College stadium. None of those things cleared Kelly's words from my mind or eased the anger.

Not until I saw Kara many hours later, sitting on a stool in the backroom of our gig, did I feel the euphoric rush of freedom gather below my feet and sweep me to higher ground.

"Hi, sweetie," she said, patting my stool.

I floated to the stool.

"Are you okay?" she asked, placing her hand on my knee.

"Kelly and I broke up."

Her eyebrow rounded slightly. "What happened?"

I told her the entire story of how Kelly dumped on me the minute I got to my apartment. How she berated me and basically told me I was changing for the worse and making a fool of myself. I told her everything down to her slamming the door on her way out with that shit-eating grin on her face like she was so self-righteous and perfect. It just felt better to paint that picture.

"What a bitch," Kara said.

"I know, right?" I went on, crafting more of Kelly's annoying insults, reveling on her faults and pretending how I was so much better off without her. The more I talked, the more I convinced myself that this was the best thing that could've happened to me. Kara agreed, and moved closer to me with each delivery, so close that a piece of her hair actually tickled my forearm.

"You are so much better off." She cradled my hand. "Just wait until you see how much more fun it is being Becca James and being single."

I'd be able to flirt, drink, and come home late. I was free. And I could date whomever I wanted to date. I could kiss whomever I wanted to kiss. I could have fun with whomever I wanted. "Can't wait."

"I'm going to help you forget all about her. You and I are going to party tonight."

~ ~

I was horny as hell, sitting in the front seat of her car after our gig. I waited while she talked with her friends. I wanted to yank her inside and throw myself on top of her. I was free, and I could do that now if I wanted.

I played with the radio while checking out the other girls. One had fake boobs and a waist the size of a coaster. The other one had hair blacker and shinier than a mink and just a smidgeon of fat bumping out the sides of her lose-rise jeans. Kara was laughing about some idiot guy with a mullet who asked her to autograph his ass with a Sharpie. The two girls were smoking long, skinny cigarettes and their smoke drifted into the open window.

Kara broke through the smoky haze and kissed their cheeks. Next thing I knew she slid in beside me and turned on the radio. "Let's get the party started, hmm?" She belted in, revved the engine and punched it into gear, peeling her tires against the pavement like a dragster. I imagined flames shooting out of the exhaust pipes as we sped out of the parking lot. I gripped the handle above me when she skidded around the curbstone and onto Charles Street. I bobbed around like a Weeble, giggling like a fool. I swung dangerously close to her each time she weaved around a slow car, one time so close that my hand landed on her leg. I slid it off and contemplated over exaggerating the next turn just so I could feel her skin in my hand one more time. I was free and could do that now. I don't think she would've minded, if I judged by the sultry smile tiptoeing across her face. She flicked a wisp of hair off her cheek, then shot down a busy street, dashing in and out of tight spots like she was starring in a Batman movie.

I never felt so scared and exhilarated in all of my life.

We didn't say a word to each other until we cleared the city and broke out ahead of the pack of cars hogging route ninety-seven. "This car kicks ass," she said. "I bought it in the spring for a steal from one of Gabby's clients. He owns a Ford dealership out in Finksburg and he owed her a favor for this party she threw for him."

"It beats my Civic."

"You want to drive it?"

"I can't drive a stick."

"We'll see about that." Kara swerved across two lanes to get to the breakdown lane. "I'll teach you." She slammed on the brakes and screeched to a stop.

She climbed out her door and a second later was at mine, pulling me out. I resisted and we got into a little tug-o-war match right there on the side of the road. I've never stood on the side of a highway before. Each time a car passed, I thought it would blow us over. I grabbed her wrist harder when a U-Haul passed by, and that's when she pulled me in tight and I got a good whiff of her perfume. Mmm, she smelled yummy. Next thing I knew, she shuffled me over to the driver's side and stuffed me in the seat.

I didn't know a brake pedal from a clutch pedal. I giggled, overcome with the thrill of it all.

Kara slid in beside me and looked directly at my hands clutching the steering wheel. "Okay, sweetie, you've got to work the shift with one of those." Next thing I knew, her fingers were spooning mine. I let her guide me to the shift.

"I'm going to need some serious instruction. I have no idea what to do with these three pedals when I only have two feet."

"Aw," she said and reached up to touch my cheek with the back of her hand. "This is going to be so much fun."

Her eyes reflected the headlight of an approaching car, and in them I could make out the slightest tease. It brimmed right on the outer edges next to her long lashes. I wanted to kiss her.

The car sped by, and Kara dropped her hand.

"This is what you do," she said. "Use your left foot for the clutch pedal, the one farthest to your left. Use your right one for braking, that's the middle pedal, and use it for the gas, too."

"Got it." I pressed each one once just to make sure.

She flicked on the interior light, and that's when I noticed she had painted her fingernails black. A little rhinestone sparkled on the tip of her left pinky. "You didn't strike me as the Goth type," I said to her.

"Hmm?"

"Your nails. I would've thought you were more of a red person."

"Aw, sweetie, there's lots you don't know about me."

We held the gaze, and I nearly wet myself.

She pointed down to the stick jutting in between us like a two-mile valley. "Tell me what this gear shift looks like."

"An H," I said. "Actually more like two H's stuck together."

"Good. You've got five gears and each sits on the corner of that letter H. That'll make it easier for you to remember your gears."

H for horny. I'd never forget.

"Now, put your right foot on the brake and left on the clutch. Make sure you keep holding down the clutch and the brake, then move into first gear." She pointed to the H with her rhinestone pinky. "That top left position."

I stalled.

"Try again," Kara said without missing a beat. "This time make sure you take your foot off the brake and slowly give the car gas, but keep your foot on the clutch."

I considered myself a fairly intelligent person, but there were way too many steps to remember and I hadn't even moved a solid inch, yet. "Okay. Let me try again."

She leaned in close to me. "It's easy, sweetie, just imagine the give and take, not too much, not too little." I inhaled her minty breath and my head swirled.

After several minutes of my intimate lesson, I successfully got moving from first to second to finally third gear. I was still in the breakdown lane. I slowly turned on the road and when the engine whined, I shifted to fourth without her having to tell me. I was in full control. Then I popped it into fifth gear and sped up past seventy all the way to eighty. I looked over at Kara, and her hair blew all around her.

I was on top of the world.

I sped up behind a car in the fast lane. Kara leaned across my lap to honk the horn, beeping it over and over again. Her hair whipped me in the face, and I loved every second of it. In between beeps, she rested her hand on my thigh. My stomach whipped around like there was a mini tornado in it. The car moved over to the middle lane and we sped by it, two reckless, single girls ready to party their hearts out.

I climbed to eighty-five and decided I'd reached my limit. I steadied it there and Kara slid back into her seat with her hand still taking up refuge on my leg. I did what I would think any girl in my position would do. I reached down and covered her hand with mine, giving it a little squeeze so she'd know I approved.

I loved being single.

"Pull over," she shouted over the wind.

I downshifted until I slowed enough to pull off and ease her down to first. Instinctively, I managed to stop her and stick her in neutral without any help. I even cut the engine. Fifteen minutes alone with Kara and I was an expert. I could anything now.

"Ah, that was amazing." I leaned back and took a deep breath. When I opened my eyes again, Kara was no more than an inch away from my face.

"You look hot tonight," she whispered.

I felt hot. So hot that I took the liberty of brushing my finger lightly across her cheek as she washed me over with her soulful stare.

"Your ass looked amazing in those jeans," she said, reaching up for my fingers. She played with them, rubbing them between hers.

I needed to kiss the woman. I inched my finger over to her lips and stopped breathing momentarily while I circled them. They were so plump and ripe. My head spun in wonderful circles. I bore my eyes into hers. "I want to kiss you," I whispered.

"Then go for it."

I did.

I went for it like I'd die if I didn't. I tingled the second my lips landed on hers. I kissed her tenderly for several seconds, and she kissed me back with a sweet mix of sensual and tantalizing sweeps. Then, she backed away and said in the most serious voice, "My turn to take over."

I wasn't about to argue. "I'm waiting," I said, my eyes still closed, sealing us in that moment.

She jumped out of the car, ran over to my side, and yanked me out. "Let me show you how it's really done." She climbed into the driver's seat and blew me a kiss.

I don't think my heart beat again until I was back in the passenger side. When she hit the accelerator, I was still tingling. And, I hadn't even passed between her lips, yet.

~ ~

Two seconds after we arrived at her friend Ella's mansion, some guy with a ring stuck in his chin handed me a vodka and cranberry. The girl he was with wore heels a mile high and reminded me of a delicate dandelion swaying in the wind. She placed a lime on the rim of my glass.

I sipped my drink and followed Kara through the foyer, past the double winding heart staircase and down a flight of basement stairs far wider than any I'd ever seen before. I was afraid to trip and spill my red drink on the white carpet.

The bottom of the stairs opened to a trendy barroom. Bottles of liquor lined the walls behind the dark cherry wood bar in the far corner. Tumblers, wine and martini glasses, and champagne flutes hung from above. The room smelled like a bar, thick with a haze of cigarette smoke and jamming with classic rock music. Several pool tables sat ready with the balls racked and little compressed chalk cubes dotting their laminated edges. A few girls were dancing under a disco ball, grinding and bending over each other like a bunch of burlesque dancers.

When I turned back to Kara, she wasn't there. I scanned the room and she was nowhere in sight. So, I walked over to some leather couches that were spread around a roulette table and pretended I was fascinated with luck. Ten or so people gathered around the table and cheered on a guy with a long, slicked-back ponytail. I plopped down on one of the empty couches and sipped my drink, opening my eyes really wide when the guy's marble landed on the right number. One would've thought the guy just won a marathon the way he jumped up and high-fived the empty air.

I sucked on my little straw, sailing the liquor straight to my head. I felt like the lanky girl with braces at the school dance, pressed up against an obscure part of the wall, trying to look like I belonged.

"Looks like someone needs a refill." Kara scaled over the back of the couch and landed right up against my legs. She smelled like weed and her eyes were glazed, polished to a shine.

I clanked my ice cubes around my almost dry glass. "I sure do. I think I'll go grab one." I started to get up and she pulled me down, resting her head on my shoulders.

"We'll let Chad get it for you." She motioned to a tall, Hollister-dressed guy standing behind us. His hair was gelled into a perfect faux-hawk. He wore a salmon button down, fitted shirt and was drinking pink champagne. "Babe, can you get us a refill, please?" She raised her empty glass up in the air, and he took it from her.

I raised mine up just like her, and he eased mine out of my hands, too. He glided around the strip teasers on the floor and walked behind the bar.

"I could go for a cigarette," she said, cradling her head back up against my shoulder.

I snuggled my neck into her soft waves, wanting to keep her against me for as long as I could.

She jumped up and reached for my hand. "Let's go bum some." She strutted across the floor. Everyone checked her out. Then, I started to strut, too, and their eyes scanned to me. We strutted hand-in-hand all the way across the room. Just knowing how much she loved the way my ass looked in my jeans made me flaunt it even more. When we got to the bar, Chad handed us each a new drink, prettied up with more lime wedges and that time tiny umbrellas.

"Do you have a couple of cigarettes on you?" she asked him.

I pulled her hand back. "Kara, I don't—"

"—Tonight, you do," she said, taking the two cigarettes along with his lighter. He skipped off, summoned for his game of pool.

She placed the cigarette between her lips and lit it with one quick flick. She handed me the other one and the lighter. "Here you go, sweetie."

I had only smoked a cigarette once in my life, if I could even call it that. My cousin, Hanna, smoked, and she used to keep her cigarettes hidden in a shoe box on the top shelf in her closet. Well, one day when I was visiting, I snuck into her room and stole one of her Newport Lights. Later, I drove out to a new housing development under construction and parked at the edge of the empty cul de sac. I attempted to smoke the butt but didn't get very far because a construction truck turned onto the street. I tossed the lit cigarette out the window and sped off.

That was my big smoking debut. My big step out on the edge of danger.

Having someone like Kara willing me to give it a try again, sent a little rush of euphoria through me. I wanted to be daring, dangerous, and on the edge. So, I placed the cigarette in between my lips and flicked the lighter. I couldn't quite get the hang of it. After three tries, Kara stole the lighter from me, and with one quick strum of her thumb, set that flame shooting up towards the end of my cigarette. "Breathe in a little bit, sweetie. It lights quicker that way."

I drew a breath in and my mouth filled with smoke. I just let it sit there for a few seconds before tilting my head up and blowing it out in a long, slow stream. I wanted to look as sexy as she, but felt ridiculous.

"Is this the first time you've ever smoked?" Kara asked.

I shook my head as though that was the silliest question I'd ever been asked. I drew the cigarette up to my lips again and took another drag. When I thought enough time had lapsed, I exhaled again. That time the smoke danced around Kara's head like a halo. I was proud in a weird sort of way that I created that.

She chuckled softly. "You have no idea how to smoke a cigarette do you?"

"It's not like I get a lot of practice," I admitted.

"For starters, breathe it deep into your lungs until it makes your head spin." She took a good long drag, making the tip swell up red hot. "Really suck it in. Otherwise, it's pointless." I waited for her to blow out the smoke, but she never did. It settled into her lungs and stayed there.

I attempted again, and that time I breathed in so deeply that I felt the instant burn in my lungs. I had succeeded. I coughed out the smoke, and Kara laughed.

"You are so adorable." She rubbed my shoulder for a few seconds and headed off towards the pool table. I took another drag, a shorter one, one that I could handle that time. My head began to spin as my lungs filled with the burning menthol. I followed Kara over to the pool table, smoking my cigarette as if I'd been smoking since I was ten years-old.

I watched as Chad struck the white ball. The triangle of balls spilled out across the table. He called to shoot a striped ball in the right corner pocket. When he sunk it, his face grew serious like a crime scene investigator interpreting blood splatter. He leaned in close to the edge of the table, staring down a row of the striped balls all lined up ready to make him the champion. When he took the shot, he missed and saved us all from having to watch his scrawny chest beat up and down for another second.

Kara chalked up her stick. I stared at her breasts when she leaned over to hit the yellow ball into the side pocket. I wanted to dive right in between them. I wanted to feel them against my tongue, drink up their beauty, savor their taste, and feast on them.

When Kara finished taking her shot, she walked over to me. Her eyes, a dreamy reverie, narrowed. A sultry tease settled into her smile. She grabbed my hand and led me to a dark corner of the room. She turned me around and guided me into a leather recliner. My heart hit the floor as she climbed on top of me, straddling me. She leaned in and started making out with me. Her tongue, furled between my lips, danced with mine. Then, she abruptly rose, leaned down, dragged her tongue softly up my neck, and walked away.

I craned my neck to watch her. She looked back at me and nodded for me to follow.

I was flying, soaring, and adjusting just fine to my new set of wings.

I was free, and I could do anything I damned well pleased to do. "Want to get out of here?" I asked when I reached her.

"I've got a better idea."

She tossed her pool stick to the dandelion lady, then led me out of the basement, through the foyer, and up the cascading staircase.

"Where are you taking me?" I asked, breathless.

"To my room."

"Your room?"

"Yeah, Ella rents me a room."

Through an arched door frame and around a sharp angled wall sat her door. She pulled me to her and lifted me. I wrapped my legs around her waist and kissed her hard. She kicked open the door, and before she could kick it shut, we already ripped each other's shirts off.

~ ~

The room spun around me. Blues, creams, and flowers danced around my peripheral view, masked in a glaze of sweet lilac and vanilla. The soft glow from the table lamp bathed her skin in amber. She pressed her lips harder against mine. I squeezed my legs around her waist. She grazed her nails along my back, kissing, sucking my neck, sending feathery shivers through me. Her soft lips caressed me in a succession of hard and soft pulses.

We kissed softly for a few minutes, both taking a moment to stop and admire the other's hair and soft skin, until she started to moan softly. She latched on tighter, clawing at my back, slowly devouring me, one eager bite at a time. She sought out my lips and kissed me hungrily. "I want you to make love to me," she said.

I kissed her harder and pushed over to the bed. She dropped onto it and pulled me down on top of her. She wasted no time. She reached up and tore the button off my jeans. I reciprocated. We tore each other's clothes off like we were angry at them for getting in our way. Bras, sandals, and buttons flew in every direction around us.

She moved underneath me like a slinky; flexible, arching, and teasing. We devoured each other, even sinking our teeth into each other's skin. Each playful bite stirred moans from deep inside. I felt like a wild animal, greedy, hungry, and uninhibited. I wanted to please her. I wanted to hear her scream out in pleasure. I skipped across her neck and started to go down, but she grabbed my head and guided me to her breast. At first I just sort of grazed her with my tongue, but she pressed my head harder.

So, I vacuum sealed my lips around her erect nipple and sucked for dear life. She arched and moaned, and even let out a little giggle. "Hmm, I can tell you've done this a few times before. Keep going." She pressed my head back to her breast. I sucked and flicked and was very close to having an orgasm myself when she started panting and grinding, and then spasmed right below me. I had given Kara Travers an orgasm. I wanted to scream that through a megaphone on top of the pointy roof.

When she relaxed in my arms, she rolled me over and pinned me to the bed. "I want more."

She rolled me back over and pushed my head down between her legs. I needed to taste her. I played with her nipples, and got high on her juices and screams of pleasure. She shuddered beneath me, digging her fingers into my hair and moaning. I was pleasing Kara Travers. And, she was every bit as delicious as I had imagined she'd be. She pressed me to her, begging me not to stop. I savored her smell, her taste, her shaking, and her ascent to pleasure.

When she slowed to a subtle rock, I climbed up and kissed her lips. She ran her fingers through my hair and smiled. "Your turn."

Not a minute later, I was bucking and screaming out in ecstasy, pressing her against my drenched, quivering body, certain I had just skyrocketed to another level, another dimension, and another world outside the one I had always known.

An hour later, I woke up to the sound of the shower. Steam, the scent of lavender, curled out from the bottom of the bathroom door. I looked around at her calming blue haven. The canopy bed, the white leather chaise lounge in the corner near the window, and the lacy curtains, all formed her private world, a world that I had somehow managed to weave myself into.

## Chapter Eight

For breakfast the next morning, we ate crepes in bed. Kara had ordered them with whipped cream and strawberries from Ella's live-in personal assistant, Rosemary. She had delivered them to our door on a silver platter. I fed Kara mouthful after mouthful, wiping her pink lips with the edge of a prim, white-laced napkin. I offered her a drink of orange juice and she gladly accepted, wrapping her lips around the rim and sipping like a dainty princess.

I could get used to this life.

"I'm thinking we should spend the day pampering ourselves," I said, placing the tray aside and straddling her.

She giggled in a low, sexy drawl. "You are a little sex fiend, aren't you?"

I grazed her neck. "This is all your fault."

"Blaming this all on me, huh?"

I kissed her, lingering on her sweet taste.

"You really surprised me last night," she said.

I stopped kissing. "Oh? In what way?"

She traced a finger down my arm. "I thought I'd at least have to take you out for a few dinners first."

I backed away to check her face, her eyes, to see if she was smiling. I stiffened when I realized she wasn't joking.

"Relax," she said, massaging my shoulders. "I didn't say that was a bad thing." A playful smirk danced across her face.

Her eyes grazed my breasts. "You were incredible. I guess that's one of the fringe benefits of escaping the prison of a relationship. You become horny as hell." She rolled over, causing me to flop on the mattress.

I stared at her bare back. A series of five freckles formed a star over her left shoulder blade. I touched the top freckle. Her skin flared below my fingertip like a burning ember.

She flipped over and traced my nipple with her guitar-calloused finger tips.

I melted. "I don't ever want to get out of this bed. Can we stay here all day?"

She rubbed my cheek with the back of her hand. "No can do, sweetie. I need to get showered. I'm supposed to meet someone over at the Harbor for an early afternoon run."

I didn't want her to go. I wanted to stay there all day, breathing her in, feeling her skin on mine, and getting lost in her hair.

She climbed to her feet, walked over to the bathroom, and climbed into the shower. The water splashed. The soap dropped. She started to hum. "You can join me if you want."

Every fiber of my being pulsated. I wondered if my legs would ever work again. I scanned the room and Kara's clothes sat in a pile on the floor. Her jeans. Her tank top. They were on the floor of the room I was in. The indentation on the pillow created by Kara Travers' head. Kara Travers was in the shower and calling for me. This had to be a dream. From the moment her chocolate eyes met mine at McFaddens, this was the exact scenario I had fantasized about, the one that had consumed all of my thoughts. And now, it was reality. In just a few short months, dreams were coming true for me. I no longer had to wish for them. They just popped up on their own, as long as I kept pushing forward.

Kara stuck her head out of the shower; a vet of steam formed a cloud around her head. She scooped up a pile of suds from her arm and blew them at me, then ducked back behind the curtain. "It's getting cold in here without you."

~ ~

By three o'clock that afternoon, I was bouncing off the walls to my condo. I was somehow supposed to wait until nine to see Kara again for a late practice. I tried passing the time by reading my newest issue of *Glamour* magazine, which ultimately resulted in my reading the same sentence over and over again. I couldn't stop floating. I'd catch glimpses of Kara's nipple, of her star freckle, of her smoldering ass resting in the cup of my hands, and I'd vibrate like an out of control dildo.

I decided the only way I would get through those hours was wine. Lots of wine. So, I ventured to the liquor store.

Standing in line behind a well-dressed business man in a tailored suit purchasing a pack of Marlboros, I gripped my jug of sangria and Kara filtered into my thoughts again. She was arching, grinding, and pleading with me not to stop. My body buzzed. I closed my eyes sealing in the moment.

When it was my turn to pay, I placed my jug on the counter.

"Will that be it?" a gray-haired clerk with a sea of cigarettes in his backdrop asked.

I suddenly felt like smoking.

Two minutes later, back in my car, jug on the floor, cigarettes and lighter on my passenger seat, a sense of power rose in me. I opened the pack of cigarettes, plucked one out and let it dangle from lips as I fidgeted with the lighter. In one clean flick, I lit it. I drew a good long drag. It traveled deep, burning and tickling my soul. My head spun, floated, and drifted like a leaf in a gust of wind. I rested my head back and blew out the smoke. I felt so alive, so free, and so invincible.

I drove down the street, smoking my cigarette like a pro and feeling every bit as sexy as I did the night before. No one could pay me enough to return to the old Becca.

I loved this new life, this new me.

~ ~

Six cigarettes and half the jug of sangria later, I puked. Then, my doorbell rang.

"You don't look so hot," Margie said, feeling my forehead with the back of her hand.

I staggered to the couch, reaching out for its arm. My stomach jackknifed before I could sit. Next thing I knew, Margie grabbed my bamboo plant, yanked out the shoots, poured out the marbles and water and shoved the vase under my chin just in time.

A few minutes later, I emerged from the bathroom feeling shaky, but less queasy. Margie handed me a glass of water. "I knew you'd be upset, but I didn't think you'd be this bad."

"Upset?"

She reached into her pocketbook. Her hand emerged a moment later clutching a bottle of prescriptions meds. "These helped me. Why don't you take them?" She handed me the bottle.

I tossed them to the side. They spilled into the crack between the cushions. "You think I'm puking because of Kelly?"

She crossed her legs and leaned back, shedding her coat and scarf. "I puked for days. I lost seven pounds that first week."

"I'm fine. Trust me."

"Yeah." She rolled her eyes. "Listen, the reason I stopped by is to ask you a favor. I'm thinking of having this Christmas party at the spa for my employees. Nothing big. Just some finger foods, a few giveaways, things like that. And I was wondering if I could ask you to swing by and play a few sets for them?"

"When is it?"

"I was thinking of having it in three weeks. I'll go with any night you're available."

"Tuesdays are good," I said.

"Great. I'll get the invitations out."

"Great."

We sat in silence staring at my collection of vinyl records. Then, "Oh, and don't worry," she said. "Kelly won't be there."

"I'm not worried. Invite her if you want her there."

"Let's get through a couple of months first," she said. "Then we'll think about putting the two of you in the same room."

"I'm going to get some crackers," I said, sliding past her. "Want anything?"

She crinkled her nose. "Have you been smoking?"

Suddenly, I was thirteen years old again, sneaking a hit of my father's whiskey. "Yeah, so? I might have smoked a cigarette before you came."

"You're smoking now?"

"It's a cigarette. I'm not shooting up."

"Well, that's just bullshit."

"You know what the single greatest joy of being single is?" I asked.

She shrugged.

"Doing whatever the hell I feel like doing without having to pass it by anyone first."

"Okay." She raised her hand in surrender. "Point taken. You obviously know what's best for yourself."

"I'll hold up just fine on my own."

"Maybe you can share your secret with me. It's been over half a year since Marc left and I'm still a mess."

"Stay busy."

"Already tried that. Ceramics class, yoga, karate, everything. What more can I do?"

Fuck someone, I wanted to say. "Just get yourself tangled up in something that gets you excited."

"Hmm." She stood up. "I'll think about it." She grabbed hold of her keys. "I'm going to take off. You're going to be okay?"

"I'll be fine."

"Three weeks from Tuesday," she said. "Please don't forget."

"I won't."

"Take care of yourself," she said.

"Absolutely."

"And don't smoke too much."

"Of course not. It's not like I'm addicted."

We chuckled over that as she walked out. I followed, stood on my stoop, and watched as she climbed into her car and sped away. When she cleared the batch of trees, I reached into my pocket and took out my pack of cigarettes. I stared at them and decided maybe Margie was right. I shouldn't smoke. It was silly, really. I walked in, went to the kitchen, opened up the trash, and tossed them in. The pack landed on top of an empty carton of eggs. I walked back to my couch, sat down, and flipped through *Glamour* again. An hour later, nausea wiped clean from my system, I stood in front of the trash again, lid opened, and reached for the pack. I decided to keep one for another day.

Not more than five minutes later, unable to think of anything else but that damn cigarette, I retreated to my back deck and smoked it all the way down to its filter.

~ ~

Kara was in the practice room, dressed in skinny jeans, long boots just shy of her knees, and a red fitted sweater that hugged her boobs. She was talking with Gabby, who was dressed in a tailored gray suit looking like she was ready to dive into a corporate business meeting. Even her hair seemed to writhe in pain from its tight bun. I snuck in, tiptoeing to the table in the corner. They were arguing. Gabby yelled, infuriated that Kara would sink so low. Kara sweet talked, seemingly amused.

My pocketbook slipped from my arm and slammed into the floor. My lipstick, wallet, and car keys slipped out. They stopped arguing. Kara smiled. I practically jumped into her open arms. Gabby pulled me off, leveraging my sweater as a means of a pulley. Another fight ensued, that time Kara was the one pulling the punches, demanding her sister grow up.

I felt overly-privileged suddenly to be a witness, front and center to that new side of Kara. Her bite, her passion, and her alpha stance mixed together gelling into one hell of defense. If I had pom poms, I'd be shaking them high in the sky, cheering for my girl.

Huffing and red, Gabby turned to me. "We've got problems," she said, her arms strangling her chest, turning blue where her fingers were digging in. Her lips tightened and buckled shut.

I winced and backed away from her a few inches afraid to get burned from residual sparks. "Something I did?" I asked.

Kara pushed forward, protecting me from her seething sister. "Take it easy, sis," she said. "So what, I got us the gig."

"Getting gigs is my job. Mine alone. What you're doing... what you did today was wrong on so many levels." She punched her hands to the air. "So incredulously, irresponsibly wrong." I half expected her head to spin.

"I don't see what the big deal is." Kara turned and shielded me from her sister's wrath.

"You're an idiot," Gabby said, her heels clicking backwards.

"I'm resourceful," Kara said, loosening her grip on me.

"A resourceful idiot." Her foot stomped, cracking the anger and exposing its raw, edgy poison.

"Admit it," Kara said, "You don't always have what it takes to get the job done."

"You fucked the organizer of Langden Ridge Concert Series. That's just plain sleazy."

Alarm bells rang, red lights flashed. Langden Ridge Concert Series was a popular outdoor concert venue that attracted hundreds of people on any given night. Jim Perry, married with four children, was the organizer. Pin pricks darted every square inch of my skin, stabbing me, and gutting me alive.

"I didn't fuck him. I made out with him. Gigantic difference there, sis." She turned to me. "By the way, it was such a gross kiss. He smelled like a pastrami sandwich that had baked in the sun too long."

I nodded, grateful for that tidbit.

"You made out with him, he promised you stage time, you left him standing by the Carousel with blue balls and one hell of a fantasy to get off on, probably in the outhouse a few hundred feet away."

Kara turned me to her. "Gabby's just jealous because she's been trying to get this guy to agree to let us play and I got the yes first."

Gabby stormed up to our faces, pointed her finger at Kara. "I'm the manager. That's the deal. I get the gigs. You perform. You disagree, I walk."

I saw our future slipping, being pulled overboard and sinking to a place too deep to rescue. I braced, determined to rein it in and tie it into an unflappable knot. Then, swooping in with her beautiful, delicate voice, Kara saved the day. "We agree, okay?" She parried her finger away.

Gabby lowered her stance, backed away, and dropped her arms down to her side. "Good. I'm glad we're clear." She spun and stomped to the door. "And just so there's no confusion, we're canceling that gig because that's not how we operate." And with that she slammed the door.

I exhaled.

Kara hopped on her stool, looped her head through the guitar strap, and started strumming. A sly smile rested on her face. "We're not canceling that gig."

"We're not?"

She extended her hand. "Hell no, sweetie." She reached out for me, pulling me in close. "What she doesn't know won't hurt her."

"You don't think she'll find out?"

"No," she said with clandestine mischief written all over her, shining like a diamond. "It'll be our little secret."

"But, what if she does find out?" I asked.

Her arm cradled the guitar. She leaned over, exposing her taut, golden skin, skin I was privy to viewing and touching. "You are so adorable when you get nervous."

I couldn't resist. I leaned into her kiss, ready to prove I was up for anything. Hell I'd play topless if that's what she wanted. She was Kara Travers. The one, the only, and the master of getting what she wanted. "I suppose one little secret won't hurt."

She kissed me deeper. "That's my girl."

~ ~

A week later, Margie called me in a panic. "Marc is seeing someone."

Kara and I were halfway to our secret gig, crawling towards the Woodrow Wilson Bridge with Daughtry's new song blaring on the radio. "Are you okay?" I covered the mouthpiece and whispered to Kara, "Drama."

"I was out with Kelly at that new Mexican restaurant on Charles Street when in walked Marc and this beautiful, tall, European looking chick."

"Wow," I said, turning off the radio, sidestepping the flash of Kelly's face and cutting right to the important question. "Did he see you?"

"No. I practically stuffed my head in my pocketbook when he scanned my end of the restaurant."

Kara ran her finger up and down my thigh. I shuddered as she stoked the tiny sparks into a gush of flames, engulfing me in an inferno. Cell phone in one hand, Kara's silky skin grazing the fingertips of the other, the world could've been caving in on itself and I would've been just as tuned out to the news.

I couldn't speak. I could hardly breathe. Silence waited patiently while Margie hung in the balance, waiting for some acknowledgement. At some point, she broke through my orgasmic ride. "We were just finishing up. They stayed and paid the bill while I scooted out undetected."

My ride halted. "They?"

Pregnant pause. Margie stammered. "Kelly and Bonnie." Her voice wavered on the fringe of regret. "Sorry, Becca, I didn't mean to mention that part."

"Kelly can do whatever," I said, snapping in half any idea she might've had that I was upset by the news. "I don't give a shit." I pictured the scene with Bonnie. She was probably a plain-looking girl sporting a brown bob wearing an argyle print sweater who sat holding Kelly's hand under the safety of a green and red speckled table. Margie would have sat across from them. Bonnie would try hard to befriend her. Margie would try hard not to like her, but fall like prey into her friendly, non-assuming smile.

"How do you do it?" Margie asked. "How do you not care? How do you turn off three years like you would a water spigot? I wish I knew your secret because right now I feel like I'm going fucking crazy. When I saw his arm around that skinny-waisted husband stealer I wanted to die. I wanted to crawl under the table and stop breathing, just die."

Kara's fingers feathered up my arm and headed south for my boobs. "Listen, you'll be fine, Margie," I said, fixated on Kara's fingers' sultry trajectory. "How about tomorrow night I come over and we talk?"

"Yes. Tomorrow night. Nine o'clock?"

"Nine it is," I said. I barely hung up when Kara snaked into my bra and started playing with my nipple.

A minute later, I hung on the verge of the sexiest orgasm ever experienced when traffic suddenly cleared. Kara accelerated, heading south. Desperate for the moment to return, I latched onto her hand, brought it up to my lips and practically made love to it as she sped on down the interstate towards our secret gig. I didn't give a shit what Kelly was doing with her life. Bonnie could have her.

I inched up Kara's arm, to her shoulders, to her neck, down her chest, and into her bra. In the dark, the glowing dashboard lights our only hinder to privacy, I drove Kara wild.

I loved living on the edge.

## Chapter Nine

We rocked the crowd as the third act on stage, weaving a cover in between two of our originals. Covered from her breasts down to her toes in leather, Kara stole the limelight. Girls and guys ogled her ass and her long, slender legs as she strutted across the outdoor stage, belting out lyrics, guitar hanging at her hips, and clapping her hands above her head in an infectious two beat count. The crowd transformed into one giant vibrato. Kara embodied the show. At one point, she curled up around me and whispered in my ear, "You play, sweetie. I'm going to work the crowd a bit." And off she pranced, flinging her hair every which way, inching towards the edge of the stage, and willing the crowd to join in her dance parade.

Gabby would've freaked, yanked her right down to the ground and forbid her to get back on that stage. A few girls reached up and grabbed her arm. I slowed the tempo, enough to grace Kara with time to get away from their prying, eager hands. She turned back towards me and winked, sashaying one hip in front of the other. From behind, the two girls had walked up and onto the stage. I stopped playing altogether at that point. They sandwiched her and danced against her to a beat all their own. Was that allowed? Kara grinded with them. Together they looked like a machine in perfect sync. I thumbed my strings, not sure where to pick up. The crowd was whistling, hooting. So, I broke out into one of our faster songs. But before I could get more than a stanza into the song, two security men appeared and pried the girls apart. One of them looked at me and signaled for me to stop. On command, I did. "You're done. Show's over."

With my jaw hung low, I looked to Kara. She plucked up her guitar from its stand and pulled me off stage, laughing over the incident. My guitar bobbled behind, whacking me in the ass.

"Ah, that was so much fun," Kara said, breathless and bending over once we arrived in the pavilion.

Several minutes later, after returning from the bathroom, I pretended to fiddle with my strings while the two girls flirted with Kara. I decided after ten minutes or so to walk up to them, join in their banter, and show Kara just how cool I could be. They ignored me until Kara finally put her arm around me. "Have you girls met Becca, yet?" She squeezed me close. I reveled. "These are two of our most loyal fans, Sherry and Dania." I offered my hand like the CEO of a corporate conglomerate. They smirked, shook my hand and then excused themselves, blaming their rapid departure on event traffic and nine a.m. meetings. They said their goodbyes to Kara with a kiss on her cheek and a pat on her ass. They walked right past me without as much as a nod. Kara giggled and waved to them. One of the girls practically broke her leg tripping over her coat.

"Fans. I just love them," Kara said.

As people passed, they snuck glances at her with their fantasies perched for me to see. Dreamy eyes, sultry nods, and puckered lips focused solely on Kara. One thing rang true, those people were absolutely infatuated with Kara Travers, the rock goddess, not Becca James the folk singer.

Kara flashed me a sidelong glance completely oblivious to her sole-propriety over fans. "I'm starving."

"I can get you a hotdog if you want. We could watch the rest of the concert if the security lets us near the stage."

She tugged at my shirt and jammed her finger around my neckline. Her eyes smoldered. A smirk reserved just for me blanketed her face. "I'm not hungry for food."

I melted into her kiss. "Those girls were so hot. They made me ravenous," she said before yanking me towards the bath house and into a full-blown state of rapture. I flailed, along for the ride, teetering on the hairline edge of a cliff. Embrace it, or fall off. I opened my arms wide and took it all in, sure the thrill would knock me off my feet.

~ ~

Kara pushed me into the biggest changing stall, kissing me while throwing me roughly up against a locker with a padlock. A polka dotted curtain, our only door in and out to the rest of the world, swayed behind her. "Are you scared?" she asked with an adorable tease resting on the edge of her voice.

"You know it."

She traveled around my skin like she was discovering it for the first time, kissing me, devouring me, and shining me up like a jewel. Her tongue pushed aggressively downwards across my chest, down my belly, and past my bikini underpants. Her fingers stroked me with just the right pressure and speed. "How did I ever get so lucky?" I asked.

"Less talking, more moaning," she said with her breathing husky and bold as she wrapped her lips around my secluded parts, elevating the intensity. I grabbed hold of her head of waves, scrunching them, twisting them, and moaning out in pleasure, despite the whispers of girls not more than three car-lengths past the curtain. I was on fire, sweltering under the heat of her tongue, shaking and ready to explode.

"Promise me it'll always be like this," I said.

My head swirled. I panted. I braced for the burst of ecstasy. It tore through me like a tornado, thrashing, unyielding, powerful, and leaving me without air to breathe. I clung to her with my heart pounding and nerves electrocuted. She rose up and kissed me on the lips. My smell permeated from her.

~ ~

On the drive back to her place, we held hands. "Did you ever think I'd become your girlfriend?" I asked her.

She cocked her head and bathed me in her sexy eyes. "I always knew we'd end up together at some point, sure. I'm not big into labels, though. It takes the fun out of it all."

"Then, no label it is."

~ ~

We slept like a pretzel, twisted and tangled. I woke first and watched Kara's mouth flutter with each breath. Rain pelted her sliding doors and the late morning light filtered through the blinds. Vanilla and musk settled around us, swirling from a set of diffusers set on her wicker table off the bathroom. I huddled closer to her, possessively pulling the silky sheets over our naked bodies.

An hour later, her eyes flittered open. "What time is it?"

I reached around her curves to get a better look at the clock. "It's eleven."

"I need to get showered."

I kissed her, holding her captive in our silky fort. "Stay here with me for a little longer."

She caressed my face. "Save me some for tonight." She untangled from me and climbed out of bed.

"Count on it."

She stared deep into my eyes. "You know what I'm craving tonight?"

I crawled up on my knees and the covers pooled around me. "Whatever it is, I'll see you get some."

She cored me with her smoldering eyes. "Spaghetti and meatballs."

"Not what I was thinking, exactly." I traced her arm with my fingers, chuckling.

"Homemade." She plucked up my fingers and kissed them. "By these hands. I can be at your place by seven. I'll bring the wine."

Margie, with her battered and bruised ego, suddenly wedged herself between us. "I can't tonight." I bit down on my lips hoping for some reprieve from the truly tragic moment. "I already made plans with Margie."

She pulled me up from the bed, swung my legs around her waist, and nibbled on my lips. "That's a shame. I guess I'll have to spend the night alone." She walked backwards with me wrapped around her, grabbing my ass and squeezing it.

"I'll cancel," I said, grinding against her as she carried me to the shower.

~ ~

An hour later, Kara kissed me goodbye. "Make sure you set Ella's house alarm when you leave. It's written on that blue book by my nightstand."

"You got it," I said. "See you at seven, then?"

"Yes. Text me your address," she said before closing the door.

I twirled and took a good look around. I stood alone in her personal turf. For the next fifteen minutes, I took it upon myself to inspect the details of her furniture, her lighting, curtains, her perfumes, her brushes, her clothes, and her shoes. Finally, I landed by her bedside and picked up the blue book and opened it to find her code. A picture slipped out the backside. Kara kissing a redhead. Both were wearing bikinis. Tiki torch flames and palm trees swayed in the backdrop. I turned it over. Chrissy and me, Bahamas. A mere two months prior. I remembered she had missed several practices. Gabby blamed it on Kara being sick.

I stared at the picture for several minutes. Up close. Far away. To the side. Upside down. Didn't matter how I positioned it, I couldn't get Kara to look any less in love with the girl. An inner frenzy ran, scratching itself through my blood and tossing me around the room in a mad search for more clues. I opened drawers and looked under her bed, her dresser, and in her closet. Hidden on a shelf behind a few dozen pocketbooks, I discovered a photo album darted with more palm trees and sandals than I cared to count. I flipped it open and spent the next hour scrutinizing their smiles, postures, and hands. I stared at a power couple embracing, loving, and so tender. I wanted to throw up.

I slammed the album shut and buried it back under the pocketbooks.

Moments later, I sat in the front seat of my car and lit a cigarette hoping it would ease the unsettled feeling in the pit of my stomach.

~~

I expected an outburst from Margie when I called to cancel our plans for the night, not the silent treatment. I was sitting in the front seat of my car in the Safeway parking lot fully prepared to defend why I was choosing to spend the night with Kara over grabbing dinner with her. I cooked up a white lie sure to settle. "Kara and I have only tonight to record our next single if we want it released on time for the New Year tour Gabby has planned for us," I said. I tossed in all sorts of spices, stirring up a steaming dish of undeniable reasons I couldn't be there for her that night. *The studio had a last minute cancellation. If we didn't record that night, we'd be looking at another three weeks.*

I flung excuses into the mix until I was sure of its virility. "I wouldn't cancel with you otherwise," I said, finally closing the lid on the pot of lies.

"Fine," she said.

"So, we're okay, then?"

"Yeah, sure. It's been six months since my breakup. I'll live to see another day."

"Okay. I promise, though, I'll make it up to you. We'll get together soon. We'll sort this whole Marc thing out." I waited for her to say something.

Nothing.

"Hey," I said, reopening the lid for one last attempt to stymie my guilt. "Why don't you send me a list of songs you want me to play for your Christmas party? I want to be fully prepared."

"Don't bother with the party."

"What is that supposed to mean?"

Dead silence.

"Margie?"

Dial tone.

"What the fuck?" I tossed my cell into my pocketbook before climbing out of my car and slamming the door shut. I pulled my hood up over my hair and ran through the parking lot, splashing through puddles and dodging rain drops the size of marbles. I shot through the doors of Safeway, grabbed a cart, and smacked straight into the path of a store clerk passing out appetizers on a toothpick.

"Want to try a Steak Diablo?" the wrinkled and worn woman wearing an apron asked me. The smell of garlic and onions curled around my last nerve.

I wanted to shove the table of Diablos over and kick the shit out of it. "No, thank you." I pushed my cart past her, then swerved to avoid a mountain of apples that some idiot stocker decided to pile right in the middle of the aisle I needed to go down. I bolted with my cart, hanging sharp lefts and rights on two wheels, banging into end caps and knocking down boxes of pasta, potato chips, bread, you name it, wondering all the while what else could ruin my day. Then, I broadsided a kid pushing one of those mini carts, and the mother shot me to hell with curses. I defended myself, storming on about her kid flying at me out of nowhere. She didn't give a shit about my defense. Screw her. I stomped my foot and pushed onward.

Fucking Margie. She picked a fine day to start being miss sensitivity.

~ ~

By seven-o-clock that night, I sat on my couch, cigarette in one hand, glass of wine in the other and waited for Kara to arrive. The smell of tangy tomatoes and basil seeped from the kitchen and intensified my hunger pangs. Italian bread was sliced, bathed in garlic butter and ready to bake. A box of thin spaghetti waited for its plunge. Two plates draped with white napkins, folded up like the front of a tuxedo shirt, huddled on the table, a vase of flowers their only company at the moment. Soft jazz sprinkled through the condo. Candles softened the room.

I even tossed a log in the fireplace to make my condo seem cozy and perfect for Kara. I patted my couch cushion, fluffing it a bit, hoping the pillows would stay firm and not sag halfway through our first glass of wine.

I wanted that night to be about getting to know each other beyond lyrics, guitar riffs, and fans. I wanted her to ask me questions, dig deep for answers, and search my condo for clues to who I was when I ducked into the bathroom. I wanted that to open the dialogue and turn to the page where I could ask her about life, about her dreams, and about that redhead. That damned redhead had shone brighter than a diamond, smiled broader than an ocean, and radiated more sex appeal than a Playboy centerfold. Why did Kara have to keep her picture so close to her bed?

I took a drag of my cigarette, then sipped more wine.

By eight-fifteen, Kara was officially late. I checked the time against my cell, my DVD player, and my computer clock. I calculated in my head how many minutes I'd wait before calling her. She could've easily been stuck in traffic, stopped for speeding, or gotten her heel stuck in a crack.

By eight-thirty, I called her and left a casual message, asking her to bring up her new Brandi Carlile CD. Two seconds later, my phone rang.

"I am so sorry, sweetie," she said, panting. "I'm running late. I'm on my way right now."

"Are you okay?"

"Yeah, so much better than just okay! I just had the most amazing two hours. I met Dan Steele, the drummer of the Skinners! He was working out on the treadmill next to me and one thing led to another and he asked me to grab a drink with him. Sweetie, this guy was gushing over me. I've got him wrapped around my little finger. If I play my cards right with him, he could help take us up another level. He mentioned touring together. Imagine? He's national. He's got a following the size of a small country. I can't wait to tell you more about it. I should be there in twenty."

She hung up before I could open my mouth to breathe. I should've been thrilled. That very well could have been the big break musicians dreamed of. But, I couldn't get the vision out of my mind of Kara flirting, touching, and kissing that Dan guy in a cozy booth in the back of a bar.

I boiled the water for the spaghetti and plopped the garlic bread in the oven. By the time I came to my better senses and erased all unfathomable possibilities of Kara and Dan from my mind, she called again. That time her voice climbed even higher. "You won't believe this," she said. "Dan just called me and invited me as his personal guest to their show tonight. It starts in an hour, so I've got to get going. I'll catch you tomorrow, okay sweetie?"

Click.

There I stood under my double-bulbed fluorescents, a canister of salt in one hand and my dead cell in the other. I screamed. I screamed so loud, I think I might've burned the cells all the way down my throat. The screams rose up, convulsing, shaking, and riveting. I flung the salt in the sink and punched my leg. I was mad. I was mad at Dan, mad at the boiling water for hissing at me, mad at the timer on the oven for ringing like an out of control train, mad at my empty pack of cigarettes, mad at my empty wine glass, but most of all, mad at myself for not being good enough, worthy enough, magnetic enough to overcome the likes of the Dan Steeles in Kara's world and all their possibilities.

Later I rolled around my bed focusing on Margie, trying desperately to stay mad at her, at her ridiculous outburst, and at her inability to understand the complexities of a musician's schedule. I sat up in my bed, fuming, needing to fight.

I called her. "Seriously?" I asked. "You're kicking me out of your Christmas party?"

"Like you give a shit," Margie said. "You're selfish and undeserving, and I can't believe you lied to me. That's right, I found out what a fucking liar you are. When you didn't answer my call a little while after I hung up on you, I called the studio, instead, to apologize. The girl said you and Kara hadn't been there since the day before. I asked her to double check the recording studios. She did. She confirmed that you are a self-absorbed liar."

I hung up this time, unable to hear another one of her sharp words. I had had enough holes poked in me that night already. All I needed was a hose down my throat and I'd look like a goddamned sprinkler system. Stick me in the middle of a baseball field and crank me up, then watch the fucking grass grow green with envy over my wonderful luck.

## **Chapter Ten**

Christmas had pedaled in without a warning. Soft, flickering bulbs tangled around thick, fluffy garland that was wrapped around every storefront. Plastic pine trees in greens, reds and whites glowed in display windows, and banners strapped across them announced once-in-a-lifetime savings. The smell of cinnamon and clove infused a sense of nostalgia as I walked the mall in search of an outfit that would blow Kara's mind.

The year before, Kelly and I had spent every minute of the season strolling the mall. The Christmas spirit had turned us into a couple of peppermint-loving, joyful gals. We had always loved that time of year together. By day we'd stroll; by night we'd sip minty hot chocolate and write out Christmas cards. Our favorite tradition was plucking a needy child's name off the Good Will Tree and then buying his dream toy. We'd go all out on wrapping those special gifts, tucking the paper just right and piling masses of curly ribbon on top. One year, I pulled a child's name who wanted a table tennis racket. One would've thought I was shopping for a diamond ring the way I searched, scrutinized, and then finally selected the perfect one. I found it at a specialty shop for gaming. It cost me over two-hundred dollars and was considered the holy crown of table tennis racquets with its high tech uniaxial light carbon blades. I had no clue what that meant, but when the man behind the glass counter talked about it with eyes ablaze and hands punctuating the words, nothing else would suffice. I imagined the little boy growing up and becoming a world class tennis table champion.

I managed to pass the tree without looking up at it, despite the frantic bell ringing of Mrs. Claus. I just didn't have time this year.

My head was still jumbled from not sleeping the night before. I walked with a purpose, though, intent on buying something that would make me feel as confident and unbreakable as I did just over twenty-four hours beforehand. Kara and I were scheduled for an interview with DJ Allen from the Allen and Jives show on 106.1. I wanted to show up looking decent for Kara. I figured a fitted black t-shirt and a pair of skinny jeans would do the trick.

I combed through Ann Taylor Loft, Saks Fifth Avenue, and Neiman Marcus, and none of them sold a plain, black t-shirt. By the time I walked into The Gap I was craving a cigarette and needed to pee. Thankfully, the buyers for The Gap had a clue. Right by the cash registers was the best-looking display of black t-shits Arundel Mills Mall had to offer. I plucked one up and handed it over to the clerk.

She smiled then proceeded to punch the register keys. I handed over my credit card. When she looked down at it, she smiled even broader. "I thought it was you! Becca James! I just saw you at the Promenade!"

I blushed. "Yep, that's me."

"Hey, this one's on the house," she said, then handed me the shirt.

"Really?" My breaths increased, and my heart banged around in my chest.

"Absolutely. Just promise me you'll wear it next time you're at the Promenade."

"Sure thing."

The girl walked away and stole another glance at me over her shoulder before heading to the back of the store.

I felt like a rock star. I had two hundred dollars burning a hole in my wallet and decided I was going to splurge and spend it on a pair of Lucky jeans. By the time I walked out of the mall later on, I slipped on my sunglasses, lit a cigarette, and tossed my bag of Lucky jeans and the free t-shirt over my shoulder. I felt so free.

~ ~

I braved four inches of freshly fallen snow to get to the radio station. My tires swerved, my wiper blades froze up, my car even slipped off the road once, and yet, I arrived unscathed.

I shook the snow off my A-line tweed jacket and stepped inside, ready to conquer the world. The receptionist, a short, plump woman in her fifties, led me through a copy room with reams of paper stacked six feet high and envelopes tiled around the floor in mosaic fashion. A handsome man in a suit sporting a Rolex knockoff licked the flap of an oversized envelope and winced, complaining of a paper cut. I followed the receptionist down a series of narrow hallways. We'd pass an occasional open door and in the closet-sized offices were sales-looking people jabbering on telephones, smiles in their voices, and pain on their faces. We stopped in front of one girl's office to let a group of men pass. She flipped through the yellow pages, holding the page with her pinky while calling someone. "Can I speak with whoever's in charge of advertising?" she asked. A second later, she slammed the receiver down and flung the book to the ground. I smiled, and she shot me a weary look.

We walked again. The receptionist turned over her shoulder pad at me. "These young ones come in fresh out of college and think it's easy to slide right into a six-figure sales position. You have to have the skin of a water buffalo to make it in this industry. I give her three days, max."

We arrived at a locked door with a window. Kara and Gabby stood on the other side with a round-faced man in a goatee. I recognized him as DJ Allen. Kara giggled, and DJ Allen practically drooled. We entered. I strode right up to Kara, riding in on the coattails of my afternoon romp into stardom and forgiving her for the night before. I moved in for a kiss. She turned her cheek to me at the last second and immediately tugged at DJ Allen's arm. "This is Becca."

He extended his hand. I quickly introduced myself and told him how excited I was that he agreed to interview us on live radio. He escorted us into the recording room and gave us each a headset. We sat on stools in front of a wall of switches and flashing lights.

I placed my hand on her knee and she brushed it off. She stood, took off her headset and took off mine. "Can I talk to you for a sec out in the hall?"

I followed her out the door. Gabby closed it behind us, leaving us alone in the hallway.

"Everything alright?" I asked her.

She shook her head in sharp snaps. "We can't be all over each other in front of this guy. We can't have him outing us to everyone."

"Why?" I asked, a trace of horror spiraled on the end of my words.

Her face instantly softened. "It's just not the impression we want to give to the fans."

I knew she was right on some level. The fans came out for a chance at that one fleeting look from her, that one smile, that one air blown kiss, that one drop of sweat to trickle down onto them, that one opportunity to gather as much of her sexiness as they could so they could go home filled with enough fantasy to get them through to the next show. If they knew I was her girlfriend, the thrill would die.

"Okay." I couldn't even raise my eye to her. I was embarrassed, scolded, and chastised.

"Hey." She reached for my hand. "You know I'm crazy about you."

Just like that, she managed to light her irresistible torch and soften the blow. My smile escaped before I turned to go back in.

Back in the studio, headsets attached, stools appropriately spaced apart from each other, the DJ announced to the greater Baltimore area that he had two of the hottest new performers with him and welcomed listeners to call in. He then started to ask us a series of questions about how we got started in the industry, who our favorite artists were, what the biggest thrill of performing was, what kind of foods we liked to eat backstage, how we prepared for a show, and whether we preferred acoustic over plugged. Kara answered them all with great eloquence. She spoke using her raspy voice, whispering her answers into the mic, never skipping a beat, and just issuing one smooth answer after the other.

That was why we were so damn successful. And why I'd have to make sure I did whatever it'd take to keep the girl interested in me.

~ ~

In February, I decided to go to Della Books and spend the gift card Joe McFadden had mailed to me over the holidays. When I first read his card, his words dug at me and scratched deeper than just the surface. He told me he was always there should I need to call him up and talk to him about my life, my career, anything. He also told me I should've been the star, the front runner, the one commanding applause, not the backup singer. He reminded me how I could stand on my own and hoped I wasn't leaning too much on that girl Kara whom he wasn't convinced had my best intentions in mind from what he'd heard. Then, he ended by telling me how much the customers missed me, how much he missed me, and how much he ached for my happiness and success.

At first I felt angry at him for assuming Kara was bad for me. I wanted to get him on the phone and tell him off, protect Kara, and justify how my life was so much better than before. Then, I realized he was probably just misguided by some drunken customer. A thousand people could've told him how great my show was, but all it took was one bad review to thwart thinking. He needed to see me live and witness the magic for himself. So, instead of the call, I sent him tickets to our New Year's Eve show at The Hippodrome in Baltimore. He didn't make it, citing in a phone message that he couldn't leave the pub unattended on such a busy night.

At the café bookstore, I sat in a leather chair. The smell of bread and coffee seeped from every nook and cranny. With the card, I ordered a mocha latte with extra cream and chocolate shavings. I browsed through the books on the coffee table in front of me. *Finance for the Beginner, How to Build an Empire, The Act of Home, Wolves, Twilight*. Atop them sat a crinkled copy of *The Washington Post*. A picture of a woman soldier hugging her baby blanketed the front flap of the newspaper. Below it, a gripping headline: Soldier Refuses to Leave her Baby.

I turned the pages, combing the ads, headlines, and photographs. A picture of a runner breaking through the formal ribbon of the Snow Ball Road Race caught my eye. His smile so self-assured, the joy exploding off the page like a firecracker. I could even see beads of sweat dripping down his face, despite the snow hiding the curbs. I looked, as was habit, at the credit. *Kelly Copeland*. Full credit. "I'll be damned."

The man sitting in the leather chair next to me looked up from his book, smiling. "Something good happen in the world today?"

I double-checked myself. Her name slanted in eloquence on the newsprint. "Yeah, I suppose it did for someone."

I sat in that leather chair for another hour examining every detail of the photo; the sharp focus on the runner's face, the waved effect of the finish line banner, and the perfected blurry treatment on the faces in the backdrop. I imagined Kelly, squatted on her right knee, left hand still as a statue at the base of her lens, her heart leaping, and her finger relaxed and ready to snap the photo.

I wondered, if even for the briefest moment, had she yearned to tell me?

~ ~

My curiosity stole every bit of reason from me when I got home from the bookstore. I didn't go home and do the things I had set out to accomplish that day. The carpets remained dirty with crumbs. The dishes were piled high in the sink, drenched in cold water with soap that had long since dissolved. My laundry basket overflowed with clothes from two weeks of wearing. My cable and phone bills stayed unopened. Nothing else mattered more than logging into Facebook to see what other important things I might've missed in the three months since I'd talked to Kelly.

Gabby managed mine and Kara's duo profile, updating gigs and fan notices, sending video links, even posing as us in a few comments. I hadn't logged on to my personal one in months. Apparently, I had over two-hundred friend requests since my last login. Messages from strangers jammed my inbox. Someone from Idaho wanted to know what shampoo I used. Someone else from Wisconsin asked if I celebrated Christmas or Hanukah. Another person from Providence wrote a ten stanza song and asked if we'd be willing to play it at her senior prom that coming spring. A few people had even asked me on a date. I also realized Kelly was no longer one of my Facebook friends.

The room ballooned to twice its size while I shrank to a mere atom, floating around in a world with too much space.

I turned to a Blue Moon to help set my mind straight. When that didn't work, I caved and snooped into Margie's profile. I needed a good dose of familiar comfort.

I read through her wall posts. I learned she had read the whole Twilight book series, and that she adored Pug puppies more than babies.

I browsed her notes. I never knew she was afraid to ride her bike as a kid and would instead walk it through the neighborhood. I also couldn't believe that she ran a marathon when she was fifteen-years-old.

I eventually clicked onto the place I wanted to click on all along, her photos. I smiled when I saw she still had our girls' weekend album posted. The three of us had taken off to New Hampshire in the middle of October two years prior. We stayed at The Red Sleigh Inn, a bed and breakfast that served up a breakfast that put IHOP to shame. We hiked Lafayette trail, a wide, flat, carriage trail, by day, searching the woods for black bears and deer, and sat in front of the polished stone fireplace with steaming cups of hot cocoa in hand by night.

Kelly had snapped a photo of me and Margie upside down on the staircase. Our cheeks were flushed red and our hair had splattered around us like old fashioned floor mops. She had skillfully captured the happy moment, with the candles on the foyer table flickering in the spokes of our eyes and all.

I ventured into her album of me performing at Rams Head Tavern with Kara. I remembered that night. I had nothing to wear. I stood in my closet for three hours trying on outfit after outfit, trying to layer shirts to camouflage my muffin top. Seemed everything accentuated it instead. I settled on a black sweater that hugged my waist more than I would've liked. But, I had no choice. It was the only thing that I could wear that fit. Now when I looked at the photo of me propped on my stool, just a trace of light from the spotlight hitting the tip of my shoe, I didn't see any fat. But, I did look awfully nervous, like I was about to throw up.

Thank God those rookie days were over.

My eyes leapt from one album to another, a momentary stroll along the memories. I eventually ran into Margie's Christmas party album, and purposely skipped over it like five times afraid to reignite my hurt. I skimmed through all fifteen of her albums, then steadied the mouse over her Christmas party album once again. I lit a cigarette first, inhaling it deep into my lungs, banking on it to soothe the rising tide swelling inside.

I didn't want to see a replacement one-man band banging out Christmas tunes.

I took another drag and clicked into it anyway. Red and green blurred in the background of every shot, Margie kissing her receptionist's cheek under a mistletoe; Margie giving a toast, looking extremely skinny in a red cocktail dress; Margie dancing with some really handsome man in a tuxedo, who stared way too intently into her eyes; and Margie posing in the center of her staff, arms entwined and smiles as bright as the Christmas lights hanging over their heads. I stopped at one of Margie cracking up, bent at her knees, a drink spraying like a ruptured volcano from her mouth and nostrils. I laughed out loud in my empty condo, wishing I would've been there. I studied the picture, her shoes, her sequins, her smooth updo, and then, I noticed Kelly in the background with her hand wrapped around a pretty girl's hand. My heart stopped.

I flashed forward through more photos until I came across one of just the two of them up close, holding each other, smiling at the camera. The girl had dark, shiny hair to her shoulders with the slightest wisps on her forehead. Her eyes were deep set, coral green, with a hint of something exotic. An electric pulse cursed through me like a firecracker, sizzling all the way from my hand to my feet.

She was way too pretty.

Then, when it couldn't get any worse, I discovered another photo that literally pulled my gut in twenty different directions. Kelly's parents were digging into bowl of food with Kelly and the girl arm-in-arm right next to them.

Later the next day, I drove to my gynecologist for a checkup. I think the only other thing I dreaded more than death was going to the doctor's. They never had anything good to say. They always found fault. You're ten pounds over your ideal weight. You need to take better care of your skin when out in the sun. You need to stretch your muscles so you can be more flexible. I knew walking in to Dr. Russo's office, that I'd get a lecture that year more than any other. Perfect Dr. Russo—with her perfect straight marriage, her two perfect honor roll students, her perfect body, her perfect education, her perfect everything—would stare me head-on and tell me I was a mess. The only reason I kept the appointment was because I needed a refill on my allergy meds, and she had been the one doctor willing to dole out the prescription without subjecting me to the torture of allergy testing.

So, there I sat, naked under a gown, boobs and vagina on highest alert, prepared to be violated. As usual, Dr. Russo was running late. That gave me way too much time to examine the room and all its unnerving medical fixings: posters detailing the anatomy of a women's breasts, a plastic model of a women's uterus, glass jars filled with cotton swabs, a vat of rubbing alcohol, a stack of sterile gauze, a red biohazard container, mitted stirrups with polka dotted red and pink circles, notices of health insurance coverage changes and payment procedures, and a rack of fitness magazines.

My legs dangled down in front of me and tissue paper creased under my ass. Then, the knock, and the cheery smile of Dr. Russo.

"Good morning," she said, owning the room and commanding respect.

I breathed and my chest rattled. "Morning."

She glanced at my chart, searching it for screw-ups that she could call me out on. "Okay, so I see you gained five pounds since our last visit. Why is that?" She cocked her head to the side and waited.

I cleared my throat. "Stress?"

"Do you smoke?"

"Nope." I said as casually and carefree as possible, fooling her to avoid a lecture.

"How about drinking?"

"Maybe a glass of wine once a month," I said, then added, "if that."

"How much exercise do you get?"

"I work out regularly." At least I did at some point in my life.

"Are you sexually active?"

"I have a girlfriend."

She nodded, "No need for birth control, then." She reached for her stethoscope, then placed it on my back. "Deep breath."

In ten minutes, she completed my exam. She sent me out of the door with a new prescription for allergy meds, then told me to keep up the good work and that she'd see me next year.

I carried the undeserved compliment out the door and all the way to my car.

I lit a cigarette and called Kara. "Hey, after the gig, let's go do something. I need time with you." I couldn't wait to get my mind off the Facebook photos, off Kelly, off Margie, and off the wad of bad feelings stuck to me like chewed bubblegum.

"I have the perfect place," she said.

~ ~

Kara's friend, Mica, lived in a four-story townhome on the Inner Harbor. Brick lined one side of wall on the main level. An open staircase adorned the middle, separating the living room from the dining room. The dining room sprawled out to the kitchen, which then opened up to a garden of holly bushes, and as Mica explained, vegetable and flower plants of every kind in the summer months.

She smoothed her black-bobbed hair, then invited us to sit on the leather couch while she served us up some cocktails. We picked at carrots and broccoli hearts as we waited. Kara pointed out an oil painting of two dancing ladies that Mica had created herself. She explained the Visionary Museum displayed it for several months. A dozen or so leather-bound encyclopedias lined a glass and brushed steel bookshelf to my left. An odd statue of an owl on a tree limb stared at me from the edge of the staircase. An orange tabby cat rubbed up against my black pants. The smell of burnt wood smoldered from the fireplace. Finally, the three of us sat staring at each other, martini glasses in one hand, cigarettes in the other. "The others should be here soon," Mica explained, taking a deep drag then blowing it out of her plump, red lips and straight up on the air to dance in the glow of her chandelier.

"So are you two fucking each other?" she asked, flicking her ashes into a crystal bowl.

I choked on my cigarette.

Mica stared straight-faced at me with her heavily lined eyes.

I looked to Kara for help, but she seemed to not even hear the question. Then, the doorbell rang.

Mica escorted four dashingly gorgeous women and three equally dapper men through the front door. Within ten minutes, the townhome filled up with a good thirty more people, and when the music started to pump, I could've closed my eyes and felt like I was in a New York City nightclub. Kara flirted around the room, hugging this one and that one, leaving me to stand like a wallflower over by the staircase with the owl statue. I helped myself to another martini.

By my fifth drink, Kara had made her way back to me and was equally tipsy. She straddled her hand around mine and began making out with me right there in front of three women engrossed in gossip about a girl named Rachel who wore fishnet stockings to a New Year's Eve party. The drinks, the music, and the onlookers, just intensified my feelings for Kara tenfold. "I love when you're affectionate like this," I said to her.

"In front of friends, I can be myself." She kissed me hard and my head swirled. I packaged thoughts of Kelly and her girlfriend to the side of my brain, as far away from that moment as possible.

Soon after, more people filtered into the party. Drinks were flowing, laughter was rising, and dancing was underway. Kara let loose and began grinding with me, humping every inch of me, kissing me hard, and showing me off to all her friends in the center of the makeshift dance floor. Before long, I found myself sitting outside on her lap under heat lamps, a circle of her friends all around. Someone lit a joint and passed it to Kara, who then passed it to me. I was drunk, but not without my wits. Kelly and I had made a deal with each other that we'd never stoop to drugs. I wasn't ready to toss that promise away just yet. I passed it right on to the next girl. Kara tossed me a disapproving nod.

"I'm doing just fine with the martinis."

A minute later, Kara was taking another hit of it. She inhaled a long drag, then planted her lips on mine and blew it into my mouth. A victim of happenstance, I inhaled it, telling myself I wasn't really smoking a joint this way. Kara took another hit and passed it over me to the girl next to me. When it came back around again, I allowed Kara to spoon feed it to me again, reminding myself that I was just an innocent bystander of second hand smoke, enjoying a fruitful kiss. After five hits like that, Kara and I fell into a giggly heap. Everything was so funny, from her eyebrows to her watch. But the funniest thing of all was when one of her friends stuck her ass in Kara's face and asked her to sign it. When that sharpie touched that girl's tight ass, I almost peed myself. Then, suddenly, another one of her friend's placed her boob in my face and asked me to sign it.

I signed it with the fine tip of that black sharpie marker. The trail end of my last name stretched daringly close to her nipple. I thought that was the funniest thing in the world. I laughed and laughed until Kara helped me out. She stole the sharpie right from my fingers and signed the girl's other boob. She even drew smiley faces in all of her letter A's.

Then, when the joint came back around, I plucked it from Kara's fingers and took a hit all by myself. I leaned into Kara, pulling up my shirt and bra, giving a show to any townhome-dwellers who happened to be looking out their windows. "Sign me."

She signed it with big letters, and drew hearts all around my nipple. We giggled all night long over that.

## Chapter Eleven

My ends were split for the first time since I had met Margie. It didn't matter if I spent five minutes or two hours primping, my hair no longer cooperated. I had contemplated walking into a new salon for about two seconds, then flipped that switch off just as fast. I couldn't bear the thought of someone else digging into my personal life.

I needed Margie.

I called the salon and immediately hung up when her receptionist answered. A minute later, I called back and apologized for the hang-up, blaming it on bad cell service instead of my ridiculous cowering. I set an appointment for the next afternoon at two o'clock for a trim and color glaze. I figured, I'd walk in for my appointment, we'd take one look at each other and giggle away the last two month's bitter ties.

But, half an hour later, Margie called.

"Hi," she said, her voice chilled to just above freezing.

"Hi," I said as chipper as possible. "I'm so glad you called." I really was. "I've missed you so much."

"I don't think I should be the one to do your hair tomorrow."

"Oh, come on, let's just forget about that little fight. It was so long ago now. I don't even remember what we fought about."

"Of course you don't."

"Look, whatever I did or said, I'm really sorry." I pitched my apology in a darned convincing tone.

Silence.

I drank some water.

I tossed a piece of gum in my mouth.

Cleared my throat.

Then, finally, "I'm still pissed," she said. "I just need some more time."

"This is ridiculous. Can't we just grab a coffee or something? Straighten this whole thing out?"

"Not yet."

"Then, when?"

"I'm just really busy at work and I'm going away this weekend with Marc."

"Marc? You're going away with Marc?"

"Yes, he invited us to go skiing in Vermont with him."

"Who's 'us'?"

Silence again, which only confirmed the answer.

"Why does it matter?" she asked.

"I guess it really doesn't."

"Look, if you really need your hair done, I can get you in tomorrow, but you'll have to wait around a bit. I'm squeezing you in between another color and cut."

I pictured Kelly and her pretty girlfriend cuddled up in the backseat and Margie and Marc holding hands in front. Then, I imagined the new girl bantering with Marc as Kelly and Margie bonded over a funny story involving one of Kelly's latest clumsy moments. "No, I'll wait. I'll give you a call next week and set something up. Have fun." I hung up before she could argue.

~ ~

I had received a notice from the post office that my mailbox was filled to capacity, and that to receive any more mail, I needed to go down and get it from them. Well, the procrastinator that I had become waited two weeks before trekking down, and that was only because I was waiting on my royalty check from the fourth quarter sales of our single. I stood in a line twenty-two people deep waiting for the one and only grumpy postal worker to hand me my pile of envelopes. As fate would have it, the one piece of mail I gave a crap about wasn't there. I looked through the pile of letters, postcards, circulars, and magazines at least ten times before surrendering to the idea that I'd have to wait another day to get my check, and therefore to get the new pair of boots I had planned to go out and buy that very afternoon for my date with Kara that night. She was taking me to a club, and we were going to get drunk and get wild with some of her friends. I couldn't wait.

On my way out the door, I stopped to buy a book of stamps from the vending machine. I decided on the Marilyn Monroe ones. For some reason, I got the inkling to weed through my mail right there on the counter for all the postal customers to witness; a bill from Nordstrom, from BGE, from Verizon; a notice that some books on music theory were long overdue from the library; an invitation to join the Chesapeake Bay Foundation; a mailer announcing that now was the best time for me to get ahead and attend a free information session at the University of Maryland.

Then, I opened one up from my doctor's office, fully prepared to see that I had underpaid my co-pay. Instead they had written me a letter, hand-signed from my doctor informing me they had tried calling me several times, but my phone number was not in service. They then proceeded to inform me that my Pap smear results were abnormal and that I should call the office immediately to schedule a repeat examination. They even sketched the situation out in terms of how urgent the matter really was. My eyes welled with tears and my knees buckled as I read that my results showed signs of cervical dysplasia, a significant warning sign to cervical cancer. I gulped, trying desperately to catch my breath. I stuffed the letter into my pocketbook, along with the other mail and ran, pushing through the door, unable to hold it for the elderly woman walking towards me. Images of me in a hospital gown flashed in my mind. The scene so bitterly etched and real; my head in a turban, my face sunken, an IV jutting out of my skin, which was hooked up to a pole with chemo meds in it, a lone nurse my only company.

Once inside my car, I managed to call the doctor's office, blinded by hysterical tears. The receptionist placed me on hold after I blurted out my traumatic situation. A nurse picked up. She verified I was Becca James and told me I needed to schedule a repeat pap. I cried. Actually I bawled, convulsing in a fit of absolute fright. She assured me this happened all the time and could be something as simple as a tampon rubbing too roughly against the cervix during my last menstrual cycle. She urged me not to panic. She set me up with an appointment two weeks from then. I gasped and ranted on about how I'd never make it that long. I begged and pleaded. My life now depended on it. She offered me a ten-fifteen the following morning.

I wanted to call Kelly. I wanted so badly to hear her tell me in her sensible voice that I was going to be okay. Instead, I drove immediately to the salon. I parked in the first spot available, handicapped, which I felt completely entitled to at the moment. I pushed open the door and ran past Angelina's fake smile and right towards Margie. I practically mowed down a little girl about to get her first haircut to get to her. Margie looked up, her eyes a soft and welcoming sight. "What's wrong?" she asked.

I yanked her away from her foil client, bleach smothered brush and all. I blubbered on past clients, the tears rained down in monsoon fashion. I pulled her into an empty waxing room. I waited while she secured the lock before I attempted to speak. And, when I did, all that blurted out were more blubbers and inaudible grunts. She squeezed me in her arms and patted my back. Pat. Pat. Pat. A tighter squeeze. More pats, then finally a momentary lapse in the great swell of tears.

"I might have cancer."

"What?" She asked like I just told her I was planning a trip to the moon.

I slid the note out of the envelope and stared at her face as she read it. Her face remained still and unaffected. "This doesn't mean anything." She folded it back and handed it to me.

I opened it back up and pointed out the word cancer. It popped off the page on a level all its own. "It says cancer."

"You've never had an abnormal pap smear?"

I suddenly wanted to punch her. "Have you?"

She cradled her hand around my forearm. "A few times." Her eyes circled around the room, hesitant. "I caught HPV from some guy I had a one night stand with a long time ago. It's a very typical STD, and it causes the abnormal paps."

"The only guy I ever had sex with was some guy in high school. If I caught something from him, wouldn't it have showed up before this?"

"I'm just saying that that's what caused mine. I had a couple of minor surgeries to fix the situation. And, I'm fine as you can see. I'm walking around healthy as can be. So, whatever caused these abnormal results, doesn't matter. You'll be fine, too."

"What if it's cancer?"

"Do you get an annual pap?"

"Yes."

"Has it ever been abnormal?"

"No."

She grabbed me by the shoulders. "Then, you'll be fine, even if it is cancer. It would be an early detection. And, cervical cancer is the most curable form of cancer a person can get."

We stood staring at each other in a sterile room with white walls and white furniture. "I'm scared."

"I know." She lowered her hands and hugged me again. "What do you say we go back to my place after I finish up here tonight? We can get some takeout, soak in the hot tub, put on our jammies and maybe play Scrabble?"

"I can't imagine doing anything else but that right now."

"Have you told Kara about this, yet?"

I hadn't even thought about it. Kara wouldn't know what to do with the news. She'd probably try to get me drunk. "I'll wait to see what the doctor says first. No need to worry her, yet."

A few minutes later when I got back to my car, I called Kara to cancel for that night, telling her my stomach hurt.

~ ~

The next morning, I sat on the edge of an exam table expecting my doctor to come in at any second and explain the grim reality of my fate. The night before, Margie made the whole process sound like a walk in the park. But, I suspected she was just trying to get me to stop crying. "All they'll do is prop your feet back up in stirrups and take another swab. Simple. Now eat another brownie." We ate the entire plate of brownies and downed a half gallon of milk.

The exam went exactly as Margie insisted, which didn't ease me any. I needed answers, but the medical staff at St. Agnes needed the exam room empty so they could tackle the other fifty women waiting for their turn to be poked and prodded and told they may or may not have cancer. When I questioned my doctor, she rushed through a clinical blurb she had obviously stated more times than she probably said good morning. Test results would be back in within two weeks, she assured. "Until then, relax and don't worry."

Well, I did worry. And, I also did what I thought at the time was a good idea. I called Kelly. She wasn't there. I didn't bother to leave a message. She called me back anyway and left me a message asking if everything was okay. I called her back and left her message thanking her for calling me and telling her not to worry, that I'd get in touch with her. We continued to play phone tag like that, never connecting in real time.

When the two weeks rolled close to an end, I drew nearer to terms with my situation, largely because I didn't have a choice. Kara and I needed to prepare for a large venue. We needed to capitalize on our studio time as well. I was prepared to tell her all about the scary what-ifs one night after we had sex on the floor of the studio, but decided I'd rather her not know the ugly details. I didn't want to become the hideous girl with a problem in her vagina. I wanted her to adore me, not pity me. Every time we kissed or fucked, I envisioned the doctor squaring off in front of my vagina with a needle and laser beam ready to attack my damaged cells. Instead, we wrote a song.

I pretended to be carefree the whole week. I tried my best to flirt back with Kara, to kiss her with intensity, and to wink at her every once in a while. I massaged her back just the way she liked it. We played with sex toys. We watched porn. Basically I did everything I could to feel sexy for her and to get my mind off the trauma and onto things that typically would've sent my body into earthquake central. We even got really drunk one night at her place and found ourselves on the bathroom floor, razors in hand. We trimmed each other's bikini lines. At her request, I shaped hers into a Mohawk and she shaped mine into a heart. She discovered a beauty mark of mine positioned right inside my bikini line. It was shaped like a star. The first time Kelly had noticed it, she had joked about it, claiming I was earmarked for fame. Kara nibbled at it, and I shimmied away not willing to share Kelly's and my intimate claim to fame just yet.

Kara had rescheduled our club date from two weeks prior when I had canceled. I had spent the afternoon at the mall, searching for skinny jeans to go with my new leather boots. Hanger after hanger, I dug deep for the will to survive the one last night before D day. I found the jeans, and I paired them off with a chunky beaded necklace, paid the clerk and then sat down on a square bench outside the mall. I smoked three cigarettes as I watched people. I didn't know how I ever lived without smoking before. It eased me in a way nothing else could.

I watched moms with their kids, hand-in-hand, skipping over sidewalk cracks. I watched older couples help each other climb the sidewalk curb. I watched single people looking self-conscious. And then I saw a gay couple, arms hooked around each other, walking in a world all their own, looking every bit as blissful as newlyweds heading off to their honeymoon. I thought about trying to call Kelly again, to hear her voice, and to hear her tell me I would survive another day without knowing. So, I did. And once again, I got her voice mail.

I walked back to my car, resolute on calling Kara to cancel. I couldn't face her like this. I drove all the way home in a fog, and decided to go anyway. I'd get drunk and hopefully forget all about it.

I laid out my clothes, then turned on the shower. I was just ready to jump in when my cell rang. It was the doctor's office. I froze, butt-naked with one leg slinked over the rim of the tub, the other balancing on the floor. Time stood still as a gazillion emotions ran through me. Cancer. Not cancer. Surgery. No surgery. Chemo. No chemo. Hair loss. No hair loss. My fingers trembled. It took three times before I could hit the answer button. And when I did, I held my breath.

"Hello," the pleasant lady said. "Can I speak with Becca James, please?"

I exhaled sharply. "This is Becca."

"I'm calling from St. Agnes Medical Center about your test results."

My temples beat. "Okay."

"Your pap smear came back normal. So, we don't have to see you again for another year."

I stuttered over my tongue. "Normal? You said normal?"

"Yes. Perfectly normal."

After thanking the lady a million times, I hung up and literally jumped for joy in the center of my bathroom, smiling, crying, and screaming. I didn't know how to contain the relief, so I ran through my condo naked, spinning, and leaping like a ballerina. First I called Margie to tell her the good news. "I told you," she said all matter-of-factly. Then, I called Kelly and left her another message, "I just got the best news of my life. Please call me so I can explain. Or tell me when I can reach you. You need to hear this. I need to tell you this."

I screamed and jumped some more. I owed God big time now!

The rush continued to pour through me as I primped for the exciting night ahead. I downed a few cocktails, smoked a couple of cigarettes, and twirled some more right up until the moment Kara honked her horn.

I sailed out of my door in my pair of heeled, black leather boots, skinny jeans, chunky necklace, and the new suede jacket Kara had surprised me with at Christmas. I climbed into her passenger seat feeling more alive than ever. My smile chiseled permanently. I told her everything—about the scare, about crying with Margie, about the nightmares I'd envisioned, and about the cathartic moment when my heart started beating at a healthy pace again. "We've got to celebrate," I said, cupping her face in my hands and kissing her hard.

She smelled like alcohol and relaxed into my kiss. With her musky perfume, her soft lips, and the rolling of her tongue with mine, how could my life get any better?

"Let's forget the club and go spoil ourselves at a fancy restaurant." I said. I craved alone-time with her, time where we could focus a little on us, away from everything and everyone.

"I've got an even better way to celebrate. One that's really going to rock your world."

I kissed her hard. "Tell me."

"Oh, no." She pulled away, revved the engine. "You think you feel alive and free right now? Just wait." She punched the car into full force, shooting off out of the parking lot like a jet engine taking to the air.

~ ~

We arrived at a gay club with a line of people a quarter mile long trying to gain access. Kara waltzed us right up to the front of the line and the bouncers let us in like we were celebrities.

"We are celebrities now," she said. "Celebrities who need to celebrate by getting toasted!" She led me straight to the bar, which appeared like a nebula with its hazy blue lights and Star Trek style stools. Kara plopped her pocketbook on the bar and smiled at the bartender, a blonde Adonis with a broad chest and a toothpaste-commercial-worthy smile. He strolled over, leaned in close to her. "What can I get for you, babe?"

Kara lit a cigarette. "Two margaritas."

"You got it." He swiveled off. Kara followed him with her eyes. "If I were into men, I'd fuck him."

I lit a cigarette in response. "I bet he'd fuck you in a heartbeat." I drew a long, thoughtful drag.

Her eyes twinkled at me. "I'd like to fuck you right now."

I placed my hand on her knee. "Are you okay with me showing you some public affection?"

She pulled me to her and started making out with me. "Right now, I don't care who's looking at us or what they're speculating. If I could fuck you right here in the open, I would."

The bartender returned with our drinks, clearing his throat. We came up for air.

"Keep them coming," she said to him. "You may as well line up another four of them for us."

He winked. "You got it." He shuffled off, looking back over his shoulder, nearly salivating when Kara licked my cheek with her tongue and giggled.

We downed our first serving of margaritas. And, in less than ten minutes, we downed the other two helpings as well. My head buzzed, tickling me down to my toes. I was free. I was healthy. I was in heaven.

"I'm going to the little girl's room," Kara said. I watched her walk away, her hips swayed like a teeter totter, her back arched slightly, and her calf muscles tightened with each step. My life was back on track. I called the bartender back over and ordered us some shots.

I downed both of them myself. My head spun in pirouettes. I wanted to dance. I wanted to float around the dance floor and embrace the bliss. I scanned the room for Kara. I couldn't see her anywhere. I mowed over the lounge tables searching for her. I circled the place, tripping over long legs and high heels. I swept through the dance floor. The hardcore techno beat and flashing lights echoed in my mind. I started to panic for a moment, scared Kara had left me alone to celebrate, drunk and horny. Then a chubby girl with spiked hair and Harry Potter glasses grabbed my arm. "Hey you're that girl, right?" She called over a couple of other girls. "This is that singer Becca I was telling you about."

Their squinty eyes opened wide. One of the girls wearing a charcoal halter with beads and glow-in-the-dark lipstick bobbed her head up and down. "Right, Becca, oh my God, I can't believe you're at Uptown Girls."

"Hey, isn't that the other girl?" the chubby girl pointed up behind me at Kara who was holding hands with Mica, the girl from the party. "I think it is. God she's even more gorgeous in person."

The third girl's mouth dropped open like Elvis had risen behind me. Kara and Mica strutted down a set of circular stairs. Mica's arm was now draped on Kara's shoulder. They were giggling, whispering, and sipping new drinks.

"I thought you left me here," I said to her when she got close enough. The room spun violently now.

"Aw, sweetie, how could you think I'd do that to you?"

She ran her finger up my arm the way she always did when she wanted to flirt. I fell into her embrace, grateful for the leverage against the spinning walls and the nausea. "Can we go?"

She reached into her pocketbook and wrestled for a cigarette. Mica lit it for her. She blew the smoke high up in the air, then leaned in to kiss me. "In a few minutes. We still need to celebrate. Let's get you another drink." She took off, pushing her way through the crowded dance floor, blowing her smoke up, latching onto my only free hand, my other one somehow entwined in Mica's.

She bought me a shot of tequila and a Blue Moon to chase it down. I swallowed it. Mica bought the next round of shots and I downed that one, too. By the next, Mica asked me to open my mouth. I did. She plopped a pill on it. "Ready to party?"

I swallowed it without ever asking what it was. Next thing I knew, we were dancing together in the middle of the crowded floor, bumping, grinding, and touching each other. The sparkly lights, the heavy music, and the sweet rush of euphoria all melded together to form a little slice of paradise for us to celebrate in.

Kara bumped and grinded in front of me while Mica held my waist from behind. "Let's have a threesome," Kara said to me, her eyes full of lust.

I nearly collapsed at the thought of something so naughty.

"It'll be so sexy, so wild," she whispered.

Everything with Kara was so sexy and wild. Kara played with my hair from the front. Mica ran a finger down the middle of my spine. Her breath hot on the back of my neck.

"Kiss Mica," Kara said to me, grinding her hips to the beat of the music.

Caught up in the euphoria, I turned and started making out with Mica while Kara watched us, leaned in to us, and grinded heavier against us. I closed my eyes and pictured Kara horny as hell, her face flexing in a moan, hungry. The hornier I pictured her, the harder I kissed Mica. The three of us floated in a crowd of equally loving and embracing women high on euphoria.

"Follow me, ladies," Kara said, taking both of our hands and pulling us towards a back hallway. She brought us into a dark room and locked the door. The rest blurred. I remembered her kissing Mica and me trying to pull her off. Then, I started to undress Kara with my teeth. The taste of cotton rested heavily on my tongue. First her shirt, then her bra, I devoured her one lick at a time. Her moans aroused me. Next thing I knew I was lapping up her juices, and then, I was being played. Only it wasn't Kara, it was Mica. I remembered pulling away, and Kara stopping me, coaxing me with her strokes, with her tongue, telling me to just relax and enjoy the ride. Next thing I knew, Kara and I were both kissing Mica at the same time. Our faces touched as Mica moaned. With the three of us entwined, we kept taking turns getting off on one another. Last thing I remembered was falling to the ground and Kara sweeping my head to her chest. The three of us piled on top of each other on the floor, panting like wild dogs in heat.

When I woke up, my head felt like it was going to crack open. I heard moaning. I felt movement. I smelled sex. I opened my eyes to Kara who was in the middle of an orgasm, her face etched in pleasure. I crawled my eyes down and landed on Mica. That was when the night crashed back into me, all the split memories blurring into one giant nightmare. My skin itched. I suddenly wanted to jump in a shower and scrub myself. I jumped to my feet. Naked, I ran around the room collecting my clothes.

"Hey sweetie, come back here. It's your turn," Kara said.

I just looked at her, and for the first time felt disgust.

## **Chapter Twelve**

I ran out into the cold morning air with my shirt on backwards. Kara's car sat by itself next to a snow mound. I dug for her keys in the bottom of my pocketbook, where she'd tossed them the night before. My cigarettes flew out and spilled all over the gravel. Fuck. I bent down, plucked them all up, and then stole a glance back at the building. Kara standing naked from the waist down, begged me not to leave her stranded. I sunk into her driver's seat and dropped it into gear faster than she could run her bare feet across the stones. From the rearview mirror, I caught her arms flying wildly above her, her hair whipping her face, and Mica running up behind her.

I lit a cigarette and blew smoke all over the place. Fuck her and her pride and joy Italian leather seats and vanilla bean air freshener. I punched the steering wheel. How could she think I'd be okay waking up to seeing Mica between her legs again? I taunted the engine until it screamed. I purposely bucked her precious car over and over again so angry at her for ruining what should've been a night of celebration.

Flashes from the night raced through my mind. Downing shot after shot. Mica flirting with Kara. Kara flirting back. Me and Mica kissing on the dance floor. Mica slipping the pill on my tongue and me being stupid enough to swallow it. How could I be so irresponsible? Did Kara take one, too? I slammed on the brake, burning her tires. Angry at her, at me, at the traffic lights, at the police car monitoring the few of us tramps stupid enough to be up at that ungodly hour. Why a threesome? Was I not enough for her anymore?

As I sped down the road, I tried to rationalize the night. A threesome was sexy, wasn't it? Did I really drink too much? I didn't end up in the hospital getting my stomach pumped. It was just one pill. That didn't make me a drug user, did it? The pill helped me to let loose, to be wild and crazy for a night, to be someone Kara would think was fun and worth spending her night with.

I looked in the vanity mirror on the visor. My eyes sunk, rimmed in black and my face pale, lacking glow. I didn't recognize myself. I hated the girl in the mirror.

I wanted to be mad at Kara, to blame her for everything that happened that night. I wanted to want to ram her car against a telephone pole, slash her tires, smash out her windows, anything to get rid of the anger swelling in me, to feel vindicated of the whore I'd become overnight. I wanted so badly to throw those feelings back at her and toss them in a heap at her beautiful face, her teasing smile, and her hungry, orgasmic thrusts.

I didn't want to know this Kara, the real Kara. I wanted the one I'd built up on a pedestal and worshipped like the goddess I thought she was on that very first meeting. I wanted her pure and unadulterated, undamaged, shining like a prism, dazzling, mesmerizing, and encompassing beauty in its rarest form. But she didn't exist like that. She never did. Last night was the real deal, Kara being Kara. She'd never be that wholesome wonder I built her up to be.

Who was I trying to kid thinking she was anyone but who she was? None of her actions were innocent like I wanted them to be – the flirty smiles she offered other men and women; the winks I'd learned to brush away as friendly gestures; the kissing of music executives—none of them.

She was simply true to herself. If anyone was guilty of being deceitful, it was me.

Who was I? In less than a year I turned into a cigarette and pot smoker, pill popper, and whore. None of those things were part of my dreams, my goals.

As I drove on, my anger started to dissipate, replaced with a calm acceptance of the lonesome road I'd paved for myself. I pulled into a gas station and filled up. As I propped my foot against the car, waiting for the gas to guzzle inward, a quiet peace settled in on me, a tranquil melding of my heartbeat finally catching up with my breathing. I drew in some deep breaths, even laughed a little.

How did I let myself get carried off so far? From that little girl playing in front of her grandpa feeling like the world owed me a stage, to a woman who deserted herself on the side of a road no one really cared to travel down.

I drove on after that with no destination in mind, just me and the road and a keen understanding of who I didn't want to be. I drove past Lucky Strike Bowling Alley, past the Exxon station, and turned into the parking lot of McFadden's just like I had done a million times beforehand. The sun shone in on its windows making it look like a gem. Joe wouldn't be in for several more hours to prepare for the rush of lunch. I parked in the back, got out, and walked right over to the heating unit by the dumpsters. I reached up into the metal case, and sure enough, Joe had left the key right where he always had for me. "In case you ever need it," he said. Man, did I need it now.

I let myself in through the kitchen. The place still smelled like burgers and fries from the night before. The stainless steel counters, polished clean, reminded me of home, of my friends, of my family, of Kelly. I strolled in to the dining area and lit a candle on the bar. The place hadn't changed. The tables still set around the round stage just as they always had. My stool still perched towards the backside of it, out of the spotlight, vacant for another backup guitarist, idealistic and naive to the real world as I had been. I peeked in the broom closet near the bar, and smiled when I saw the Yamaha guitar. I walked on stage with it strapped around my shoulder and picked at a soft melody.

I began strumming lightly. The steel strings carried me into a state of peace like a lullaby.

*I've lost myself, blinded by stardust*
*Traveling in a dream weaved up in lust*
*Why is it I can't see your true colors*
*All shiny and new?*

I sang to the empty room, my voice crying out to the rafters above, to the dartboards against the far wall, and to the imagined fans there for just me. I sang freely, the sole voice vibrating through the air.

I continued strumming and making up lyrics. I swirled in a monologue of truth and innocence, giving in to the song the way I wished I could do in real life.

When I finished playing, I placed the guitar back. I sat at the bar and lit a cigarette, inhaling deeper than ever and burning my lungs. I exhaled slowly and watched the smoke haze around my face. I caught a glimpse of myself in the backbar mirror. I took another drag and watched as I pulled my face in and narrowed my eyes to just barely slits. I blew out the smoke and it hung in front of me like a dirty, smelly cloud, one that I was completely addicted to. I couldn't get out of bed without lighting one first. I couldn't have a drink or a cup of coffee without one accompanying me. The four inch roll of chemicals controlled me, caged me in a cloud of filthy lust. I inhaled one last long and bitter drag and then crushed out the half smoked cigarette in a glass. I watched myself exhale the last bit of smoke I'd ever allow between my lips again, knowing that, sadly, quitting smoking would be harder than quitting Kara.

~ ~

I met up with Margie that night after she closed up her shop. We ate Chinese food at our favorite spot. She told me her and Marc were officially back together again and that he surprised her with a vacation package to Rome the very next week. She was glowing.

A few minutes later, she told me she was three months pregnant.

I screamed out in joy and three waiters ran to my rescue. They ducked away as soon as we both sprang to our feet and hugged.

"She's going to be a mommy!" I yelled out to the restaurant. A few people cheered, others kept right on eating.

Once we sat back down and started eating again she told me all about how wonderful things were between them now and how excited Marc was to find out they were going to have a baby. "He already bought the baby furniture. You should see it. It's beautiful, shiny wood, with all these intricate carvings. He bought this mobile to hang above it that has the cutest butterflies. He's amazing. Even more amazing than ever." Her eyes glimmered in the soft lighting. "We want you and Kelly to be the godmothers."

She was smiling at me, waiting, and probably anticipating another round of exuberant jumps. She had no idea what a dumb choice I'd be for such an important role. I suddenly felt like the recipient of an honorable award that I had no right claiming. Dumb luck for the child to be stuck with me for a godmother.

"That's quite an honor, truly. But, I'm not worthy," I told her.

She bit into a spicy shrimp. "Not worthy? Just eat your fried rice and say yes."

"You don't want me saying yes. Trust me." That was when I spilled out all the ugly details. "Last night I got drunk, smoked two packs of cigarettes, took drugs, and fucked two women at the same time." I sat back, placed my egg roll back on my plate and stared into her shocked eyes.

"I don't even know what to say." She gazed down at her fingers and twirled her wedding ring around a few too many times. She couldn't look at me. "Why would you even admit that?"

"I thought I could." I waited for her eyes to soften and that don't-worry-about- it-of-course-you-could look to come across her face. When it didn't, I panicked. "I'm ready to quit all that. I'm done being that person. I promise."

"You're so screwed up," she said with her face as firm as stone.

"I know, but—"

"You need to get your act together before you hurt yourself." She slipped out of the booth and walked out of the restaurant door without looking back.

I tossed a fifty on the table and ran after her. Her heels pitter-pattered against the pavement as she tore off towards her car.

"Are you just going to leave me stranded here?" I yelled out to her.

She kept on pounding the pavement toward her car. "I can't deal with you right now."

I ran up to her and blocked her from getting in. "I can't have you mad at me. Not now."

"Don't you get it? You're acting like a fool and I don't want any part of it. I've got my own thing going on right now and the last thing I need is you to roll into this good place I'm at with a cigarette dangling from lips and half a quart of vodka swishing around in your belly. I don't want to be around you."

"You're making me sound like I'm some sort of animal," I said.

"Aren't you?" She pushed me out of her way and climbed into her car.

"Oh, come on. Don't be an ass." I punched her window, demanding she listen to me. "You can't just leave me alone in a dark parking lot."

She opened her window a slit. "You're out of control."

"Well, so weren't you that night I first witnessed you on the brink of cheating," I said, my words charged and full of rage.

"Of course I was," she said, her voice taking up refuge behind her door window. "See that's just it. I was completely out of line and look how far that got me." She looked straight ahead out her windshield.

"Well, that doesn't give you the right to get all uppity up on me, judging me like I'm a nasty contestant in a reality television show. So, what? I'm a little screwed up. You sure proved we all are."

At that she sped off, spraying some mud up at my ankles. I chucked her the bird, and it felt so right waving it up in the air at her. To that, she broke hard. Her brake lights screamed red. She stayed put. So did I. Then, finally, she reversed and pulled right back to where she was less than thirty seconds ago. Then, she opened her window a little more. In the dim, foggy light I could see pain etched on her face. "We are all screwed up in one way or another. But, Becca, I don't want you to be."

That honest phrase, along with her sad expression, opened my spigot. I broke out into sobs. "Neither do I." My words stretched down to the pavement, swollen by my tears.

Margie unlocked the passenger door. "Get in."

I hobbled over to the door and slid in, spewing tears everywhere. I cried into my hands. "I'm so screwed up." Margie shouldered me, drawing me in to her like a wounded child. She even patted my back and rocked me. I kept on babbling. "I don't want to be a druggie or a smoker or a shit-faced loser or a slut who sleeps with every girl she sees."

"Shush, it's okay. So, you made a few mistakes."

I cried into her shirt, wailing. "How am I going to get out of this mess?"

She pushed me back, wiped my teary face with the back of her hand. "I'll help you."

I buried myself against her again. "I don't know if I can get over these vices. I'm dying for a cigarette, and I don't think I'll ever be able to perform on stage again without downing a strong drink. And I have to walk-away from Kara. I am so dangerously obsessed with her, and because of her my life is spiraling out of control. I'm addicted and I don't know how to let go. So, how can you possibly help me out?"

"We'll figure out a way. Don't worry."

~ ~

Once I returned home after my blubberfest with Margie, I realized that Kara had finally come to get her car from my parking lot. I still had a message on my cell from her that I'd yet to listen to. I wasn't ready to hear the pissed off side of Kara until then. I tossed my pocketbook, void of cigarettes now, and filled with Nicorette gum instead, onto the couch and decided I was ready to listen to the insults, the yelling, and the destruction of mine and Kara's romp—a romp that I could now only describe as a complete and utter chunk of gluttony sprinkled with a shaker full of mistakes. I braced for the anger.

"I came by today to pick up my car. I was hoping to see you," she said, her voice still dripping a sexy vibe. "I guess you're going to make me wait until practice tomorrow night, huh? You can punish me all you want." She paused dramatically, adding tension to her tease. "I know I was a very bad girl the other night. So were you. Everything about you that night was so hot." She moaned. "I'll see you later, sweetie."

~ ~

I trotted through Vibrations leaving a fictitious wake of confidence trailing behind me, but even my pinky toes shook as I moved closer to our studio. I wanted to be strong, to have her flirts bounce off me like a bumper car, but truthfully, I doubted my strength ever since melting from her voice message. I chomped away on my Nicorette gum and entered. There she was a vision of beauty draped on the stool like one of those goddess statues you only see in the finest of art museums. Her soft, smooth skin and pouty lips still managed to cut my breath short.

She looked up from her Hummingbird, her eyes landing on mine, fluttering there for a few seconds, holding me captive. Then, she stood, arched her back slightly the way she did whenever she wanted her way. "Come here," she said. "I want to show you something."

I inched towards her, keeping my guard fully secure, trying my best to envision her old and wrinkly with a few teeth missing. Of course that was like trying to envision the sun burning black. An impossible sight even if make believe.

"I got another tattoo yesterday." She placed her guitar down on its stand. "Want to see?"

She started to slide off her yoga style pants, exposing her voluptuous hips.

I swallowed the urge to touch her and to run my finger up and down her skin. "Kara, I think we should just start to practice."

She intended differently. Between her thighs, inches from her bikini line, sat a two-inch replica of her Gibson Hummingbird. "Mica did it for me."

Even the strings were drawn to perfect scale and the color match was exquisite. I leaned in closer. "Wow, it's beautiful." I inspected the shadows and midtones, blown away by details. "Does it hurt?"

"A little." She cupped her fingers under my chin and lifted, drawing my eyes to hers. "I wanted to remember that night. I've never seen someone look hotter than you." She bent down and kissed me, and I didn't fight her off. I joined and couldn't stop, an addict faced with a full spread of fixings to keep me smiling for days.

"Did you really think I was hot?" I asked her, wanting to hear her say it again.

"Sizzling," she said into my mouth. "You have no idea how wild that drove me."

With all barriers evaporated, all guards disarmed, all sense of anger and confusion magically dispelled, I devoured her long into our practice session, feasting like a queen bee to a song too beautiful to quiet, wondering how I could ever consider giving that delicious gift of ecstasy away. I floated away with her that night on a cloud of lust, drunk on her juices and high on her moans.

Later that night, I listened to a voicemail from Kelly telling me she was returning my call. I didn't call her back that night.

~~

The next afternoon, I decided to surprise Kara at her home. When I knocked on the front door, her friend Ella answered and told me she was up in her room. I climbed the winding stairs, walked through the arched doorway to Kara's wing, armed with an elaborate bouquet of green viburnum, Dutch tulips, eucalyptus and quince blossoms. I opened her door and found her lounging on the white velvet couch with another woman. She didn't jump up, didn't pull her hand away, and didn't try to hide. They were entwined, Kara in a camisole, the woman stroking her skin.

"Hey you," Kara said, her eyes opening wide, obviously surprised to see me. "I thought you were Ella." She lifted her head from the woman's chest, as I stood holding her flowers like an idiot.

The girl sat up. "Kara, you didn't have to get me flowers!"

Kara giggled at that and unwrapped herself from the girl's arms. She walked over to me, arms fully extended to receive the gift I'd spent hundreds on. "Sweetie, they're for me," she said to the girl in response.

I wanted to throw up. I dropped the flowers, and they landed on her feet. I stole a closer glance at the girl. Her red hair, her pretty, fawn-like features gripped me in a fit of jealousy just as they had the first time I saw her in the photo album.

"Who is she?" I asked Kara, my face on the verge of a full inferno, my voice quivering on the precipice of hysteria.

She reached out to touch me, and I stepped out into the hall to avoid contact. "She's an old friend," she said.

Her old friend got up from the couch and waltzed over to me, hand extended ready to shake mine. "I'm Chrissy. And you?"

"I'm her girlfriend." I hugged my arms around my chest where a solid lump, the size of my fist, lodged.

"Well, '*girlfriend*,'" the girl said, her voice dripping with sarcasm, "Kara is just full of surprises today."

"Sweetie," Kara rubbed the girl's arm, "Do you mind waiting in my room for a minute?" The girl smiled up at her like an innocent doe before kissing Kara's bare shoulder and sauntering back into the room.

I slammed the door and leaned against it, bracing for a panic attack. "Did you fuck her, too?" I asked, now digging my nails into my sides to take away some of the pain coursing through the rest of my body.

"What the hell is wrong with you, Becca?"

That was the first time I'd ever heard Kara snap. She stood with her hands on her waist, defiant and demanding an answer.

I snapped. What was wrong with me? "You think because I allowed us to fuck another girl together, this is how things will always work now?"

Kara shook her head, obviously disappointed with my outburst. "Whoa." She mimicked the moves of a traffic cop holding me back with one hand. "I'm not trying to start a fight with you. I hate fighting." She waved her hands in front of me like a mad scientist trying to call sanity into being. "What happened to the cool, go-with-the-flow girl?"

I stood my ground. "I caught you with another girl. She could be your girlfriend, too, for all I know. What the fuck is going through your head?"

Kara pursed her lips tight and looked to her left, obviously in search of the right words that would make it all go away. "I had no idea we were on such different pages."

"What are talking about?"

She looked at me again, her eyes suddenly full of understanding. "You wanted me to be your girlfriend."

"You *are* my girlfriend," I said.

"You expected me to be monogamous."

"That's what partners do."

"You thought I was going to be your last first kiss, didn't you?" she asked, her face contorting into pity.

I just nodded to that, not wanting to bury myself any deeper.

"I bet you wanted to have babies with me eventually, huh?"

I stared straight into her sorry eyes.

"You thought I'd be the one."

"You don't think you are?" I asked her, desperate for her to let go of her bravado and silly flirtatious needs and just climb back up onto that pedestal I'd built for her.

"I'm not that girl." She walked into my arms and I let her. She smelled like musk and softened like putty in my arms.

"You can be if you want to be," I said.

She lifted her face to me. "That's not who I want to be. I love women. I love flirting with them. I love kissing them. I love fucking them. And I love doing all of those things with you. But it's just that I will never be that woman you need me to be. I wish I could. But, I can't. I don't want to be."

"Then why did you start this in the first place?" I asked.

"I'm sorry, sweetie." She traced my cheek with the back of her hand. "I never would've pursued this if I didn't think you could handle it."

"I don't want to share you," I said.

She stood there silent, unrelenting.

I dislodged from her. "I'm just going to go now." Dazed, whacked over the head with her blunt point, I walked away leaving a trail of my shattered ego at her feet.

~ ~

I was driving back to my condo, chomping desperately on a piece of Nicorette gum, when I hit a squirrel crossing the road. I ran right over it. My tires thumped. I looked back and it was flattened, spent, done with life. No chance to get even with its enemies. No chance to right any of its wrongs. No chance to redeem. In one miniscule second nothing else mattered to that squirrel. I killed it, and no matter how hard I tried, I couldn't blame it on anyone but myself.

I pulled over to the side of the street because I was shaking. A few cars passed and swerved to avoid the mess in front of them. I turned off my radio and buried my head in the steering wheel.

I really needed a cigarette.

I had kept one hidden in my glove compartment just in case. I wanted it so badly. I reached over, tossed a pile of napkins off to the side and dug it out. I placed it between my lips and let it dangle there while I searched my console for a lighter. I'd allow myself one quick drag as a consolation for what I'd been put through. One drag and I knew I'd feel better. My sense of balance in the universe would be restored and that nagging pounding at my temples would finally rest. I flicked my lighter and watched the flame grow tall. I inched it up to my cigarette and braced it within millimeters of its tip. I wanted this. I deserved this. I needed this.

Before I could light it, I saw Kara's face as she lit my first cigarette for me. I immediately retracted. If I lit it, I'd be defeated again, fooled by my own insecurities.

I called Margie. "I need you," I said to her. A blow dryer whistled in the background.

"What happened?"

"I need a cigarette, and I'm seconds away from lighting one."

The blow dryer cut off. "You're in control. Not the cigarette," she said.

I stared at it, brought it up to under my nose and sniffed, taunted by its fresh menthol fragrance. "I don't know if I can do this."

"Please do because I miss the old Becca. I want her back."

I swallowed, pushing the craving as far down inside as possible. "I'll try."

I tossed my phone down, mildly upset that Margie could have such powerful effects on me. I caressed the cigarette between my fingers and cursed at it. It seemed the sensible thing to do. I wanted to be angry at something. I needed to be angry at something because only then would I maybe feel less stupid at how far out of control I'd let myself get.

I sniffed the cigarette again, wanting to blame it for my weakness towards it. But, perhaps more than the cigarette, I wanted to blame Kara for how I'd turned out. I wanted to be angry at her. I wanted to want to toss her a guitar case full of insults and curses. I wanted to want to point my finger at her and call her a slut. I wanted to want to punch her across her pretty face. But how could I? She was just being true to herself, a concept I'd long since forgotten.

I tossed the cigarette out my window and drove off. Within seconds, that action lifted me, empowered me, and granted me a sliver of hope that all would be okay in my world. A sliver was all I needed at that point.

## **Chapter Thirteen**

I placed Tangerine Twist on the glass counter of Tony's Repair Shop.

Earlier that morning, I had pulled Tangerine Twist out of the closet and sat with her propped on my knee. I examined her injuries and decided now was the correct time to have her fixed. I had rubbed her pickguard, smooth, sleek, still shiny after almost a year in the closet. Not until then had I felt right holding her in my arms again. A guitar that beautiful deserved a rightful owner, deserved respect, and deserved to be cradled by the hands of someone my grandpa had wanted me to be.

I now wanted to be that person. I was ready to get Tangerine Twist prepared.

When Tony whistled in awe of her beauty, I knew I'd made the right choice in coming to him. As others had told me, Tony was the only one I should allow to touch Tangerine. His hair, sleeked back into a tight ponytail, glimmered under the overhead lights. He asked me about her, about her story, about how she came to be so important to me. I told him everything, even down to the sparkle in my grandpa's eye when I first played her for him. He assured me in two weeks, she'd be as good as new.

When I walked out of the door, the bell jangled above my head. I turned back, waved, and begged him to take good care of her. He winked in reply, and that was enough to assure me she was in good hands.

Once outside, I walked down the street, breathed in the fresh spring air with its earthy scent and sweet grass, and smiled heartily. I felt alive.

~ ~

I had just returned home from the repair shop, popped six different vitamins, and eaten a nutritious spread of egg whites, twelve grain bread, and almond butter when Kelly called me. I didn't know how else I could explain how I felt at that moment other than in complete awe of the intricate workings and impeccable tuning of God.

"Hi," I said, as though we'd only just spoken the other day and not six months ago.

"Hey, Becca," she said, her voice coated in sweetness. "I hope it's all right that I called?"

"Of course, yes, definitely." I paused. "It's great to hear your voice."

"It's been while."

"Yeah, it sure has."

"Do you have time to get together?" she asked.

"You want to get together with me?" I asked, excited and confused. "Is everything okay?"

She laughed. "With me? Yeah. Everything is fine. I just wanted to catch up, hear about all the good news you left messages about, and see how you were doing."

"Did Margie call you?"

"Yes."

"What did she tell you?"

"That you could use a good friend right now."

"Sounds like something Margie would say," I said with a bite of friendly sarcasm.

She chuckled again, her laughter refreshing, unrehearsed, and ebbing from her in delicate laps. God, I missed her.

"What do you say we meet up for a run in the park?" she asked. "I'm open today if you are."

"A run?" That time I chuckled. That day was only the second day I hadn't started out with a cigarette for breakfast in almost a year. "I think I might have to start out a bit slower than a run. Possibly a jog."

"A slow jog, then," she said.

"A very slow jog."

"Okay then. Two this afternoon at our usual spot?" she asked.

"See you then." I was just about to hang up and added, "Hey Kel?"

"Yeah," she said.

"Thank you."

We hung up and I plopped down against my couch pillows. A calm sense flowed through me, bathing me in nostalgic comfort. To have Kelly back in my life would be perfect now. I'd spoil her silly and treat her with the respect and dignity she had always deserved from me. I'd be that woman who would take care of her, nurture her, love her completely and ensure nothing but happiness and good fortune surrounded her that time around. With her by my side, I could heal properly and become a responsible person again with values and stakes in a bright future. I could build a future for us full of love and hope. I'd buy us a big Victorian house with five bedrooms, enough for me and Kelly and each of the four kids we'd always dreamed of having. We'd spend nights singing and playing guitar as a family, the Copeland-James family. Maybe one of our kids would play piano and another one a fiddle. I'd see to it that we got our chance to vacation across America the way we had always planned. We'd rent an RV and drive endlessly over the course of an entire summer from one end of the country to the other, witnessing the miracles of mountains and lakes and valleys. When I toured, the whole family would come along. Kara would have to deal with them laughing and climbing all over her as we practiced. And, Kelly would not be jealous of what Kara and I had in the past because she would not ever know the exact details. I'd protect her from all that reality and make sure she knew how much better a person she was than Kara could ever hope to be. She could never know how much I enjoyed fucking Kara. Ever. If she knew how much I got off on Kara, our relationship would never work no matter how much I'd try to convince her that Kara wasn't really that great to start with. She could always see through my lies. If she asked, I'd tell her that yes, we fucked, and that Kara was completely selfish. She was selfish outside the bedroom after all. So, that part was not a lie.

I stared at my ceiling fan, watched it whirl around and around. My heart ballooned bigger than my chest walls could hold. Kelly, her sweet and innocent smile, her love for all that was calm and pure, was all I wanted now. I was done with my reckless life. I wanted Kelly and all she could offer me in the ways of a good wholesome life. She had come back into my life right when I needed her most. That was no coincidence. That was what my grandpa always referred to as fate. I couldn't wait to get back on fate's path. I fell asleep on my couch for a bit dreaming of a life that I now wanted more than Kara, more than cigarettes, and more than fame.

~ ~

The day couldn't have been a more perfect one for a jog in the park. I opened my window, allowing the mild mid-March air to filter in and tickle all of my senses. When I pulled into the parking lot, Kelly was stretching her calves at the rock by the front of the path. She had on a pair of black running shorts, which hugged her long toned legs. She wore a lime green tank top that showed off her sleek arms. Her hair was pulled back in a messy twist, just the way I liked it.

I jogged up to her and she smiled broadly. "Hey," she said, opening her arms wide. "Come here." She pulled me into her embrace and hugged me tightly. She smelled just like she always did, refreshing, innocent, and youthful, like morning dew. She squeezed me tight and out of nowhere a release sprouted from deep within me. Some pent up emotions that I didn't even realize were hidden suddenly surfaced; a fear of some sort that I had to have her back in my life. I fell into her as if I was gripping the edge of a cliff. And, then, the release poured through me. I began crying. The tears just rained down. Great sobs created out of relief to be in her arms again, out of humiliation for all I'd put her through over the past year. She cradled me and I sunk deeper against her. "It's going to be okay," she said.

I nodded and sniffed back the rest of my tears. "I know it will be. It's just been a little unnerving, you know?"

I pulled back from her arms and took a good look at her. It had been a long time since we'd seen each other and she was definitely in the best shape of her life. "You look great." She wiped my tears away and smiled. I added, "I'd say ten years younger."

"Thanks," she blushed. "I guess losing some weight will do that."

She looked just like she did when we first met, fit and glowing, even down to the sparkle in her eye. "How did you lose it?"

"Eating clean and lots of exercise." She stood tall and reached for her camera case, which was perched on the rock next to us. "I'm actually thinking of signing up for a triathlon." She zipped her case shut and strung it from her neck. She started off into a light stride down the wooded path. I fell into place beside her.

"You're going to get on a bike? Are you kidding? I begged and begged for you to go biking with me for years."

She laughed. "Yeah, I know. Bonnie thought it might be a nice thing for us to do together."

Stab. Twist. A sobering pain I deserved. "Ah, I see."

She stopped walking and reached for my arm. "Tell me how you are doing."

"I've been good." I nodded my head up and down to emphasize. "Yeah, things have worked out really well for me over the past year."

She smiled. "Don't lie to me."

I tried to look past her and off to the bridge down the path, but her eyes, like magnets, drew mine back to hers. "Okay, so I've had a rough patch. But, it's getting easier."

"Margie told me a little of what's going on, that you're struggling with a few things. She also told me about your pap smear scare after I begged her to tell me what was going on with you after all those messages."

I stared into her eyes, which brimmed with sympathy. I wanted her love, not pity. "Is that why you called me? To make sure I was okay?"

"Yeah, of course. I was worried about you."

I nodded and fell back into a brisk walk. She followed.

"Let's talk about you," I said, trying not to fumble. "Tell me what's going on in your life. How's the photography?"

She cleared her throat. "Well, okay. Photography. Let's see... I landed a shot in *The Post*."

"I saw," I said.

"You saw?" She broke out into a huge smile.

"I did. I randomly opened up to it one day. You must have been on cloud nine."

"You have no idea." She walked and the smile grew larger. "Well, actually, you probably do." She chuckled. "After that, I was shadowing this award-winning photographer around and he let me take some pictures for him. He's been contracted to photograph a book for the Governor and right now he's on the Marinetime section. We've been shooting the harbor down in Annapolis. We even went sailing to get more authentic." Her smile lit up her face. I don't think I'd ever seen her face so bright and rosy.

"You're beaming."

She just kept going. "I'm taking this new photography class that's making me look at things differently. Like see that weeping willow?" She placed her hand on the small of my back. Her touch comforted me like a cup of tea on a really cold, wintry day. "Before, I would just snap a picture from this front position, but now," her hand slipped away and she grasped the camera with both hands, squatted down and shot upwards. "Now, I've learned that unusual angles are more interesting and give a picture more depth."

She looked so pretty to me all scrunched down to her ankles. So natural. So pure. "Can I see?"

She showed me the picture and it really was interesting. The tree looked as though it sprayed branches all around it like a messy splatter of paint on canvas. "That would look great in a frame."

She giggled. "You should see my walls. Snapshots framed everywhere." She skipped off.

I caught up to her. We walked in silence for a few minutes more. I admired the majesty of the trees and the beauty of the weeds that grew up around them. I especially liked the way the ivy wrapped itself around the trunk, trusting and loyal for eternity.

"So, did you really start smoking?" Kelly asked, breaking the silence and getting right down to it.

"I did," I said, embarrassed. "But, as of a few days ago, I haven't smoked a single cigarette." I showed her my patch. "Withdrawals are tough, though."

"I can't believe you ever started. I thought you always hated smokers."

"I led you to believe I hated them. But, secretly, I've always been curious."

"It's weird thinking of you lighting up a cigarette."

"It was stupid, I know." I kicked a stone and it sailed through the air landing on a bed of weeds. "I did some pretty stupid things, but that's all behind me now. I really want to focus on good things and making everything right again." I stopped and placed my hands on her shoulders. "I'm so sorry I was such a selfish person to you."

"You did act pretty selfish. I didn't even recognize you. It was sad. It was like you died."

"But here I am again. And, I want to make it all up to you."

She smiled crookedly and tilted her head. "That's not necessary. I understand you were going through some sort of growing period. You needed to spread your wings and see what it felt like to fly. I was holding you back. It was hard for me to let go of you. But, what choice did I have, right?"

"I'm so sorry." I rubbed her cheek with the back of my hand, soothing away some of the hurt I had caused.

"I think we both needed that little push," she said. "I was falling apart before we broke up. I couldn't stand myself. I was pitiful, lying around moping all day, nagging you, blaming everyone else but myself for the life I'd sowed."

"We've all been there," I said. "I'm sure I was no help. Which is why I want to make things right again."

"You already did. Don't you see that?"

Some birds sang above us in the tree canopy. The trickling water in the stream down the hill played in harmony with the rustle of the leaves and the faint cheers of baseball fans in the field on the other side of the stream. The earth was so sweet with life. I could taste the fresh sprigs with each breath. Love danced on Kelly's face, a love that was meant for me, waiting for me to return.

I cupped her face in my hands like a chalice. Then, I kissed her, and she responded. Passion, love, and beauty bloomed between us. Shivers of delight danced through me. Touching her, smelling her skin so close to mine, I could've swept her up and laid her under a tree and made love to her all afternoon long. I instantly fell in love with her all over again. "I love you so much," I said into her mouth.

This time Kelly was crying. I wiped her tears as they rolled down her cheeks.

"Why are you crying?" I asked.

"Because what you are doing to me is so unfair."

"Unfair? How?" I cradled her in my arms, swayed her side to side.

"I just know I'm going to walk away from you feeling way too much guilt."

"Guilt? Why? We've already agreed I was the idiot here. Not you. Never you. Why would you have to feel guilty?"

"Because I'm not free to love you anymore."

She pulled out of my arms and walked away, back up the path we'd just walked on together. Her hair bounced and flopped in a beautiful, highlighted mess. Her honest spirit shone on everything but me. "Why not?" I yelled out to her.

"Because," she swung around, spraying tears onto the greens below. "While you were out probably fucking Kara Travers and ignoring me, I fell in love with someone else. Someone who respects me and loves me back the way I deserve."

"Bonnie?" My voice shimmied out of me in nothing more than a stifled whisper.

"Yes," she said and broke into heaving sobs. "Yes, Bonnie."

"Break up with her," I said, moving towards her slowly, with great care not to scare her off.

"You're too late, Becca. I moved in with her. My family comes to dinner at our house every Sunday. My mother helped her pick out my engagement ring."

Her ring, shimmering in the sunlight, pierced me, stole my breath, and cut off all circulation to rhyme and reason.

"Why does she get to be part of your family?"

"Because, she showed me that my fears were getting in the way of me being able to experience the fullness of the life that I wanted. She taught me that the only way to live was to leap."

I cringed. "So that's it then? There are no more chances for us?"

Tears leaked from her eyes. She just stood there and shook her head no. We stood amidst the brush crying out like wounded wolves, eventually clinging to each other. Crying for our losses and our gains, for the shadowed line that separated us from ever being able to freely love each other ever again.

## Chapter Fourteen

The first thing I did on my way back to my condo was stop at the convenience store to buy a pack of cigarettes. I wasn't even through the swinging door when I lit it up. I smoked a quarter of it by the time I plopped in the front seat of my car. I inhaled like a drug addict desperate for a high, figuring I had no good reason to quit now. My life sucked. I had lost Kelly forever due to my own self-serving interests.

I drove down the street past Cindy's Snowball stand, which had a mile of moms, dads, and kids waiting in line for shaved ice drowned in fruit syrup, and wondered what the point of anything was anymore. That would never be me in line. I'd never get to watch my kids freeze their brains or hear them giggle as they tasted the sweetness of life with their little hands folded into mine.

I got halfway through the cigarette and felt sick. I pulled over into a ditch by the side of the road and threw up, cigarette still smoldering in my hand. A car whizzed by and honked, teens yelled out something inaudible to me. What a pathetic loser I'd become.

I sat in my car for a few minutes staring at a patch of woods and wishing I could just disappear into them and start over on the other side.

But instead, I drove off back to the park to finish the walk alone.

I ran through the woods, crying, tripping, falling, and hacking. I feared standing still, afraid I'd sink and never be able to breathe again. I needed to change the scenery. I needed to step outside of everything I knew. I needed to get away from my mistakes and failures. I couldn't just waltz back into everyday life. Nothing was the same anymore. Everything had changed in a flash, except me.

I returned to my car hours later, soaked in sweat, stained in tears. I didn't even remember driving back to my condo. I pulled into my parking spot and before stepping out of my car, I called Gabby and told her I was taking a vacation. She forbade me, citing we had a show to perform in four days. I told her I was already out of town and unable to make it back. She rambled on about my contract and how I was legally bound to show. I told her to sue me then. She assured me if I didn't show, she would. I told her I wouldn't be back for two weeks. She told me I'd better get my ass back to the studio that afternoon. I laughed, told her I'd see her in two weeks, and hung up on her.

I needed at the very least those two weeks to figure out how I'd make it through the next seven decades of my life.

~ ~

Two hours later, I shoved every piece of underwear I owned into my suitcase along with enough sweats, shorts, and t-shirts to clothe a small nudist colony. I tossed it in the trunk of my Civic. I asked my neighbor, Gerry, an old man with grey hair poking out of his ears, to collect my newspapers and mail for me. I brought him up to my condo and showed him on which shelf he should stack everything. He looked around my condo and insisted for the fiftieth time that his was way bigger and nicer. I agreed. He asked if I'd like him to fix anything while I was gone. I begged him not to and reminded him about the hole I still had in my bathroom floor from the last time he attempted to fix my leaking toilet. He stood in the center of my living room with his hands bracing his weakened hips and said, "Don't forget your cell there on the table." I told him that where I was going I didn't need one. He asked where I was going, and I told him I didn't have a fucking clue. His eyes grew large. "Then, at least take my road atlas. I've got one in my place."

"No thanks," I said. "I don't care where I end up."

He just shook his head and walked out of my door. "Well, alright then. You take care out there."

I locked my deadbolt and handed him the key. "I'll see you in two weeks."

A few minutes later, I filled up my tank, loaded up on water and munchies, and headed west on Interstate 70.

~ ~

I drove for the rest of daylight following I-70 just stopping for gas and to pee. I sang. Then, I listened to some health expert talk about the obesity crisis in America on talk radio. At one point I turned off the radio to concentrate on the chirping of some creatures, which might have been tree frogs or cicadas. When a family of deer crossed in front of me on a stretch of road snaking through Columbus, Ohio, I decided to stop for the night. I chose a room at the Red Roof Inn and ate a hamburger and a massive pile of French fries at the diner next door. The waitress poured me a fresh cup of coffee and plopped a Splenda down on the table. "How about a slice of apple pie, sweetie?"

I cringed at her use of my pet name. "Just the check, please."

Later, with my belly full, I plopped down on my hotel bed, flicked the television on, and watched an episode of "Fringe" where the lead character escaped into an alternate universe. I didn't remember what happened next because I dozed off and dreamed I was her, standing in Battery Park in New York City. The twin towers still colored the skyline behind me. I was her, playing guitar and singing a Melissa Etheridge song. A large crowd gathered around me, tossing coins in my case. I felt sad to be far away from home, away from everyone I knew. When I finished the song, to the dismay of those gathered, I collected my coins, zipped up my black guitar, and walked away. I felt tethered to a deeply painful loneliness. I had nowhere to go, no one who expected me, and no one who cared. I was walking alone past the cafes and fancy office buildings of the budding financial district and crying, wondering where I'd lay my head that night. As I rounded a corner, a man jumped out at me, and I screamed. I screamed so loud, I woke myself up. I sat up in my hotel bed sweating with tears streaming down my face. An episode of *Law and Order* blared on the television.

I didn't sleep anymore that night. Instead I got up, showered, brewed some of the courtesy coffee, and read the issue of *Glamour* I'd purchased from the convenience store.

My mind wandered from the articles to reality and back several times. I reread sentences three and four times, trying desperately to squash the images of Kelly and Bonnie, Kara and me fucking, my empty condo, my life with no gigs, me smoking cigarette after cigarette alone in a dark barroom, and me delivering pitchers of beer and plates of burgers to four toppers brimming in laughter and good cheer.

Ohio was not far enough away. I needed to go further west. I needed to rack as many miles as I could between me and that old life. Then hopefully, I could just pop it like a blister and wait for it to heal.

~ ~

The next morning, I ordered an extra-large cup of coffee from the diner and drove off back down I-70.

I drove down some long and winding stretches of highway, sometimes the only one on the road for miles. A deep welling of hurt and dread suffocated me and held me down at the bottom of a ditch I'd fallen into, turning the walls to a texture too slippery to climb. I shivered and drove onward, finally realizing I'd have to eventually surrender to my punishment. I'd have to face it head on, staring at its sharp edges that protruded out at me at every angle. I cried out in writhing pain from its blinding power and numbing sting. I felt it necessary to shout out promises that the next time I was granted blessings, I'd take better care of them. "Just stop the pain and I promise I'll never be a selfish idiot ever again," I said, begging and pleading with God to stop the excruciating jabs, promising that I'd learned my lesson.

I sobbed so hard, I could barely see the pavement in front of me. I pulled off the side of the road to allow a year of regret to break free, run from me, and get as far away from its source, energy, and creator as possible. The world stood silent and still around me. Not even the wind dared to interrupt my confessions, my cleansing, and my apologies to God.

Eventually, I cried out everything in me, and then just like that, ended on a sigh, a knowing nod, and a soft chuckle of recognition that I'd hit the lowest part of life I could hit. The time had arrived to start new, try over, and resurface one tiny pull-up at a time.

The sun was climbing higher in the eastern sky behind me. It sparkled like a tiny glimmer of hope, offering me the first tug. I latched onto it and let it lift me. I'd take an inch if that's all it had to offer. I'd take any amount of hope God was willing to shell out to me.

I rolled down my window and exhaled a year's worth of bad energy, then I breathed in what I hoped would be the first of many fresh breaths. I watched as the wind rustled through the trees again and the leaves waved. I savored the air's fresh sprig of hope, forgiveness, and change.

I started my engine and pressed the gas, anxious and ready now to embrace whatever it was God had in store for me.

~ ~

My Civic partnered with me all the way to the Rocky Mountains in Colorado, at which point, it fizzled out and refused to go further. I pulled into a dealership at nine a.m. They had just turned on the coffee pot and laid out a platter of powdered donuts when I walked through the door looking disheveled, tired, and desperate.

"My car is sputtering when I try to climb the mountain," I told the man dressed in a Nike polo shirt. His name Earl was embroidered right above his right shirt pocket. "It died out right at the sign for Estes Park. I turned it around, popped it into neutral, and it made it all the way down. Of course, it seems fine now."

"Sounds like a head gasket issue," he said with a nod. He placed a clipboard in front of me. "If you can just complete this paperwork, we'll take a look and get you on your way."

I didn't have a freaking clue what a head gasket was. I began filling in my name and address. By the time I got down to my payment information I stopped. "How much do you think this is going to run me?"

"It all depends what we find when we get it up on the lift."

I hated being a woman in that situation. The man saw a distraught female whimper into his shop and thought he'd be a richer man. "I want an estimate. That's it." I placed the clipboard on the counter and dropped the pen down on the incomplete paperwork.

He snapped his head to the side. "Sure thing. Come back in about two hours and we should have an answer for you."

"Two hours?"

"Busy morning for us."

"But, I'm the only one here."

"Two hours. That's the best I can do."

A few minutes later, I walked down the streets of Denver trying not to look like a tourist. I slipped into a diner shaped like one of those old style steel trailers. Mini juke boxes were propped up on the wall near each table. Elvis blared out of most of them. The only seat available was a small table squished near the waitress stand. I sat down, ordered a cup of coffee, and braved the clanking dishes, the complaining wait staff, the sizzling coffee pots on their wet bases, and a screaming two-year-old pleading with his mom and dad for chocolate milk, banging his little fists against the table like it was a drum.

"Ready to order?" a girl about twenty asked me, staring down at her notepad instead of at me.

"Three egg whites scrambled and wheat toast. And coffee, please."

She pushed off back to her stand, muttering something to the other waitress and then wiping the counter frantically with a rag she had plucked up from under the station. She came back, poured my coffee, and left me without as much as a smile.

I missed home so much. I had only been gone a week, but it felt like a year. I sipped my coffee and thought seriously of returning to Maryland and everything familiar. Screw this making a clean break shit, I thought.

A man sitting at the counter across from me got up, tossed a couple bucks down, and asked if I wanted his newspaper. "Sure," I said. He sailed it in a high arc, and it landed perfectly in front of me. He tilted his head to me and scampered off.

I flipped through the pages and noticed nothing different happened in Denver, Colorado than in Baltimore, Maryland. Same shit, different city. Carjacking, house break-in, armed robbery, car accident claiming four lives, etc. I tried my luck at the crossword puzzle, filling in almost half of it by the time my breakfast came.

I ate slowly listening to Frank Sinatra and Kenny Rogers. Later, when the waitress dumped my check on the table and walked away without a thank you, I decided once my car was fixed, I was going home. I could easily avoid people for a while.

I showed up at the dealership fifteen minutes before their two hours were up. The same man greeted me at the counter, his face turned down into a weary smile. "I've got some good news and some bad news."

"Good news first, please," I said, not sure I could handle what he would throw at me.

"We can fix this today. We have the parts in house. So, in about four hours you can be on your way up the Rockies and camping by dusk if that's what you intend."

"Bad news?" I asked.

"It is definitely your head gasket."

"How much?" I asked.

"With labor and parts, it'll run you $4,800."

"What?" That was more than my car was worth.

"We take all major credit cards." He offered me an apologetic smile.

"I'm getting a second opinion. Let me have my keys."

"Okay," he handed them to me. "But, if we don't start it now, you're looking at a minimum of three days before we can get to it. We're closed tomorrow and Mondays are our busiest oil change day. So, earliest we could get you up and running is Tuesday."

I walked out feeling like a two ton truck was strapped to my back. A few minutes later, back in the driver's seat, I drove out to the main street and decided to go right. My car bucked slightly on the turn, and then straightened out as I headed down Twelfth Street in search of more abuse from another dishonest mechanic. My gas gauge read almost empty. I pulled into a full-service gas station. I rolled down my window and asked a blonde man wearing a Coors baseball hat to fill it. He wore an oil stained blue jumpsuit and sipped a bottle of green tea. He sipped and washed my windows. "Do you know an honest mechanic around here?" I asked him.

"Sure I do," he said, a smile as clean as freshly laundered sheets smoothed across his friendly face. "Me."

I looked over to his two-car bay seething with grime and rusty machinery. "Oh, what the hell," I said, figuring it couldn't get much worse. "Have time to check out my car? It's got some kind of head gasket issue. At least that's what the dealership just told me."

"I'd be happy to. Why don't you have a seat in my office over there?" He pointed to a door with a flower wreath on it. "I'll have a look and see what's going on."

I stepped out of my car, grabbed for the newspaper I'd collected from the restaurant, and trailed off to the office. I entered and smelled pine right away. A basket of shaved wood sat on the counter, the source of the pine fragrance. A tiny note was attached to the basket that read, *we love you, Daddy*.

I sat on a flowered cloth sofa. Two eyelet covered pillows graced each end of it. A dainty vase with fresh carnations hugged the east end of a corner table, while race car magazines and an issue of Vanity Fair sprawled the front of the table. A Thomas Kincaid-style picture, cross-stitched in shimmery metallic, hung above the opposite wall. A couple dozen greeting cards decorated the wall behind the counter. I squinted to read them. They were mostly thank you cards, a few birthday well wishes, and a couple of customized cards touting the world's best mechanic across the front of them. A wooden cross with Jesus carved onto it hung above his counter. Next to it a hand-written sign in black magic marker read *Jesus keeps me honest*.

I prayed that was true because I surely didn't have five fucking grand to just hand over to the guy.

I read the newspaper. I flipped to the entertainment section and landed on an ad for a local pub's open mic. The winner got $500 and all the burgers he/she wanted for an entire week. I turned to a story about a ten-year-old

Denver native headlining on Broadway as Annie. I was just about to read another story about a dog named Woof who performed on stage at a nursing home when the mechanic entered.

"I don't think it's your head gasket," he said.

The sun could've been playing a trick on me, but I swear I saw a halo around his head.

"I don't know what it is, yet, but it ain't your head gasket. From what I can see, it's in perfect condition. If you'd like, I can take a closer look at your car and see if I can find out what's causing the issue?"

I wanted to hug him at that point. "Thank you, and yes, please take a look at it."

"The only problem is I am going to need a few days. I am just about to close for the day. I am closed on Sundays, so I won't be able to get a look at it until Monday if that's okay. If you're looking for a place to stay, I'd recommend the Ramada Inn right around the corner."

I nodded. "I guess what choice do I have, right?"

"I wouldn't suggest driving it too far without knowing what's causing the sputtering. I'd hate to see you out on the Interstate by yourself all broken down."

I wasn't sure what to make of the guy's nice act. Was it just a ploy to sneak into my hotel room in the middle of the night to rape and murder me? "If you don't mind, I'm just going to drive over to the hotel and empty my suitcase. Then, I'll drive back here. It shouldn't take more than half an hour."

"Take your time. I'll wait for you." His smile seemed too perfect.

I backed out of the door and waved.

I thought of driving more to find another mechanic just in case the guy turned out to be a Charles Manson-type, but there it was three-thirty on a Saturday. I looked down the road and saw a Holiday Inn. I'd get myself a room there instead.

Forty-minutes later, I returned to the mechanic and handed over my Civic to him, really hoping he was the nice guy he intended for me to believe he was.

~ ~

I sat in my hotel room with the contents of my car spilled out in front of me – my guitar, my suitcase, my pillow and blanket, my books, my snacks, even my road atlas where Kelly and I had bookmarked all the places we planned to visit someday. I stared at the phone on the nightstand. I wanted to call and retrieve my messages so badly. Had she called me? Had she called to tell me she'd made a big mistake the other day? The suspense scratched at me like a playful kitten seeking every ounce of my attention.

Finally, one hour and forty-three minutes later, after downing several Cokes from the vending machine, I caved. I called my cell to get my messages. Three messages from Gabby wondering where I'd been. One from Kara calling me sweetie three times and telling me she would see me when she sees me. Two from Margie. One reminding me that I had an appointment to get my hair colored and the other to ask why the hell I didn't show up to said appointment. One from Vibrations asking if they could switch our practice time to another day because they needed to renovate the practice studios. And a final one from Kara again telling me that we were featured as one of the 20 up-and-coming artists of the week on iTunes.

I combed through the messages again, deleting them as I moved onto the next, figuring maybe I might've missed her message somehow. But, when the recorded voice told me I had no new messages, I sunk. Kelly hadn't even tried to call.

~ ~

The next morning, I woke up and ate more egg whites and wheat toast from a different diner. I also spread some strawberry jam on my toast. A dollop of excitement for the day. The little kids in the booth behind me kept tapping my shoulder. I turned around and dazzled them with a funny face. They giggled and collapsed into a joyous ball on the vinyl seat and started anew in thirty second intervals. Thanks to them keeping my spirits raised I was able to get down my breakfast.

I walked back to my hotel room after that, plucked up the morning edition of the *Denver Herald* from in front of the door, and then slept for another three hours. I woke to the sound of a couple arguing outside my door. The man told the women she had acted like a five-year-old in front of his parents, and she balked back that he should've stood his ground and told his parents they were living together. Their argument trailed off into mumbles as they walked onward. I rose and peeked out the window at the bright day. The morning frost had long since burned off the patio furniture below. The small patch of ice I'd almost broken my neck on earlier that morning had long since evaporated. I flipped on the television to the weather channel. The reporter said that the sun would catapult the temperature to a mild forty-two degrees by that early spring afternoon. I hated cold weather. My car couldn't have wimped out in the desert instead?

I stepped out of my room and leaned on the railing overlooking the closed-down pool area. A few people had scattered around the tables despite the chill. A pretty woman, about thirty, cuddled under a blanket on one of the lounge chairs reading a book. She played with her hair, rubbed her neck, and arched her back. At one point, she looked up and smiled at me, holding my gaze for a moment beyond casual friendliness. Momentarily turned on by that, I felt the familiar rush rise up in between my legs. She broke our stare and withdrew back to her book. I leaned harder into the railing, temporarily paralyzed in a fit of lust. She looked up again, and that time cocked her head slightly and offered me another smile, that one more seductive. She coyly lifted her eyes from me and returned them to her book. Completely turned on, I walked back into my hotel room, closed the door, and fingered myself right there on the floor until the release I'd ventured to claim only moments ago came rattling to me in one hell of a bold thrust.

I lay there with my pajama bottoms turned down, panting, shuddering, and freaked out by my horny impulse. I climbed up to my feet and sat down on the edge of the bed, then stared back at the spot I'd just finger-fucked myself in because of a strange woman's smile. If I really loved Kelly, why would I ever subject her to me, the pathetic, relentlessly horny girl who melted at the sight of a tight ass or a simple smile from a hot girl?

I looked at the phone again. Why was I so sad that she hadn't called me? So many months had slipped away without her calling me, and now it'd only been a little over a week and my heart turned to lead in my chest. Did I really love her or did I love the idea of being in love with her? Did I just simply miss having someone love and care about me? Did I just miss the safety and comfort of being with her? Was I afraid?

I didn't want to be that lonely lesbian eating a slice of red velvet birthday cake alone in the booth of a greasy diner on her fortieth, her fiftieth, and her sixtieth milestones.

I did love Kelly. I truly felt my heart come alive that day in the park, and I also felt it rip apart when she told me about her fiancée. But, what an ass I was to think I could just springboard back in and erase Bonnie from the picture. Kelly hadn't called me to tell me she still loved me. She called me because she was being true to her nature and showing concern for me the troubled person, not me the love of her life.

Kelly was selfless, always looking out for my best interest. Maybe I really wasn't her best interest. Maybe Bonnie was. Maybe Bonnie had a clue who she was and what she wanted from life.

God knew I didn't.

I couldn't trust myself right now. How could I ever insist anyone as special as Kelly should risk trusting me? What did I have to offer her that could trump what Bonnie could?

I needed to keep the miles between us. I needed to just quietly go and stay out of her way so she'd have a decent chance at a life she deserved, a life I wasn't sure I could give her. What if another pretty girl entered? Could I resist? Would I want to? If that woman would've strolled up and seduced me, would've I resisted? Probably not.

Who was I? What did I want? What was I willing to give? That was what I needed to figure out before I ever dared fall in love again.

I picked up the phone and dialed Gerry to ask him to look after my place for a lot longer than the two weeks. He asked me how much longer. I told him indefinitely. He asked me if he should drink the milk in my fridge so it wouldn't spoil. I told him to help himself. He pointed out that the chicken thighs and pork tenderloin in my freezer would only keep for six months. I told him he'd better eat those, too, then. The next phone call I made was to Margie. I asked her to pick up Tangerine from the repair shop and keep her safe while I was gone. She asked if I wanted to take her two-thirty appointment on Tuesday to make up for the one I missed. I told her I'd reschedule. She insisted I set a date right then because her book was filling up past June at that point. I asked her if she was booking into the following year yet. She laughed and asked if I was serious. I told her I was damned well serious, thanked her in advance for keeping Tangerine safe while I was gone, and hung up. Next call I needed to make I'd have to wait a little longer to do. I wasn't quite ready for it.

## **Chapter Fifteen**

At eight o'clock, I decided I couldn't watch another second of television. So, I tore the ad about the open mic night from the newspaper and hailed a cab. The driver drove with his window cracked a few inches, which allowed me to get a face full of the chilly Denver air. My hair blew every which way. We passed the mechanic's garage, the Ramada Inn, the dealership that tried to rob me, and a few dozen shopping centers.

"Do you play any Dylan?" The cab driver asked me.

I patted my guitar case. "I play everything."

"You know, they always give the $500 bucks to someone with a musical instrument." He looked at me through his rearview window. "Maybe you got a shot."

I fought the urge to tell him to turn around and drop me back at my safe hotel. I didn't want to perform alone. I didn't want to test my ability. I didn't want that night to be the night I faced my fears. I didn't want to be roaming around a strange city in search of myself. But, there I was. "Yeah, maybe I do."

Once I arrived, I paid my cover charge and walked straight up to the bar with my guitar strapped to my back. The bottle of Bacardi teased me from behind the cute bartender. My mouth watered for a taste of it, for a zap of its power, and for a whiff of its intoxicating, mind-numbing qualities. "What can I get you?" the girl asked.

"Club soda with lime," I said, forcing my back on the temptress that could so easily make that stupid road trip down self-discovery lane much less complicated with its one quick chug.

She darted back over to me with my second-choice drink. "Should I start a tab?" she asked with a teasing wink.

I chuckled, handed her a five, and told her to keep the change.

"If you're interested in the open mic contest, you'll need to sign up with Al over by the end of the bar." She tilted her head in his direction.

"I'm not sure yet." I sipped my dry drink.

"Why don't you let me pour you something a little stronger than that, then?"

I raised my glass up to her in a cheer. "I'm good with this."

I sat at the bar for a while and watched as the crowd expanded. A few lugged guitars on their backs like I did. The only difference was they walked straight to Al fueled by confidence. I counted that fifteen people had signed up by the time I was ready to order my third club soda. "You sure I can't spot you a little gin in this?" the bartender asked me again. She sure did tug at my command center a bit. Seemed the only thing that would quench my thirst would be a shot of that gin, which was why I refused again.

A little while later, a group of thirty-something's gathered to my right and ordered up a shit load of drinks and shots for themselves. They were laughing and carrying on, slapping backs, cracking jokes, hooting, and hollering. I overheard them telling the bartender they were celebrating their fifteen-year escape from high school. I would've had to surmise from their good looks and chummy ways that they were the popular clique that, back in their days, everyone wanted to belong to. Two of them had signed up for the open mic.

Al walked on the small stage and announced ten more minutes for sign-ups. That's when one of the clique guys, a tall blonde with a hulk sized chest, asked what I'd be singing that night.

"I'm not going to sing. I'm just here to enjoy the show."

"Bullshit," he slurred. "Why did you bring a guitar with you, then?"

"I just don't feel like it, that's all."

He squinted through drunk eyes at me. "You scared?"

"I'm not scared."

"I bet you have a pretty voice," he said.

The bartender wiped the counter in front of us. "That's exactly what I'm thinking, too. She's too scared, though."

"I'm not scared," I said to them both, wishing I wasn't.

"What are you drinking," he asked.

"Nothing."

"What is she drinking?" he asked the bartender.

"Nothing that's going to help her get on that stage," she said.

"I don't need to drink to get on stage." I pushed my empty club soda away.

"I don't believe you," he said. "Do you believe her?" he asked the girl.

She looked at me and winked. "She'll have to prove it to us."

Something in her eyes clicked a switch in me. Call it a challenge; call it a weak spot for a hot babe; call it foolish; but, I embraced my arrival at destiny's door. "I'm in."

He turned towards Al. "Hey, buddy, sign her up."

"My name's Becca," I yelled out to him.

Five minutes later, Al walked on stage and invited me up to join him. My throat, dry as the desert, burned. The brave flicker had abandoned me.

"I'll be cheering for you," my new friend, said, then added, "even if you suck."

I nodded before climbing off the stool and heading up to the stage. Whistles and cheers flew. A strobe light flickered. Strangers tapped my shoulder blades as I passed them on my way across the floor.

"Let's hear it for Becca," Al said, welcoming me to his side. I had done this a thousand times with crowds that made that one look like mere sprinkles of salt on a chef's buffet table, yet, my stomach rolled and I wanted to throw up. I hadn't performed solo in front of a crowd since my grandpa's funeral. I didn't have Kara strutting her stuff, taking the heat off of me. I didn't have her sultry voice backing me up in case I forgot the lyrics. I looked out to a sea of strangers and wondered how many of them would've scaled the stage if I had been Kara, the face of our duo, the headliner, and the one everyone came to see, instead.

"Hey," I said into the mic like I'd said into a million mics many times before, trying out my voice and testing the acoustics. "This song is called 'Back to Start'."

The crowd silenced and the lights dimmed as I began to strum. The stares freaked me out, bringing me right back to the funeral. So, I closed my eyes and pretended I was alone in my music room playing a song I'd written for Kelly. I imagined that time that Kelly was sitting in front of me instead of in my living room with her head buried in a photography book. She was smiling and swaying to my words, with happy tears rolling down her cheeks and love apparent in every one of her breaths. The sun was filtering in at just the right angle, making Tangerine Twist appear angelic. Her steel strings filled our senses with all that was selfless, pure, and beautiful. The tone was pitch-perfect, the emotions raw and real, and the connection surreal and consumed in wanderlust. I imagined love at its most fragile and reverent state, and unleashed it from my heart to hers, to the air around us, to my neighbors, to my city, to the stretches of Interstate 70 I'd just traveled down, and all the way to the strangers in front of me. As I sang, a deep love enveloped me, protected me, and carried me through. I ended with my head bowed, and one last strum that reverberated through the still pub.

Later that night as I soaked in the hotel tub, my heart still swelled in awe of the overwhelming ovation I'd received. I thumbed through the five hundred dollar bills again, feeling more proud of myself than ever, even when a venue full of fans applauded. That night was different. That night, they cheered for me.

~ ~

The win from the night before stirred a pinch of confidence in me. I could become a traveling singer with no ties to anyone but me. I was ready to make that call I'd avoided the other day, and in those few seconds it took me to dial, I convinced myself that I was certain of that call.

Gabby's voicemail picked up, which I hadn't planned for. She never left more than twelve inches between her and her cell. The only obvious reason she didn't answer was that she didn't want to talk to me. I acted out once, and already she probably had a new duo partner lined up. The two of them probably sat in the booth of an unknown pub and reeled in another want to-be musician. I doubted I was her first choice. She was always so matter-of-fact with me, like I was a lowly street criminal and she was my court-appointed lawyer. In the long run, I was sure she couldn't wait to get rid of me.

"Give me a call, please," I said, "I don't have my cell with me, but am checking messages, so let me know when I can call you back." Then I hung up and prayed when she called back I'd have the guts to tell her that I wasn't going back for at least a year. I couldn't face Kara yet, and I most certainly didn't want to accidentally run into Kelly, or God forbid, Bonnie on her arm. And I didn't want to have to absorb every ounce of fucking sunshine Margie squirted from her joyous pregnancy talks. I wasn't ready to handle any of that yet. Maybe ever.

I could make it on my own. Last night had proved that. The crowd loved me. I didn't forget my words. The size of the venue was controllable. So what if only a few dozen people ever heard my songs. Sell-out crowds and radio interviews were Kara's thing. Not mine. I was just along for the ride.

All the success was just a by-product that brought too many life-altering temptations.

I was ready to move on. Just as soon as my car was fixed, I was heading further west. I had a new plan. I'd keep traveling around the country, plugging little spots with less than thirty people like the one last night. No attachments, no material possessions. Just me and my music. Nothing more to tie me down and gut me. No more of that. I was set to race down the freeway and tell the world to watch out, Becca was free and not stopping. Ever. Nothing could ever hurt me again if I kept moving past it.

That all sounded like a superb plan the longer I let it marinate, and right up until the moment I returned back to the hotel from the mechanic that Tuesday morning. All I had to dish out to him was eighty-two dollars and fifty-three cents for a thermostat. I entered the room whirling on some good vibes, reinforced with the notion that good people still existed. My plan was to gather my stuff, head out on the road, stop at a Hallmark along the way to buy my mechanic-angel the nicest greeting card I could find for his mighty fine collection, and then get on with my new life as a nomadic musician. But, when I got to my room, I made the mistake of calling to retrieve my messages again.

"What are you doing?" Kelly said in the message. "You're giving up your career? You're running away from it? That is the dumbest thing I've ever heard. How dare you? You let this career ruin us, and now you walk away from it? If you have any respect for what we had, then I hope you will think long and hard about giving up on your dream. Your fame and fortune are the only things that bring any sense to our breakup."

I paced the floor with a firestorm of anger exploding in me. What right did she have to be angry with me? Our breakup wasn't my entire fault. What about her bad moods, about her never wanting to show me affection, and about her always hiding me from her family and friends? How dare she blame our breakup on me and my career! If she had made me feel like I was someone worth loving maybe I wouldn't have had to go fuck Kara Travers and become a chain-smoking idiot. She had every little thing to do with that, too.

I called Margie from the hotel phone immediately. "Why did you tell Kelly I wasn't coming back?"

"Because you're a fool," she said with a snap of impatience. "You don't listen to me. I could tell you a million times what a mistake you're making and you let it roll off your shoulders like I was commenting on the weather. You're a selfish person, Becca. You get all these great things that happen to you and you don't appreciate them. You're acting like a two-year-old on the verge of a tantrum, running away like this. You screwed things up in your life and you think it's over. I'm just trying to find a way to convince you to face the fucking music and get over yourself. You've got a booming career. Don't fuck it up by crying about all your weaknesses. We're all weak. Just pick up the pieces, put yourself back together again, and deal with it before all your opportunities wash away forever."

I had so much to say to her, but all the words crashed into each other in the back of my throat, slipping and sliding on the invisible obstacles of my checkered reality. So, I hung up and smashed the phone against the nightstand instead, cracking the wood and denting the earpiece. Just when I thought I had it all figured out, more shit flew in my face and caused me to crash yet again.

I called Kelly, fully intent on ripping on her, setting her straight, and telling her the reason I was all screwed up was because of her inability to love me the way I should've been loved. If she had only cuddled more, kissed me in public, invited me to family dinners, and showed me off to her friends the way she was showing off Bonnie, I wouldn't have to traverse the country to find a new me. I waited for her to pick up. By the third ring, she picked up and said hello.

"Kel?"

"No, Kelly's in the shower. It's Bonnie. Who's this?"

I panicked and hung up, happy I wasn't using my cell. Minutes later, numb and feeling like I was breathing through a straw, I slowly rose, gathered my belongings, and headed off to my car. I started on down the road and landed at a traffic light before the entrance to I-70. Left would bring me west. Right would bring me east. Going west would be easier. I could just start over like planned and not have to face any of the pain waiting for me back east. I could stay bitter with Kelly and heal my wounds by citing she had no valid point or say in my future. Over time, the calluses would harden over any snippets of untruth, making me feel right again. She could go off and marry Bonnie, have a herd of kids, and build an in-law apartment for her parents. I could eventually convince myself that she wasn't worth the fight. I'd write enough songs and meet enough people to overshadow a few years spent on her. That much I could control.

When the light turned green, for some stupid reason, I chose to risk that control and veered off to the right.

I may not have been certain about too much those days, but I was certain that I needed to set a few things straight in that direction before I could travel the other way.

~ ~

I returned from Denver wanting to set the story straight with Kelly and Margie. I wanted them both to know I could make it out there on my own without their help, guidance, or love.

First, I would hand Margie the three thousand dollars I borrowed from her a year ago and tell her I wasn't so selfish after all, and not such a fool, either. And, I could straighten myself out just fine without her help. Oh, and I'd add that maybe she should just ask Bonnie to be the other godparent. Then, I would go to Kelly and tell her I wasn't quitting the duo for her. I would be the bigger person and save her from the real truth behind that decision.

Was that what they wanted for me? To make me feel like fucking shit? Did Kelly really want me to still perform with Kara? It took me seventeen hundred miles, six tanks of gas, a new thermostat, two speeding tickets, and dozens of cups of diner coffee to realize that her not even caring about me staying in the duo with Kara was what hurt me the most.

Before braving them, I decided to pay Tangerine Twist a visit.

Tony had just finished polishing her that very morning, he told me. He was just about to call me to tell me. "You saved me a call."

"You saved me space on my voice mailbox," I said, anxiously awaiting to see my baby reborn.

"Hang on, I'll go grab her." He scooted to the backroom, tripping over an empty box on his way.

Moments later, he carried her to me. She was beautiful and glistening.

"She's all tuned up and ready." He handed her to me, and when I touched her smooth body, a storm of emotions soaked me down. I ran my hand over her, in awe. "I can't even tell she was ever destroyed."

"I worked hard on her. Especially after your friend said how important she was to you."

I looked up at him, confused. "Friend?"

"That girl who came by a few days ago to check on her. She said you had asked someone to check on her."

"Margie." I nodded. "I didn't think she would come by."

"Margie?" he asked. "That wasn't her name."

"Yeah, her name's Margie," I said.

"No, her name was Kelly."

I swallowed hard, trying to suppress the second wave of emotions before they all but knocked me down to the ground. "Kelly? Are you sure?"

"Yeah, positive. Said so on her check."

"Her check?"

"Yeah, you're all set. She said she owed you. He fumbled under the counter and pulled out an envelope. "She asked that I give this to you."

Kelly had written my name on the envelope. I shoved it in my pocketbook, thanked Tony five times, placed Tang in her case, and walked out to my car. I drove off without reading the contents of the envelope. I needed to simmer and balance out before I could read it. I wanted to imagine whatever it said, it was something that would bring ease to the plaguing feelings that had taken refuge in the pit of my stomach since back in Denver. I didn't want it to be anything that would dig at me even deeper. I couldn't handle more rejection and pain from her. I just knew it would be a goodbye of sorts, and I wasn't prepared for it. I didn't think there would ever come a time when I would be prepared for that.

I drove all the way to McFaddens, parked, and opened the envelope there in the parking lot. It was a blank page with one line scrawled across it in Kelly's unmistakable handwriting.

*You deserve to be happy too.*

And just like that, she had offered me permission to move on with my life. And then, more than ever, I didn't want to.

## Chapter Sixteen

I entered the bright kitchen smelling of garlic and Worcestershire sauce. "Got time to share a beer with an old friend?" I asked.

Joe looked up from the sink and a big smile spread across his face. He dropped the wash bucket into the sink and ran over to me. "Ah, is it really you? Am I imagining this sight before me? A big hotshot now, huh?" He rubbed my head the way he always did, mashing his big hand against my hair. "Give me a hug." He pulled me into his arms and squeezed. His hair smelled like a carnival, delicious and fanciful. "To what do I owe this great surprise?"

"I need to ask you something," I mumbled into his shirt.

"Anything," he pulled away from me, held me at arm's length, and looked me up and down. "You still look like the same Becca James. Do you feel any different?"

"Joe, stop." I put up my hand in defense of hearing any more undeserved platitudes.

His face folded as his eyes softened. "Everything all right?"

"It's a long story." I looked around at the empty bar. In another hour, patrons would start pouring in for a taste of Joe's signature beer-battered burgers and fries. "I was just hoping I could steal you away for one minute to ask you something."

He examined my face like I had a secret code inscribed on it for just his baby blue eyes to read. "Looks like you might need more than a minute." He cupped his hand on my back and ushered me to a couple of stools by the back door. "What's on your mind?"

I waited for us to both settle on our stools then asked, "How come you never asked me to perform solo when I worked for you?"

His face ironed out as if steamed and starched. "That's a strange question. Why would you ask me something like that now?"

"I just need to know, Joe, that's all."

He cornered his eyes up to his left as if the ceiling above the walk-in fridge was feeding him the right words. "I've always been honest with you, haven't I?"

"I'm counting on it that you still are."

He looked me square in the eye and held my hands in his. "What are you hoping to accomplish from my answer?"

"Choosing the right path."

He exhaled. "Okay, look, people from all over Maryland know your name by now, right?"

I nodded.

"How do you not know your path, yet, then?" he asked, suddenly looking a decade older to me.

"They only know me when I'm standing next to Kara."

"Why is that a bad thing?" he asked, shrugging.

"Joe—" I sat up taller. "Just tell me, as a casual observer, untrained in the ways of music, why did you never once ask me to carry McFaddens for the night?"

He looked down at our entwined hands, stirring with a patriarchal duty just as any great role model would. "Look, kid, you've grown since those days. I know this. I've seen the YouTube videos. I've heard your song on the radio. You're not just a back-up singer anymore."

"What was it, though, that kept you from asking me to perform alone? Did you doubt me?"

"I never doubted you." He pointed his finger at me. "You did that yourself."

We sat staring each other down in silence for a few thoughtful moments. Then I asked what I really needed to know from him. "Do you think I have what it takes to make it on my own?"

Joe stood up, straddled his arms at my shoulders, and said, "If you have to ask me that, then my answer is pointless now isn't it?"

He walked towards the door leading to the pub and turned before going through it. "If you want to perform here, ever, then you better just charge your way up to that stage and take over. You hear me?"

"Loud and clear," I said.

"I better see your butt up on my stage rocking this place before I retire, then, you got it?"

He walked out the door, leaving me alone in his spotless kitchen before I could commit to what he so obviously wanted me to say. "Got it," I whispered to the back of the swinging door.

~ ~

I sat outside Kelly's office building, hoping she kept the same schedule I remembered. When the doors flew open at five p.m. and she walked through them, my heart leapt, then sank just as fast when I noticed her hand holding another girl's. Our eyes met as she passed the flagpole. She stopped and nearly fell over. "Becca?" she asked, "Is everything all right?"

"Yes, everything's fine." I walked over to them and extended my hand to the girl. "You must be Bonnie?" I asked.

She dropped Kelly's hand and closed in on mine, confirming. "Yeah, that's correct." She spoke in a southern accent, something that took me by complete surprise. She looked like more of a New Yorker, someone fresh off the scene of *Sex in the City*, with her trendy clothes, polished hair, and shiny lips.

"I'm sorry to just show up like this," I said, my stomach flipping and spiraling down. I turned to Kelly. "I was hoping we could chat for a minute."

Kelly looked to Bonnie, offering an apologetic smile. Bonnie stepped backwards, excused herself, and said she'd wait in the car. "It was nice to meet you," I yelled after her. She turned and nodded, looked me up and down once, and left me alone with her fiancée.

"I just wanted to thank you for taking care of Tangerine the way you did. It wasn't necessary for you to pay for her repairs."

She shrugged and cocked her head to the side. "I wanted to do that for you."

"I just came by to tell you that I'm not quitting the duo for you."

"Thank God," she said. "I know I was a little harsh in my message to you but I couldn't just let you throw your career down the drain because of me. I wouldn't blame you for wanting to get far away. Believe me, I wanted to do the same thing the other day in the park. It's painful and sad what happened to us."

All the anger I'd felt for her on those long stretches of naked roads snaking across Indiana, Ohio, and western Maryland vanished and evaporated in the sunny smile she now offered me. I had planned my reaction down to the tiniest detail, but never anticipated being taken down a few hundred notches by her warmth, her sincerity, and her love for me as a person still. God, how I wished Bonnie wasn't a few hundred yards away, and that Kelly wished it, too. Otherwise, I might have revved up the nerve to grab her in my arms and kiss her again just like in the park. Only that time, I wouldn't let her slip away.

"It is sad. It's hard running into you and her together like this. I figured if I wasn't in the same state, I'd never have to worry about that. But, a lot is at stake with my career, you know? It's not easy for me to just walk away from it like I thought maybe it would be."

"No one's asking you to," she said, reaching out and reassuring me with a quick latch and release of my arm.

"It's not easy to stay, either, you know? I've got a lot to lose either way."

"No. The only way you'll lose now is if you give up on you. This isn't about us anymore."

"How can it not be?" I asked.

"We're engaged," she said, staring into my eyes as if willing for me to understand the levity in that. "We have a dog now."

"You have a dog?" That fact sucked all the oxygen out of my lungs instantly. A dog to Kelly was not something to toss outside in a backyard, to send away to a kennel when vacation called, or to give back because a mistake was made. A dog was a responsibility bearing the same weight as a child.

She nodded. Her chin quivered. "Her name is Zoey and she's a Husky mix. We adopted her last week from a shelter."

"Oh my God. A dog?" Visions of her and Bonnie running, cuddling, and sleeping with Zoey played in my mind. "So that's it, then. It really can't be about us anymore."

"It doesn't have to be so final. We could still be friends."

"Friends." I laughed at that and walked away from her. "I'll adopt a dog of my own and we can have play dates."

"Why do you have to make a joke of this?" she asked.

"Who said I was joking?" I yelled out over my shoulder. I turned away a split-second before the hot tears forged paths down my cheeks. A final, devastating blow, I felt like I had lost control over the last constant in my life. It was over, and there was nothing I could do about it.

~ ~

Like a soldier on a mission, I marched on numbly. My next stop was to Kara. Ella welcomed me in and told me Kara was upstairs.

I knocked on her door. She answered it wearing nothing more than a fluffy towel and a smile so genuine I could've sworn she was thrilled to see me standing before her. "Wow," she said before throwing her arms around me. "I am so glad you're back. I wasn't sure how I'd get through this night without you."

With that, my walls crumbled.

Her musky smell intoxicated me. I fell into her embrace just as desperately as I did the first time she paid me attention.

"Come in and have a seat while I get dressed." She steered me to the lounger. "I have to warn you that Gabby is super pissed at you. She's probably going to threaten you with a lawsuit, so just be prepared to tell her to go fuck herself." Kara misted some spray on her neck and dropped her towel. She plucked some cream from her nightstand and began to massage it onto her golden legs. Her boobs, firm and round, hung in front of her as she bent over and her nipples were erect and teasing. "Just tell her you're back, don't let her bully you. Make up something like you had to bury a great aunt or something like that." She walked over to the mirror and posed, checking out her ass. "Honestly, I need to get my ass to the gym more."

"Kara." I waited for her to stop staring at her perfectly toned ass, which took a few more seconds than would be considered normal under the circumstances. "Don't you even want to know where I was?"

She drifted her eyes from her ass to me and paused. "You don't need to explain anything to me, sweetie. I'm just glad you're back." She walked into her bathroom and came back with a pack of cigarettes. She lit one for herself and blew the smoke out in a long, sensual stream. Then, she handed me one.

"I quit."

She stared at me with eyes as big as pancakes. "Smoking?"

"Were you afraid I was talking about something else?"

She took another drag, not taking her eyes off me. "I figured it'd be a matter of time."

"A matter of time before what?"

She walked over to me and caressed my face. "Before the party ended."

She looked sad, delicate, and fragile. I ran my fingers against the soft plush below me curious as all hell to know how she operated. "Do you ever get mad?"

She inhaled another drag. "What's the point?"

We sat in silence, her smoking the cigarette and me wanting desperately to wipe off that dubious fold of desperation creased on her forehead. "What kind of a gig is happening tonight?"

"Just a small gathering, if you're interested."

I moved over to her, then sat down beside her and held her hand. I didn't feel a spark or a twinge, but I did feel warmth and compassion. "You think maybe Gabby will be less likely to throw something at me if I show up and help you out tonight?"

She rested her head on my shoulder and offered me a puff. One friend to another, I let her place the cigarette between my lips, and I took a long, deep drag. I let it settle in me and swirl around for one last romp. "I quit smoking you know."

She chuckled and crushed out the cigarette in an ashtray. "I knew it was the smoking you were referring to," she said, turning her head to me and brushing my cheek with her soft lips. "So, thanks, then, for having your last memorable drag with me."

She peeled her lips away from my skin, walked her naked body over to the bathroom, and closed the door to get dressed.

~ ~

On my way downtown that night, I called Margie and apologized for being so ornery, and to let her know she was right once again with everything she said to me that night on the phone. We were finishing up the conversation when Margie made one last comment. "Yeah, well, just between you and me," Margie said. "Bonnie isn't as beautiful as she appears to be. She's a fake. Her hair is thin and pathetic and no longer than two inches all over her head. Kelly begged me to help. So, I talked Bonnie into putting a shitload of extensions in there. She looks pretty, but we all know what's underneath."

In some warped way that made me feel better. And later that night, when I sat beside Kara in front of a small crowd of hundreds of people at Meriweather Post Pavilion, that little tidbit of gossip helped me smile a whole lot bigger. And much later, when Gabby and I shook hands over my decision to stay on until my contract ended in two months, I thought of those extensions and a little spark jolted me. I knew deep down that those twelve inch black swatches glued to her scalp wouldn't be able to fool Kelly forever.

~ ~

I learned from Margie, after several vain attempts to get her to leak information, that Kelly and Bonnie took Zoey to the Mayfield Dog Park every Saturday morning at ten. So, on the Saturday following our chat in the parking lot, I asked Gerry if I could borrow his dog, Sam, a pug with a ticklish belly and thing for big dogs. Gerry handed Sam's leash over to me and reminded me he was a humper and that most doggy parents at the park weren't too thrilled with that trait. I assured Gerry that I'd diffuse any such situation.

My stomach flipped when I first saw them, the Norman Rockwell family. I didn't have to fabricate a way for us to run into each other. Sam found himself a new girlfriend and bounded toward them.

When Sam first humped Zoey, I thought Bonnie was going to kick him clear across the dusty field. But, then Kelly stepped in to save Sam's manhood by picking him up and rubbing noses with him. It was love at first sight for Sam, and not half as awkward and uncomfortable as I had anticipated. We spent the next two hours watching Sam and Zoey chase each other around the acre of land. When Bonnie walked away to clean up after Zoey, I took the opportunity to tap Kelly on the arm and tell her she looked adorable in her new mommy role. She blushed the way she did when we first met, and I had told her she had the prettiest hair in the world. Before Bonnie returned, Kelly turned to me and said, "I'm glad you were persistent with Margie."

"Wait, you knew?" I said, that time blushing myself.

The curve of her lips gave me my answer.

For the remainder of the morning, I made it a point to fabricate a good two dozen lies about my 'girlfriend' Kara. From the sparkle in Kelly's eyes, I could tell she had clued on to my tactics. Within the first forty-five minutes, Bonnie relaxed and we actually had some genuine laughs. I even got to the point where I stopped picturing her two inch wisps of hair collapsing under her extensions.

In the weeks that followed, I met up with them at the dog park, and I started to recognize that nice quality Margie had talked about in Bonnie. She was a decent person with a genuine interest in Kelly. But, I wasn't going to let that stop me. I eventually sweet-talked my way into getting Kelly to agree to meet me for coffee one day without Bonnie. We met at Café de Paris, a cozy French bakery that had marble round tables and soft, cushy chairs. They also had the most delicious crepes that literally melted against the roof of my mouth.

That first meeting alone we sat for hours until our asses got so numb we could barely walk once we stood. We talked openly about things between me and Kara and her and Bonnie. Over the course of the next several weeks, we ate more crepes and drank more French coffee than even those who lived in France probably did. Our meetings climbed to three a week. Under the soft murmurs of Baroque classical music and the simmer of hazelnut, I slowly found myself falling madly and deeply back in love with her. She counseled me on whether I should re-sign with Kara for an additional year. When I told her the offer, which was that we'd be touring national venues, she slapped the table and told me I was crazy if I didn't re-sign. I told her I already had. The papers were sitting on my kitchen table, and I was just waiting until Gabby broke the vein in her forehead before easing her mind and handing over my signed papers.

"You really have it all, don't you?" she asked, cupping her hands over mine.

"Not everything," I said, brushing her cheek with the back of my hand.

Then, without looking up at me she took a deep breath and asked me a question that cut like a bullet through my chest. "Did you enjoy fucking her?"

"That makes me sound cheap."

The pain sat on her face in clear sight. I prayed to God in those few seconds following, begging him to reverse time and erase the question altogether. But as her face grew more red, and her lips thinner and straighter, I grew defensive.

"I wasn't about to lie to you," I said. "You asked me a point-blank question." Dishes clanked behind our table and the pastry chefs were laughing over something that fell. "I mean you enjoy fucking Bonnie, right?"

"Of course. She's my fiancée."

We sat with our hands tangled in our laps. The weeks of bonding unraveled faster than we could stop it. The waiter came and cleared our plates and asked us in his fake accent, which we always thought so adorable up to that moment, if we'd care for our usual chocolate dessert crepe with two spoons. "Just the check, please," Kelly said, still looking at her hands on her lap.

"Don't marry her," I said, clenching my teeth and bracing for disaster.

She looked up and glared at me. "She's never once hurt me."

I had nothing of value to say to that. "Maybe because you don't love her enough to care."

She shook her head side-to-side, fighting back what I suspected was an ocean of frustrated, disappointed tears.

To that she stood and walked out. I never felt so undeserving of happiness as I did in that moment.

## Chapter Seventeen

In the days that followed my disastrous finale with Kelly, I sunk back into self-pity mode. I did not turn to drugs, alcohol or cigarettes, though. Instead, I turned to the very thing that destroyed my life to begin with, sex. I fucked Kara in the shower, on the couch, and even once on my balcony while a group of unsuspecting friends were grilling burgers below us. "You are so horny lately, sweetie," she said to me on our way to our biggest event, yet. She leaned over, watching the road out of the corner of her smoky eyes, and whispered. "I love this side of you. You're so wild."

Before I fell back in love with Kelly, those words would've landed me in a swirl of bliss. Now they dropped to the ground like fallout ash. I needed to numb the pain, not increase it. "That's me, wild."

"So listen," she said. "Gabby asked me to remind you to bring your contract with you tonight. Did you bring it?"

"I'll get it to her."

"She's going to be pissed."

"You always make your sister out to be this angry venomous person with steel nails just waiting to punish the person who dares to mess with her. You do realize that she's harmless, right?"

"This is really important to her," Kara said.

"She's made her mark. She'll be just fine now."

"She's pretty amazing. Without her, we'd still be playing little pubs." She lit a cigarette. "By next year we will be playing even bigger venues." She twirled her finger around the palm of my hand.

Her smoke stung my eyes and burned my lungs. Her finger scratched at my skin. Could I take another year of Kara and putting up with her reckless ways? I tugged my hand back and buried it under my legs. "Can you open your window?"

We drove in silence for a few more hundred yards. "Let me ask you something," I said. "How many girls have you fucked since I found you with your ex up in your room?"

To that she giggled. "I don't count them, sweetie." She pulled her lower lip into her mouth.

"Aren't you afraid of growing old and lonely? Of having no one to love you?"

"I don't believe love is all it's cracked up to be," she said, drawing a thoughtful drag. "People fall in love, get fat, and cheat on each other. Why would I choose that?"

"So, you really don't care if I one day just up and left you?"

She dozed on that prompt longer than I'd ever seen her give weight to any thought. "I'd miss the sex. And of course, your harmonies."

"Well that makes me feel all warm and fuzzy."

"Why are you asking me something like that anyway?" she asked.

"I told Kelly that I enjoyed fucking you. She didn't take it too well."

"You spoke to Kelly?"

I detected an undeniable trace of concern on her words.

"Yup. But probably never again thanks to my coming out clean and sober to her. I thought being honest would help us grow closer."

"By telling her that you liked fucking me?"

"I know. In hindsight that was not very strategic."

"Well, that's love for you. An institution set up to fail."

She didn't speak another word for the next twenty miles, and I didn't try to prompt her again. We built our steel palaces around us and let the cruel world harden our skin. By the time we entered the gig, I doubted even a bullet could've gotten through to us.

I chomped on a dried-out ham sandwich backstage at the gig, and then checked my cell for the umpteenth time to see if maybe Kelly had called me back after all the messages I'd left her. I stared at a picture of her in front of the Whale's Tale in New Hampshire, willing for her to call me and reassure me she understood that Kara meant absolutely nothing to me anymore. That she was just someone to help see me through those nights I knew she was with Bonnie. That she was just another bad vice I could quit.

The bread crumpled in my mouth like rotted paper. I swallowed it anyway, trying to fill the void. I felt hollow, like I had no heartbeat, no blood, and no feeling other than the swooshing of emptiness against my insides.

The only other time I had that feeling in my life was when my grandpa died—that dreaded numbness. You could be walking down the street and run into a million dollars jutting out of a sewer grate and not even care, because the only thing you wanted more than the money was having your loved one back.

My heart hung in my chest like a fifty pound dumbbell. The weight of all that drama in my life hunched my shoulders forward so far my spine actually ached. If that was the price to pay for being honest, I couldn't imagine what it would cost me to feel whole again. I'd never be able to prove that she could trust my feelings were true.

"Where's the contract?" Gabby asked, sneaking up around me with a Coke in her hand.

"Relax," I said. "It's on my dining room table."

"You're past contract now. I need you to get it back to me. Tonight, you can drive back with me and I'll get it from you."

"I'm supposed to be going out with some friends, so I'll get it to you tomorrow."

She withdrew her fangs and sidestepped past me. "It's going to be a big year for you two. Just want to make sure we're all ready for it."

My cell rang. It was Margie. "Hey," she said. "We're here. Where are you?"

"Backstage. Come back around and have a ham sandwich with me."

Five minutes later, Marc and Margie walked hand-in-hand up to me. "You look like shit," she said to me and messed my hair. "What did you do? Forget to plug the straightening iron in?"

She reached into her pocketbook and pulled out a bottle of her trusty pomade. She rubbed it in my hair, pulling me back and forth with each swipe. "Have you talked to Kelly?" I asked.

Marc cleared his throat. "Is there a bathroom back here I can use?"

"Yeah, somewhere back behind that wall." I pointed him in the right direction.

When he left us, she stopped messing with my hair. "You really fucked her up again."

"I didn't want to lie."

"When are you going to learn that some things you must lie about?" She smacked my arm. I smacked hers back. We went back and forth a dozen times.

"So what did she say?" I asked.

"That she's still in love with you."

The weight in my chest suddenly lifted and my stomach turned over. A flood of adrenaline rushed through me, greater than any rush I'd ever felt with Kara.

"But—" Margie started.

*But.*

That one word sliced me like a knife.

"But, she's bent on doing everything in her power to get over you. She's marrying Bonnie, Becca. That's it."

"What if I quit?"

"You'll just piss her off more."

"So what do I do?"

"Move on." She gathered her pomade. "Let Marc know I'm in our seats." She walked away.

When I sent Marc on his way, I tuned my guitar. Never did I think music could bring me so much pain. Music was that one constant that kept me straight, and yet, now I walked a crooked line with it. I had a springboard under my feet ready to catapult me and Kara out to the nebulous world few musicians ever reached. We were at that point where our feet were as low as they could go before springing up and feeling the winds of fate take over as our driver. We had our fans right where we wanted them. We performed like tuned strings on a fret board. One couldn't work without the other.

Why couldn't I just have lied to Kelly, said no, I had not enjoyed sex with Kara, and it was just cheap sex? I've never been able to lie to her. She brought out the integrity in me.

I stared down at my phone one last time before Gabby and Kara walked over to me.

"Full house, sweetie." Kara curled her arm around my shoulder and hugged me.

I rolled off my chair and picked up my backup guitar. I'd still yet to bring Tang to one of the gigs. She was too brilliant, and I was unwilling to tarnish her. "Let's get the show started."

Kara and I walked out on stage together, holding hands as usual. The spotlight followed us. I sashayed beside her, one clumsy diva step at a time towards our stools. The crowd cheered, but it was lost on me that time. I didn't want to be there anymore than I would want to be standing in the checkout line at the grocery store.

Kara waved to the crowd, and they cheered louder. I loosened my grip on her hand, but she tightened it and raised our arms up together, united. Then, I adjusted my mic.

Kara whispered a hello into the mic in her usual sultry voice. The crowd whistled and hissed to life like the flame of a match. The cheer intensified before fading out and allowing me to interject. "Hello, Baltimore," I said. My voice echoed around me and ignited hotspots throughout the stadium, flickering, and then burning like a brush fire in a brittle hay field. That kind of power wasn't real. Kara and I were an illusion, and the audience was too stupid to not recognize it. I was no better a guitar player that day than a year ago when I played backup covers at McFadden's. I set the mood, Kara sparked the candles ablaze. She swooned and flirted with their inner desires. Men and women would never get enough of Kara Travers and the sex she sold.

Kara cradled the mic and then curled her eyes up at me.

My stomach didn't flip anymore when she did that.

"We're going to start off with one of our new songs, "Wild Ride." Kara broke into strumming the melody of the song we wrote the night we fucked on the floor in the stage closet.

I tore my eyes away from her and then looked out at the swell of people churning out in front of us. I joined in, and when we hit the bridge, an earthy sound vibrated around us, cocooning us together in a union too intimate for observers to see. Kara stood up and swooned up beside me. Her hair tickled my face and her breath smelled like spearmint, cooling my hot cheek. I felt like I was fucking her all over again, only that time I wanted nothing to do with it.

That was our act. To keep the guesses flowing. Are they fucking? Are they not?

What did I expect Kelly to do as my girlfriend? Bear witness to that night after night? Kelly the helpless, innocent bystander vulnerable to Kara's every move, and I expecting her to trust me even though I hadn't done a damned thing to deserve that. Kara would've been prancing around me while singing and swaying, stealing Kelly's dignity from right out under her.

We continued to sing in harmony, her low, me high, all the while her breath caressed my neck. I didn't want that anymore. I couldn't fake it for the crowds and for the act. My skin crawled and my body ached, this time to be away—as far away as possible—from the emptiness that had become my life.

I wrestled for a few inches of freedom, but Kara just smashed through my personal space like it was hers for the taking. She consumed me like a fire ate air, hoarding it close to capture its energy so it no longer could stand on its own. My knees buckled, even though my ass pressed into the stool.

Kara finished the hook of the song and curled up around my shoulders like a fur stole. How could I expect Kelly to give up the safety of Bonnie for someone as reckless as I was? I couldn't even find my chords at that point. I stopped playing all together and just sat there like a big idiot letting Kara take advantage of me for entertainment's sake. The crowd applauded when Kara pulled her lips away from me and cat-walked to the edge of the stage, reaching for her fans' adoration like she was Miss America. They were all here to see her flaunt. She mesmerized them into believing the sexy girl strutting her shit on stage was the real deal. They couldn't see that under her pretty face and stunning body, she was nothing more than a scared girl afraid to be a thing of the past. Her looks and fame defined her. Without them she'd be just as ordinary as the rest of us.

If only I had realized this long before that moment.

~ ~

When we ended our set, I walked right up to Gabby and Kara and told them I quit.

Gabby just stared at me. Tears welled in her eyes, and her strong jaw clenched. Kara cradled my upper arm and shook her head side to side. "You don't mean that, sweetie."

"I'm sorry, but I can't do this anymore. This isn't me. This is just me trying to be someone else. And, I don't want to be that person anymore."

"Well, you can't just walk away from all of this," Kara said. "We're under contract."

"Technically she can," Gabby said. "I still haven't gotten her signed contract back."

Kara visibly strained for air. She stared right at me, trying so hard to reach me the way she used to be able to do. Her eyes had no sparkle left in them, though. Her chin quivered. "But, we're a team."

I hated to see her weak. I didn't want to see that side of her. I'd rather witness a car wreck than see her mouth twist up in pain. I hated that it had to come down to a choice. "You're brilliant on your own," I said to her. "You don't need me sitting up there with you. You can get any girl who plays a guitar to do that. You're the real star of the show."

Tears started to well up in the corners of her eyes. "I need you, Becca."

For the first time since we had met, Kara Travers was real.

I placed my hand on her arm. She shrugged it off.

I reached down for her hand and squeezed it. "You don't. And, now it's my turn to find a way to light my own way."

Kara smiled weakly at me. "I knew you were going to do this to me one of these days." She kissed me ever so gently on the lips, leaving one last taste for me to cherish. Then, she turned and walked away. Her sandals barely clacked against the floor, she walked so softly. She melted before me like an ice sculpture in the blazing desert sun. I felt empty for a moment as I watched her transform from my hero into an ordinary person.

Margie came up from behind me, hugging her hand to mine, waiting patiently until I was ready to move on.

## Chapter Eighteen

A month later, after I completed nursing my wounded soul with lots of Margie talks, playing Tangerine Twist, and reading self-help books, I opened my eyes and saw the sun. It shone brightly and offered me the hope I needed to move forward.

In the spirit of redemption, I sent a bouquet of flowers and a basket of dog treats to Kelly, Bonnie, and Zoey. I didn't expect a response, just a personal reprieve. What I got from those two women secure in their love was a lesson in trust, honor, and forgiveness in the form of a dinner invitation.

I respectfully declined.

~ ~

I asked Margie and Marc to join me at McFaddens not soon after.

And, just as Joe had challenged me to do, I stormed the stage at McFaddens. Margie and Marc sat at a table close to the stage. I climbed the steps, straddled Tangerine around my neck, and gave Joe a hug.

"Are you ready?" Joe asked.

"You bet."

He walked off the stage, leaving me standing to face the large crowd. They silenced in a flash.

After working out the nervous kinks and momentary lapse back into stage fright, I dug deep and launched into my solo debut. As I did, Joe stuck his fingers in his mouth and whistled, high and loud.

"This is a song I've been working on for quite a while," I said.

I winked at Joe before closing my eyes and breaking into the lyrics, singing those words like I was singing them to save my life.

*Falling fast and headfirst,*
*I thought I'd swirl in the sunburst*
*Take up refuge in the beer,*
*Paint the world with a cheer*
*All the time praying for a turning point,*
*For a taste of my faithful tangerine twist*

Once I got into a comfortable rhythm, I opened my eyes and set them on Margie, centering on her strength. Her eyes latched onto mine. The diamond sparkles in them danced around, swaying to the music I played in honor of her always wanting what was best for me, in always being my friend, and in always being true. In those few minutes, a lifetime of feelings erupted in the form of a new joy for what was to become of my life and career. I didn't know exactly where I was heading in life, but I sure knew how to get there now. I closed my eyes and reached for those notes that, up to that point, I could only dream of hitting. They stood before me urging me to reach up with everything I had and claim them. And, so I did. I lunged towards that high 'A' note, catapulting towards it from a place deep in my soul. My falsetto voice climbed to an octave I'd never been able to scale before, landing so softly and perfectly on the last note. I held it there for as long as my breath lasted.

A single clap broke the silence, which was then followed up and pummeled like dominos by a thunderous ovation, the likes I'd never created on my own before. I must've thanked them a thousand times. Each time I did, they grew louder. Joe broke into a smile so wide it took up his whole face. I cradled Tangerine in my arms, feeling my grandpa's spirit, and feeling, at last, deserving and free.

The End